Landlord Wars

USA TODAY BESTSELLING AUTHOR

JULES BARNARD

JULESBARNARD.COM

LANDLORD WARS

Also by Jules Barnard

Landlord Wars

Never Date Series

Never Date Your Brother's Best Friend (Book 1)

Never Date A Player (Book 2)

Never Date Your Ex (Book 3)

Never Date Your Best Friend (Book 4)

Never Date Your Enemy (Book 5)

Cade Brothers Series

Tempting Levi (Book 1)

Daring Wes (Book 2)

Seducing Bran (Book 3)

Reforming Hunt (Book 4)

Stay informed! Join Jules's reader group for writing updates:
julesbarnard.com/newsletter

Chapter One

Sophia

THE TALL, CHISELED MAN AT THE FRONT DOOR EASED his navy-suit-clad shoulder against the doorjamb, his hand tucked into his pants pocket. "You're the new tenant? Sophia, is it?" He took in my frizzy hair, then glanced into my San Francisco apartment, his attention snagging on something. "Your pink panties are hanging off the couch."

My face heated and my eyes widened. I'd blindly thrown things out of the way this morning in my haste to make it to work on time, so this wasn't entirely surprising. Still, did he need to point it out?

I lifted my gaze from his broad chest and stared into his blue eyes, which perfectly matched his tie. "Who did you say you were?" He hadn't, but I was being polite. I'd only just moved in, after all.

"This is my building." He peered past me again, and I moved to block his view. Not that it helped; he was a head taller and could stare over me even while slouched. "I was told you're an interior designer." He studied my face in what felt like a search for cracks. "I assumed you'd be organized." His tone carried an assholian blend of disappointment and irritation.

My lips parted as the verbal gut punch hit my most tender insecurities.

This guy didn't know where I'd come from. He didn't know my past. I breathed through my nose, calming myself, and tried to think through how a person without my past might react—and found I was still pissed. Anyone would be.

Was he equating the scattered panties...to my entire life? "Is there some sort of requirement in this building that demands tenants act like professionals in their own homes?"

He fixed me with a condescending look. "If it's going to offend your roommate, then yes."

I shared the Victorian apartment with a guy named Jack, who worked from his bedroom office and wore sweatpants and a baseball cap turned backwards most days. He wasn't the fastidious type. Granted, he was neat. Me? Not so much, between a midweek move and work.

So maybe the landlord had a point. The panties might offend Jack—if he ever emerged from his bedroom. But since I'd moved in two days ago, Jack had said nothing about the mess. Either it didn't bother him, or he was giving me space while I unpacked because he was kind.

Clearly, kindness was something this landlord guy struggled with.

On the other hand... Was I being rude to my roommate?

I gave my head a light shake. My tidiness was none of this man's business. "My roommate seems happy with the living arrangement. Besides, I didn't know landlords went through their rentals with a white glove."

His eyes flashed with...annoyance? Intrigue? I couldn't

tell, possibly because I hadn't had much practice reading the emotions of assholes. "I'm the owner," he finally said.

Was there a difference? My gaze narrowed. "In other words, *the landlord*."

His lips turned up on one side, and for a moment there, he looked amused. "Sure, if that's how you prefer to think of it."

He was dressed expensively, and his nearly black hair was combed to hot-guy perfection. The crystalline blue of his eyes reminded me of a tropical beach I'd never be able to afford to visit. But if he was the rich owner of the building, why the hell was he landlording?

Either way, he was acting like a lordly ass. Henceforth, he was *Landlord Devil*.

A week ago, I'd thanked my lucky stars when I found this apartment. Had it been a mistake?

I looked him up and down, my vision snagging, annoyingly, on his broad shoulders. "What did you say your name was?" A girl could never be too careful. And I hated the territorial look in his eyes, even if he did own the place.

"You can call me Max."

As in Maxwell Burrows, Inc.? The name printed at the top of my sublease agreement?

I plastered on a stiff smile and put my hand on my hip. "Did my deposit and first month's rent go through okay?"

Of course they had. I went to business school after getting my design degree, thinking it would give me a leg up; thus, I was anal retentive when it came to money. Mostly because I had none. Still, there had to be a reason he'd stopped by, and I'd just as soon get him out of my new space. He was ruining the vibe.

Could landlords dictate the orderliness of an apartment? Was it sexual harassment to point out pink panties? I realized my finger was tapping my hip nervously, and I flexed my hand to make it stop.

I smoothed the front of my royal-blue sheath dress, which hung on me like a sack after the weight I'd lost over the last few weeks, and offered a smile—this one less stiff than the last since I was trying to make an effort.

Landlord Devil didn't flinch. In fact, he appeared bored and glanced at his fancy gold watch. "Just make sure you don't cause any trouble."

The tendons in my neck stiffened, and my jaw clamped down. *Trouble?* Moving away from home was the first selfish thing I'd done in years. I was responsible to the nth degree, and this man had the gall to suggest I wasn't?

Visions of strangling him flashed before my eyes. I squeezed them shut. I was under too much stress. This guy was annoying, but not worthy of homicide. Yet.

Landlord Devil glanced up, and his lips twitched as though he sensed my inner rage.

I took in a deep breath and willed myself to remain calm. "The, ah, mess you mentioned will be tidied as soon as I'm able to spend a weekend putting everything away."

Note to self: stuff unmentionables inside bedroom once Landlord Devil leaves.

I'd been working at Green Aesthetic for six months— not long enough for me to get time off due to emergency relocations when fancy apartments become available. Waiting until the weekend to finish unpacking would have to do. "Did you need anything else?"

His eyes narrowed, as though he didn't trust a word I said. "I came by to welcome you to the neighborhood. I live upstairs."

My chest spasmed, and I choked. "Oh...that's...nice."

He lived upstairs? *Shit.*

Max glanced past me once more. Given the twinkle in his eye, he was taking a final look at my panties. "Enjoy the rest of your evening."

How was I supposed to enjoy my evening with a judgy asshole living above me?

————

THE NEXT MORNING, the living room was back to tidiness —because I'd stayed up late hauling moving boxes into my bedroom and putting clothes away in my new IKEA chest of drawers that had taken me two hours to build. I was a people pleaser, even for lordly asses like Maxwell Burrows. It was a problem.

I held my cell phone to my ear and rubbed my temple. "You can't come over tonight," I told Elise, my younger sister, as I sorted socks in the dresser drawer.

The sound of chomping came through the receiver. Somehow, Elise subsisted primarily on a diet of corn chips yet still had muscle tone. It was super annoying. "Why? What happened?"

I wished the reason she couldn't come over was because my bedroom looked like a tornado had blown through it, but that wasn't it. "I met my landlord."

"And?"

"He's nosy."

The crunching ceased. "I can stay with Mom tonight," she said.

Up until now, I'd been living at my mom's, along with my sister, in the outer Sunset neighborhood of San Francisco. I'd averaged four hours of sleep a night while commuting from home and helping my boss at Green Aesthetic catch up on overdue projects. Victor, the owner, had needed a designer-manager for over a decade. Hence the reason I was overworked. But working with Victor was a steppingstone to bigger things, and I adored him, even if the paycheck didn't leave much after my expenses.

For a while there, I worried I'd never be able to afford my own place, given the housing costs in San Francisco. Those had been dark times. But all that changed the day I happened upon Jack's listing for a bedroom plus private bath inside his apartment in a Victorian building.

By some miracle, I'd been checking the online listings in Jack's neighborhood seconds after he posted. Given its location a few blocks from my work, in one of the nicest neighborhoods in the city, I never thought I'd be able to afford a place in Russian Hill.

I never figured out why Jack had listed the room so inexpensively. He'd mentioned something when I applied about wanting to pass on the discount, which I hadn't quite followed, but I wasn't about to tell him the price should be double. I'd been so excited when he offered the room to me that my hands had shaken for days, up until Jack dropped the key in my palm and I officially knew it was mine. Dozens of people had to have applied to rent it. But I was the first, according to Jack, and I had met his requirements.

Only that wasn't entirely true. Jack had wanted a single renter (as opposed to a couple or two friends sharing a room) who didn't own pets. I didn't have a pet, but I planned to stash my sister in my room as often as possible.

"I wish you only had to stay at Mom's for one night," I told Elise. "But it's not that simple."

Our mom was as sweet as they came. She also had major issues that had traumatized me and Elise growing up. Even if my mom refused to get help, I could finally pull my sister out of the stressful living situation as often as possible.

As soon as Jack had offered me the room, my mind formed all sorts of fantasies where Elise stayed with me instead of living at Mom's full-time. According to the sublease, Elise could crash seven days consecutively, but she couldn't stay indefinitely. It wasn't a perfect solution, but it was better than the alternative: Elise living under Mom's roof until she graduated from her nursing program and got a full-time job. And now I was terrified of what Landlord Devil would do if he discovered I was going to take advantage of the sleepover clause. He'd hated my panties being out of place; what would he say if he saw Elise staying here on a regular basis?

"I'll continue to pay Mom's mortgage," I told my sister. "You'll move out soon. I promise."

I could afford to support my mom and Elise. Sort of. Sharing this room with my sister part-time at Jack's apartment was supposed to be the transition piece in the overall plan. And then Maxwell Burrows had shown up and freaked me out with his threat about *not causing trouble*. Which had me worrying I *was* being troublesome.

I pinched the bridge of my nose. My hyper-responsibility issues might have begun while growing up with Mom, but I sure as hell didn't need to drag this shit around with me forever. There had to be a way to make this new housing situation work. I would not let the landlord intimidate me.

"So the plan is still on for me to stay with you most of the month?" Elise's voice rose with optimism.

Now that I heard it out loud, it sounded ridiculous. "No, actually. There's been a small snafu where the plan is concerned."

I sank onto my queen bed and tipped my head against the beige-upholstered headboard, the pulse of a headache brimming behind my eyes. "Guess who lives in the flat above mine?"

"Paul?"

"*What?*" The unexpected reminder of my ex triggered my gag reflex. "Not Paul. Landlord Devil."

I gnawed the corner of my thumbnail. Should I move? Find a place where Elise and I could both be on the lease? But no affordable apartment I found would be as nice as this one or even located within city limits. I'd be returning to longer commutes and rationed sleep. As the breadwinner, that was problematic. It was no good when your weight fluctuated due to stress and exhaustion. If I got sick, who would pay the bills?

I took a deep breath and let it out slowly. Then I breathed in and out again. There was no room for anxiety. I had to get that shit locked down, or the house of cards would collapse.

"Wait, who is Landlord Devil?" Elise asked.

"He's the asshat who runs the building."

There was a pause, then, "Don't most landlords live onsite?"

Leave it to Elise to get to the crux of the matter. "He's not only the landlord. He's also the owner."

"Oh. *Ohhh*...yeah, that's no good. Not if you're trying to stretch the boundaries of your contract behind the owner's back." The munching continued, and she let out a heavy sigh. "Look, Soph, I can get a job. Really."

My hand clenched at my sister's blasé attitude toward taking on another job. "You already have a part-time job," I said with a strained voice, "and you're still in nursing school."

She made a carefree sound. "I can get another job. I'm ready to move out too, you know."

"Yes, sir."

"Add something about maintaining household orderliness."

There was a pause, then, "I'm not sure that can be dictated."

"Word it in such a way that it can."

If I'd known I'd have to deal with rude, social-climbing tenants, I never would have agreed to Jack subletting the second bedroom. He'd insisted, and I'd caved because his intentions were good, but there was nothing I hated more than greedy, self-centered people.

"Ms. DuPont called again this afternoon," my assistant said. "She wishes to schedule a lunch appointment with you."

My ex might have had a change of heart after months of separation, but I hadn't. "Tell her I'm not available."

———

Sophia

I CRAWLED up the last steps to my apartment, sweat dripping down the middle of my back, and breathed through the pain of a throbbing heel blister. In an attempt to maintain some form of sophistication, I'd been wearing heels to and from work. The walk to work was only four blocks, but September in San Francisco could be the warmest time of the year, and my swollen feet were paying for it.

I opened the front door. "Hello?"

Jack was standing in bare feet, shorts, and a faded black hoodie pulled up over his head in the kitchen on my left, his body bent at the waist. The light from the mostly empty fridge illuminated his face.

He straightened and looked over, shoving the hoodie off his head. "Hey, how was work? You don't happen to have any food around, do you?"

I kicked off my heels. "Are you foraging incognito style? What's with the—" I waved at his head.

He flashed me a goofy grin, his light, wavy brown hair falling over his forehead. "It fits my mood. I'd hate to have to come face-to-face with a delivery person."

I hefted my computer bag onto the marble counter that separated the kitchen from the living room, with expensive-looking rattan stools for seating. The barstools and the rest of the furniture in the apartment didn't match Jack's faded sweatpants style, but it was sophisticated and nice, and I wasn't complaining. "I've been meaning to ask—did you pick out the furniture in here?"

He laughed. "Why? Doesn't it look like me?"

I shook my head sheepishly.

"I did not pick out the furniture in the apartment. My best friend has much better taste than me, and I couldn't be bothered at the time."

Best friend? Must be a girl. Even my rich ex-boyfriend didn't have taste this good, and he had a diamond-encrusted Dubai First Royal MasterCard his mom got him for his twenty-fifth birthday. There's a lot of stupid shit you can buy with a card like that, but it can't buy good taste.

"You're welcome to whatever food I have," I said. "I wouldn't want you to have to venture out into the wild."

He kicked up another smile. He was handsome, with an athletic build and a playful disposition. Before my ex, I would have found it awkward to live with a man that good-looking and not trip over my own two feet. But ever since my breakup, I hadn't been able to muster up any energy toward the opposite sex. So Jack was safe. I appreciated the easy smiles, though. Made living with him pleasant.

Landlord Devil, on the other hand, whose preferred expression was a sneer, was a whole other issue that I hoped would get better in time. Fingers crossed.

"I know, right?" Jack said. "Why return to the land of the living when I can stay in for a week or two?"

Despite the easy smile, I got the sense Jack was hiding from something. He stayed in way too often for a good-looking guy in his late twenties. "Hey, what's the deal with Max Burrows? He slipped this letter under our door this morning." I reached for the piece of paper I'd stuffed in my bag and handed it to Jack.

Dear Sophia Markos,

Please abide by House Rules during your tenancy:

- No loud noise between 10 P.M. and 8 A.M.
- No pets.
- Notify landlord of needed repairs within 24 hours.
- Apartment and common areas should be kept clear of debris and strong odors, and maintained in an orderly fashion.

The Management

MAX HAD double-underlined that last part, the ass.

Jack's eyes quickly took in the letter, and his face drew down as though he'd smelled something rotten. He looked up, balled the paper, and tossed it basketball-style into the trash, where it hit the side and fell on the floor. "Ignore him," he said and picked up the note and dropped it in the trash.

I paused for a moment, trying to make sense of it all. "Why's he so uptight?"

Jack shrugged. "That's his normal first impression. Also, I might not have chosen the best roommate last time. But that has nothing to do with you. I'll talk to Max."

That was a relief. "Thank you."

I lowered myself onto one of the rattan barstools and squeezed the bottom of my foot, rubbing circulation back into it. The blister wasn't as bad as I'd feared, but it hurt like a bitch. I tipped my chin up in his direction. "You look very cozy over there in your sweatpants. Seems like you spend most of your time working from home. You ever need to go in to work?"

He stretched his arms over his head, his mouth gaping in a yawn. "I'm not conventional when it comes to routines. I get my best work done between the hours of midnight and four in the morning, and no one I work with cares."

"No wonder I never see you." I limped into the kitchen and washed my hands before pulling out a forties-era green mug I'd found in a vintage shop on Polk Street and my favorite fruity tea. I filled the mug with water and placed it in the microwave, then punched in a cook time before turning around.

"There's something I wanted to run by you." My hands began to sweat. Rocking the boat went against the grain, and I felt like I was already screwing this up.

Jack reached into one of the upper cabinets and held up a bag of kettle corn. "This up for grabs?"

"It's all yours." The microwave beeped, and I flinched. I was acting like a scaredy-cat, and I needed to relax. People asked for favors. Especially when they lived together. Like grabbing the mail or emptying the dishwasher. This was no big deal. "What do you think of my sister staying the night?"

Now that Landlord Devil wasn't intimidating me with his power suit, I decided it wasn't up to him who stayed in the apartment. It was up to Jack.

Jack tore open the top of the popcorn and poured the contents into a large bowl. "Yeah, sure."

"For a few nights?"

He shrugged.

"Or a few weeks?"

He stopped what he was doing and looked up. "You want your sister to move in?"

I bit the inside of my lip. "Not move in, because that's against the sublease. Maybe stay for several days out of the month?" I offered him a shaky smile.

Jack set the bowl down. "Sophia, I don't mind if your sister needs a place to crash. Not sure I'd be up for a sorority of girls at the place..." He shook his head as though to clear it. "On second thought, that's probably fine too." He grinned.

My eyebrows rose. Jack didn't come across as a player, but what the hell did I know? "It's like that, is it?"

He chuckled. "Not exactly. But lately I've been antisocial for various reasons, and I should probably get over it."

There was a story there I hoped to hear one day. "You're doing better than me. It's been almost a year since I broke up with my ex, and I haven't gone out once."

He nodded. "We're a perfect match. We can sit around and cry while watching romantic comedies."

I chuckled and pulled out the steaming mug. "You paint a charming picture, but I'm trying to have a life now that I'm living here." I dipped the tea bag in the mug and limped back to the barstool.

"What's wrong with your foot?" he asked. "You hurt yourself?"

"Women's fashion hurts me."

He shook his head slowly. "Why do women wear high heels?"

"Because men think we look hot in them?"

He held up his hands. "I personally don't care."

"You say that now, but if a woman walked in wearing a miniskirt, with long legs in heels..."

"I'd marvel at how she balanced and think of nothing inappropriate." His look was expressionless, which gave him away. He was trying too hard, and I saw right through it.

"Sure you would." I held up my bloody heel, careful not to flash him in my work skirt. "We do it with a pound of flesh."

He cringed. "Got it. Keep in mind, we'll look even if you wear comfortable shoes, so don't blame us." He scratched his stubbled jaw and seemed to consider something. "How old did you say your sister was?" His tone held interest.

Oh, hell no. "Stay away from my baby sister!"

He grinned devilishly. "Noted. Besides, I'm damaged goods with all the baggage I've got going on. I'll take the kettle corn and resume my video-game marathon with strangers in the privacy of my bedroom."

I laughed and watched him pad down the hallway. We had the perfect setup with en suite bedrooms on opposite sides of the hall. I never heard Jack once he entered his room.

The tension from a long day of work eased from my shoulders. With Jack's support, my sister staying the night was doable.

Chapter Three

Sophia

THE NEXT EVENING, I MET UP WITH ELISE AT OUR favorite dim sum restaurant to celebrate my new apartment. This was gonna work, even if I had to ass-kiss the landlord until my lips were chapped. At least Jack was willing to let Elise stay over.

I dug into my massive multipurpose bag that was function over form, carrying my laptop, shoes, and beauty essentials, and searched for a scrap of paper. I'd scribbled the reservation confirmation on it and shoved it in here, but now I couldn't find it. The situation was made worse by the fact that I hadn't cleaned out my bag in a week, and everything I owned was inside.

I glanced at the hostess, who was clad in a black dress and stylish glasses halfway down her nose. "I'm so sorry. I have the confirmation here somewhere."

Nom Tea Parlor was the best dim sum in town. You booked reservations online for lunch and dinner or you didn't get in. It was also expensive as all get-out. Moving in with Jack was a big deal for me, so I'd been skimping on other luxuries, like afternoon mochas, to celebrate the occasion. Which was also why I'd booked a table days ago. If only I could find the darn slip of paper with the confirmation code!

"Name?" the hostess asked.

I rattled off my name.

The hostess scrolled a computer screen then said, "I don't see it here."

Wearing a moss-green lantern dress she'd picked up off Shein for about fifteen bucks, and dressed to honor the occasion, Elise nudged me in the side with her elbow. "There's a line behind us."

Perspiration prickled beneath my arms as I dug around in my purse. "I know, I know."

"Well, do something," she said, "or we should leave. Someone just walked in, and you don't want to see who it is."

The hairs on the back of my neck stood on end. I looked behind us, exactly what Elise had warned me not to do.

My chest constricted, closing off airflow.

"Paul just walked in," she said needlessly, her wavy dark-brown hair partially blocking my view because Elise didn't know personal space. But I didn't need the full view.

Paul was making his way to the hostess, and he looked like a K-pop star, with his glossy black hair lightened to a reddish brown. He was wearing a black T-shirt that was tight on his biceps and slim at the waist. Knowing what he spent on clothing, the shirt alone must have cost as much as I earned in a day. More importantly, he was holding the hand of his new fiancée.

I'd been told his fiancée was exactly the nice Korean girl his mother had dreamed of for him. Apparently, she came from a wealthy family who was richer than Paul's, and that was saying something. It was a wonder he ever dated me knowing I was making my way through graduate school on scholarships and student loans. Not exactly rich-girl material.

Paul's family owned a popular café chain in town, but in graduate school we were all on a level playing field. I hadn't wanted a boyfriend at the time; relentless financial stress will do that to you. But Paul brought me lattes before class, and even though I don't drink lattes, I'd appreciated the effort.

Clearly, I'd been deeply deprived of male attention because there were plenty of other things I'd overlooked.

I pressed my lips together and closed my eyes, feeling my chest loosening. This was the best week. The very best week. I had my own space in a swanky apartment, and I was getting better sleep than I had in years. I would not let my ex's presence ruin this day.

"Excuse me?" the hostess said, peering from above silver-framed glasses that matched her hair. "I can't find your name, and if you don't have your reservation number, I'll have to take the next customer."

The sound of someone clearing his throat came from behind, and I stiffly looked back.

Paul was standing right behind us now. Tension lined his eyes as he clenched his fiancée's hand. "Sophia... Is there a problem?" He looked over his shoulder at the growing line. "Maybe you should step back and let someone else through."

"You know her?" his fiancée murmured.

Shame swept through me, and I stepped aside in jerky

movements, wishing to be smaller. I wasn't with Paul anymore, yet somehow, I still managed to embarrass him.

I'd lost the reservation number. For most people that wasn't the end of the world, but the truth was, I couldn't afford this place. I'd wanted to live like the *haves* instead of the *have-nots*, even for an hour, and I'd just been bitch-slapped into reality courtesy of my ex, a guy I hadn't seen in a year.

I looped my arm through Elise's and moved to leave, when a man said, "Ming, she can have my reservation."

My head swiveled in the direction of the deep, cultured voice a few feet behind Paul...to find Landlord Devil staring at his phone.

He glanced at the hostess. "A call just came in that I need to take."

Landlord Devil placed the phone to his ear and turned his back to us.

"Of course, Mr. Burrows." The hostess smiled and motioned me and Elise toward a pair of double doors and the restaurant that resided just beyond. "Right this way."

I looked at Max, but he still had his back turned. Though I caught Paul giving Max a sidelong look, and his expression was annoyed.

Was Paul disappointed that Landlord Devil had rescued me like a suit-clad knight in shining armor?

Elise nudged me forward, and I followed the hostess numbly.

Max and I hadn't made eye contact once, which led me to believe he hadn't known it was me blocking the line. Just some random woman. And for a moment, I could see him in a different light—one less harsh. Maybe he wasn't entirely awful. Maybe we'd just gotten off on the wrong foot.

Catching my stiff composure as we made our way

through the restaurant, Elise said, "I think he's in the other dining room." At my confused expression, she added, "Paul."

I rubbed my temples. "It's fine. I was just... I haven't seen Paul in a long time, and that was embarrassing as hell."

"No shit. He didn't even have the courtesy to say hello. Just *get the fuck out of the way*. But holy hell, the hot businessman? Yes, please! I'll take some of that." She waggled her eyebrows.

I stared in horror.

"What?"

"That businessman was—*is*—my landlord."

Her nose crinkled. "Landlord Devil?"

"Correct."

She looked toward the double doors that were now closed, and nearly ran into an older couple leaving the dining area.

"Watch where you're going," I mumbled.

The hostess stopped near a table and gestured for us to sit.

Elise leaned in and lowered her voice. "Well, he seemed okay. And he's a freaking smoke-show, Soph. Why didn't you tell me?" She pulled out her chair and sat.

Too many unsettling thoughts were running through my mind to respond to Elise's question. I jerked out a chair and slumped into the seat. Maxwell Burrows *was* good-looking. Of course I'd noticed—in the split second before he criticized me the night we met. Then all pleasure at a handsome face had dissipated. But he hadn't been an asshat just now, and I wasn't sure what to think.

"He probably didn't know it was me at the front of the line," I finally said.

"Max is his name?" Elise's mouth twisted and she shrugged. "Either way, more dim sum for us." She clinked her water glass against mine, and I focused on the delicious menu instead of on the two men who'd reminded me of all the reasons I was cautious when it came to relationships.

Chapter Four

Max

FLEET WEEK IN SAN FRANCISCO WAS THE BANE OF MY existence. The planes I enjoyed, but the people coming into the city for the parade of ships, music, and airshows? Them I could do without.

I stood on the sidewalk in front of my building, and a horn blared. Some BMW dickhead had stolen a parking space on the cramped San Francisco street, and a Tesla proceeded to road-rage the hell out of the other car. The scenario epitomized my mood.

The other day, I'd run into Jack's new roommate at a restaurant, and I hadn't been the same since. She'd been distraught after she couldn't find her reservation number, so I'd given her mine. Seeing her upset was unsettling, and I'd had the unprecedented urge to...help. I hadn't felt settled since, wondering why I'd gone so far.

Juggling a paper bag of groceries in my arm, I checked the time, irritation brimming beneath my skin. Just before the rooftop party (now in full swing), my mother had asked me to meet her downstairs and escort her up. The party was in celebration of the finished building renovation, and I was officially late.

Not like my mother needed an escort. She had my dad, after all. But she liked the pomp and circumstance. And to inconvenience me.

Just as I was about to call and tell her I needed to entertain my guests, a town car pulled up.

Recognizing the driver, I moved forward and opened the back door, lending a hand to Kitty Burrows.

"Darling." She stretched up and kissed me on the cheek.

My dad stepped out next, followed by someone who hadn't been invited, and yet somehow had managed to show up anyway.

"Gwen?" Perfect. All I needed was my ex to make the discomfort and frustration I couldn't seem to shake complete.

The slim blonde that exited was exactly the type of "good society" my mother wanted me to marry into. Gwen DuPont was highly educated, beautiful, and from a family with more money than the state of California. I'd known her my entire life, and for a while there, I had thought I would marry her. Until I figured out what a terrible idea that would be.

This had my mother written all over it.

"Max," Gwen said, leaning in for a too-intimate hug.

My hackles rose. "What's going on?"

My mother snorted. "Maxwell, don't be rude. You two kids greet each other while your father and I go up. Someone needs to host."

I ground my molars. There would already be a host had my mother not insisted on my waiting for her downstairs.

I let out a sigh. The only way to get out of a Kitty-induced trap was to plow through.

My parents entered the stairwell, and as soon as they were out of earshot, I leveled a look at the woman in front of me. "Why are you here?"

———

Sophia

AFTER PUTTING in a few hours at the shop this Saturday, I was almost to my apartment, prepared to unwind with a glass of wine before heading up to a rooftop party Jack had invited me to, when I froze.

Landlord Devil was standing at the steps to our building, and he wasn't alone. A stunning dark blonde, wearing a classy, knee-length yellow summer dress, was beaming up at him.

The devil had a girlfriend?

I didn't know why I'd never pictured Max with a girlfriend. I supposed it had something to do with the affection aspect—the Max I knew was as cold as a marble statue, and he wasn't disappointing me now.

Max's full mouth was set in a hard, straight line as he peered at the beautiful woman in front of him.

Interesting. The most I'd gotten out of Max was a smirk or a lip twitch. But gauging from his body language—stiff shoulders, hard frown—he was not happy with this woman.

Trouble in paradise?

I wanted to relax, but now my anxiety had reached a high, and I wasn't even the cause of Max's ire this time. I was tired and wrinkled, with a waffle-sized coffee stain on my skirt, and running into Max had not been on my list of things to do today. Or any day for the next month.

He had, very strangely, helped me at the restaurant a few days ago, but the more I thought about it, the more I was convinced he hadn't known it was me. Every time I'd glanced back, he'd been staring at his phone. That moment of chivalry had to have been a fluke. An excuse for him to take a pressing call, like he'd said to the hostess.

I swiveled my head left then right in search of an escape, but it was no use. No way could I walk past the warring lovebirds without being seen. As a matter of fact, if Landlord Devil bothered to look past the blonde, he'd catch me standing there like a Nervous Nelly.

Oh, for the love of God, this was ridiculous. Maybe he wouldn't notice me walk past with the beauty queen making eyes at him.

I tipped my chin down and headed briskly toward the building...and caught the tail end of their conversation.

"I made a mistake, and you blew it out of proportion," the blonde said.

Max let out a tight sigh. "Regardless of how things went down, it's over."

I froze like a deer caught in the headlights. Crap, *crap*! Max was dumping his beauty-queen girlfriend? On the sidewalk?

And his tone wasn't gentle.

Figured.

The generous businessman he'd presented at the restaurant wasn't the real Max. Landlord Devil was back in full force. A part of me was disappointed but not surprised.

Max took that moment to stare straight at me.

His expression was startled. And then his eyes narrowed and shot darts of blue fire my way.

Did he think I was eavesdropping?

Great, just great. "Don't mind me," I said, and speed-walked past them.

The woman looked over in annoyance. She glanced between Landlord Devil and me and frowned.

Holy shit, how did I get myself into these situations?

I raced up the steps and into the apartment, dropping my bag in the entry before I splayed my back against the closed door, breaths coming out in puffs.

Jack looked over from the kitchen, where he seemed to spend a good portion of his time. "Rough day?"

I lifted my back off the door. "Not my best, but it just got worse. What's going on with—"

A knock sounded behind me, and I jumped several inches.

When I stood stock-still, refusing to answer, Jack sent me a questioning glance. He finally took me gently by the shoulders, moved me aside, and opened the door.

Max entered the apartment without an invitation, his gaze searching. Until it landed on me, eyes blazing.

He'd followed me here? Because of what I'd witnessed downstairs? Crap!

"I was just grabbing some beers," Jack said, returning to the kitchen, oblivious to the tension in the room. "Did you pick up the chips and salsa?"

Landlord Devil didn't respond. He was too busy glaring. Though he did it with style, one hand in his pants pocket, the other holding a paper bag. He was wearing a pressed light-gray suit today. Did the man never wrinkle?

Jack glanced between the two of us. "Sophia, this is Max. He owns the building. He's also my best friend."

The taste of acid choked me. *First Max lives upstairs... and now he's my roommate's best friend?*

How was I supposed to avoid this man?

Max's heated look fixed on me, as though he were trying to read me. "Were you listening to my private conversation?"

"What?" I said, shocked. I mean, I knew he might have suspected that, but why did he always jump to the worst conclusions?

"Max?" Jack said. "What are you talking about?"

Max didn't move his gaze off me. "She was eavesdropping out front."

"I was not eavesdropping!" I crossed my arms. "You were standing in front of the building. There was no way to avoid overhearing you dump that poor girl. Maybe you should have chosen a more private location?"

Landlord Devil's jaw clenched tightly, and Jack moved between us. "Whoa, man, she's right. If you didn't want others to overhear, you should have had your conversation someplace else. Who were you talking to, anyway?"

Max looked distractedly at Jack. "Gwen."

Jack nodded as though it were all clear now and turned to me. "Gwen and Max broke up several months ago, so he wasn't dumping her." He looked at Max. "Were you? Did you guys get back together?"

Max set the paper bag on the counter and ran stiff fingers through his hair, ruffling the silky, dark locks. "We did *not* get back together."

Max had been angry earlier and even a moment ago, but now he just looked stressed.

Jack entered the kitchen and grabbed a beer from the fridge. He popped the cap off and handed it to Max. "You look like you could use it."

Landlord Devil reached for the bottle, took a deep swig, and his shoulders noticeably lowered.

I glanced down the hallway. Should I go to my room? Was this another private conversation I shouldn't be privy to?

Jack tipped his chin up at me. "You want one, Sophia?"

I glanced at Landlord Devil, unsure of my welcome. But I didn't need to worry, because Max wasn't paying attention to Jack's offer to join them for a drink. He was scanning the living room, shifting his critical eye to something new.

My body froze, and a sense of fight or flight made my heart race. I'd straightened up the boxes in the living room after that first unannounced visit from Max. But that had been a week ago or more. Since then, I might have left one—or several—mugs scattered about the room, as one does.

Landlord Devil's eyes landed one by one on each of the mugs. "You have a problem putting dishes away, Sophia?"

His low tone caused a frisson of awareness to sweep through me—until my brain registered his words.

Somehow the jackass knew the mugs were mine. Then again, Jack didn't seem like much of a hot beverage person. "I'm a tea drinker," I said lamely. "I tend to forget where I put my drinks, or forget I already have one. Haven't you ever lost your keys?"

His eyebrow rose. "My keys, yes. My coffee, no."

"It could happen." Okay, I was a rare case. Even my sister made fun of me.

Max's grumpy expression didn't change, and I shifted my jaw in annoyance. He didn't live here; he had no right to judge me.

My apartment was a gem, it truly was, but Landlord Devil was a plague. Just how often would he stop by?

Ignoring Max and his open hostility, I focused on more pressing matters. "Jack, is this a dressy event? I wasn't prepared for dressy. But considering Max's suit..." I looked over and caught Max's shocked expression.

"*She's* coming?" he said.

Jack finished pouring chips into a bowl and shuffled items around on the overloaded tray. "Dude, what is wrong with you today? Sophia's my roommate. Of course I invited her." He looked at me and smiled. "Ignore him. He's a grump, but he means well."

Max and I snorted at the same time.

Max's mouth went taut, and the tension in the room grew tenfold.

"And no," Jack said as he pulled cheese out from the fridge before closing the door with his foot, "you don't need to change, Sophia. Come as you are."

Jack was dressed in jeans and a T-shirt, so I took him at his word and retreated to the sanctuary of my bedroom. Hopefully Landlord Devil would be gone by the time I returned.

A few minutes later, Jack called out, "Sophia, you coming?"

I grabbed a sweater in case the rooftop grew cold and met him near the door. Thankfully, Max had already left. "Can I help with anything?"

"Do you mind carrying this?" He juggled the tray of food in one arm and handed me a bottle of wine.

"Not at all," I said.

We exited the apartment and made our way up a set of stairs, passing what had to be Max's flat, as it was the only door on the entire floor, and headed up one more narrow flight toward the rooftop. "How did you meet Max?" I asked. Jack was so easygoing, while Max was an uptight ass. It made no sense these two had connected, let alone become best friends.

31

Jack let out a slow breath. "I guess you could call it luck," he said and shook his head, chagrined. "I don't know if you've noticed, but me and Max don't normally run in the same circles. I never would have met him had circumstances been different."

Luck? I wasn't sure meeting Max was lucky. "I might have picked up a clue or two."

He scratched his jaw. "The short answer is I'm a good test taker. I got into a private school on scholarship after I scored high on a test the city gives every seventh grader. Max sat next to me in math at my new school, and while the rest of the students treated me like I was beneath them, Max was friendly. He was nothing like the stuck-up prep-school kids we went there with, and over time, he became my best friend."

Jack glanced off as though confused. "I don't know why Max was giving you a hard time earlier. I'm really sorry about that. He's usually smoother in social situations. In fact, it's a good thing we've never been attracted to the same women, or I would have lost out every time."

He was grinning as though he'd said something funny, but I begged to differ. Max had the charm of a python while Jack was good-looking and kind. "I'll take your word for it. Landlord—I mean, *Max* really is your best friend? Above everyone else?"

Jack laughed. "He's one of the best people I know."

Max had behaved like an arrogant jerk the first night I met him, and he'd been a total dick just now. But he had given up his restaurant reservation when he didn't know it was me, so at the very least, he was mercurial.

Or just a total ass when it came to me.

Chapter Five

Sophia

I STARED AT THE DISTANT VIEW OF ALCATRAZ AND THE Golden Gate Bridge from the building rooftop and shifted the bottle of wine in my arm, careful not to drop it. The prominent view from the home I'd grown up in was of my neighbor's recycling bin in the Sunset District. This wasn't a bedroom window, of course; it was the rooftop. But still, holy hell, I'd climbed far in just over a week.

Plexiglass walls protected me from the wind on the rooftop, and there was plush outdoor seating beneath heated lamps for comfort. The lamps weren't in operation this afternoon, because we had a perfect blue sky, but I kept my sweater close in case the fog rolled in and the temperature dropped thirty degrees. Other than San Francisco's unpredictable weather, this place had paradise written all over it—with one fatal flaw.

Who builds a rooftop garden without *a garden?*
Landlord Devil, that's who.

Not a patch of green filled the roughly two thousand

square feet of outdoor space. Luxury furniture? Sure, sure, had that. Sleek built-in barbeque and firepit? Yep, had those too. But no plants.

Given Max's penchant for orderliness, he'd probably find plants too messy. But as a greenspace designer, I felt the absence of vegetation in this idyllic setting like a knife to my heart.

My palms felt itchy, and my back started to sweat. The need to fix this atrocity hijacked my focus, design elements flashing before my eyes. I'd add a large-leaf philodendron and pops of maroon, and maybe even some string lights for ambiance. It would be glorious. Hypothetically speaking.

I let out a gust of air. My dream rooftop garden wasn't to be. I'd never be able to touch this blank canvas, and I blamed Max. Not only was he *Landlord Devil*, but apparently he was Stingy Plant Devil too.

Jack walked off and set down the food, while roughly fifteen of the best-dressed people I'd ever seen stood around in light blazers and early fall party wear, chatting and drinking wine. The beautiful woman Max had dated was among them.

Jack had lied. It wasn't a casual get-together. Or at least not my definition of casual.

I should have considered who else might be here. Max owned the building, so of course these weren't your run-of-the-mill folks enjoying the flight show, and now I had to mingle with them.

I walked over to where Jack had set down the platter of food and added the bottle of wine to the collection, clutching my cable-knit sweater to my chest. Why had I spent so much time alone this last year? I'd forgotten how to mingle with strangers. And definitely not ritzy ones.

"Sophia." Jack waved me over to where he was standing

beside a handsome couple sitting on one of the couches. "Come meet Max's parents."

I blinked, taking in the older couple. Jack wanted me to meet Max's parents? What fresh living hell was this?

I sighed. I was already disturbed by the lack of plants up here; might as well round things off in a conversation with the people who'd raised my uptight, arrogant landlord.

I walked up to Jack, and he proffered a glass of wine. "Red okay?"

"Yes, thank you." I took a sip from the glass Jack handed me while he passed another to Max's mother.

"This is Karl and Kitty Burrows," he said.

Kitty was blonde with very few wrinkles, wearing a cream pleated shirt dress and expensive-looking loafers that had metal buckles on top, while Karl Burrows had a full head of salt-and-pepper hair, dark eyebrows, and sparkling blue eyes. They were sitting, but by the looks of it, they were around average height, while Max stood well over six feet.

Max's parents were an attractive older couple, and it was clear where Landlord Devil got his looks, if not his height. "It's nice to meet you," I said automatically.

Kitty Burrows looked me up and down. "You're Jack's new roommate?" She glanced at her husband. "Hopefully this one is better than the last," she murmured under her breath.

Karl Burrows chuckled. "Be nice, Kitty." He smiled warmly at me. "Pleasure to meet you, Sophia."

My back stiffened. I was already off on the wrong foot with Max's parents. Why didn't that surprise me? I turned to Jack. "What happened with your last roommate?"

Jack's jaw stiffened and he glanced off. "I should probably see what Max is up to."

Had I said something wrong? Already?

Kitty gestured to the chair opposite her. "Have a seat, Sophia."

Clenching my wineglass, the sweater draped over my arm, a sinking feeling settled in my stomach. I was certain I'd touched on a sensitive subject for Jack, and I felt terrible. Would it be rude to leave early? I hadn't been this uncomfortable in forever.

"You didn't hear about Jack's last roommate?" Kitty turned to her husband. "Didn't Jack date the woman?"

"He did," Karl said.

Kitty flicked her fingers dismissively. "Yes, well, our sweet Jack dated this young woman, who started out as his roommate, and she completely ruined the apartment before she broke things off with him. Can you imagine?" She tilted her head as though pondering. "I suppose she never actually broke things off. She simply disappeared."

"I'm sorry to hear that." How awful. No wonder Jack hadn't wanted to talk about it. Was this woman the reason he rarely left the apartment?

Kitty lowered her voice. "She thought Jack was as wealthy as our dear Max." She shook her head. "That woman was a gold-digger," she said in a hushed tone.

I glanced at Jack, who had gone up to Max and was laughing at something he said.

The corner of Max's mouth lifted into a smile and his blue eyes flashed with mischief as he took in Jack's reaction to his comment.

Whirls of sensation ran up my back. Max was beautiful, and he knew it. When one of his naughty smiles escaped, it made me forget all the reasons I disliked him.

But the lapse in memory was brief. No way would I let my guard down around Landlord Devil.

"That must have been hard on Jack," I said, thinking of ways I could be a better roommate. I would not leave my mugs around for more than twenty-four hours. Those suckers were getting picked up every night before bed.

Kitty's chin turned down. "Max was livid, and Jack ended up staying with Max while my son had the place remodeled top to bottom to repair the damage."

That explained why the apartment looked like something out of a decorator's magazine. "The damage was that bad?"

Kitty pursed her lips. "The woman had a party when Jack and Max were out of town on business, and she managed to scorch the kitchen cabinets with her drunken friends. Don't get me started on what she did to the furniture. My Max paid for everything." She reached across and touched my leg, and I nearly flinched at the unexpected contact. "Please don't hurt our Jack," she said imploringly.

What in the hell? "I would never hurt Jack." Or anyone, for that matter. But what she implied was that there might be something between me and Jack, and there absolutely wasn't. "We're just roommates," I emphasized.

Kitty sipped her wine, staring at me over the rim of her glass. "Jack has a reputation for dating his roommates. It's best you remain friends."

I nearly choked on my wine. "Jack is more like a brother than a guy I would date."

"But he's handsome, no?"

Was she setting me up or warning me away? "Jack is very good-looking," I said diplomatically. And it was true. But I meant what I said about only seeing Jack as a friend.

"Mom," came a deep voice from behind me, and this time I jerked so hard I nearly doused my white blouse in wine. "Gwen wants to talk to you about the gala."

I twisted around to find Max standing behind me, his towering height making me feel small and insignificant.

When the hell had he walked up?

His gaze dropped to my face, and the look in his eyes said he was not happy.

Had he heard me tell Kitty Jack was handsome? It would be just my luck he'd walk in on that part. I sighed, resigned. I should never have come to this landmine-filled party.

Kitty stood. "Yes, yes. So much to be done for the gala." She turned to me. "As one of San Francisco's first families, we're kept very busy." She smiled and sashayed away.

First family? It sounded like she was comparing herself to royalty.

Karl turned to me. "What is it you do for a living, Sophia?" I'd almost forgotten he was there. He was more of the silent type.

Max gulped his beer, hovering and generally unnerving me.

"I'm an interior designer who specializes in indoor greenspace."

Karl tipped his head back a notch, bemusement filling his features. "That's a profession?"

"Dad," Max warned.

I glanced up, startled. If I wasn't mistaken, Max had just called his father out over a rude comment.

It wasn't only my casual clothes that made me different from the others at this party. Even my profession didn't measure up.

I often worked with wealthy clients, but there was a hierarchy in those relationships that was mutually understood. I was the service provider, to whom they offered a modicum of respect in exchange for my expertise. But here, on this rooftop, with these people? I was an interloper pretending to fit in.

"There is a profession for indoor green design, yes," I said in response to Karl's comment, while rubbing out a smudge on my wineglass. "I consult with businesses on how to make their interiors more inviting through green décor without it looking overdone. I also consult on layouts for parties, weddings, and upscale shops. Green design is as important these days as outdoor landscaping."

"Interesting," Karl said and looked at his son. "I suppose I never thought about it before."

"When it's done well," Max said, "you wouldn't notice."

Max's head was turned away as though he were barely paying attention, but he was. He'd defended me a moment ago, and he'd just done it again.

"Is there upward mobility?" Karl asked.

I twisted my lips. "Not in the way you mean, with me conquering the world one plant at a time. But there is in the sense that I'd like to run my own green design business one day. We'd cover all levels of plant furnishings, from corporate to small shops to private homes, and even galas like the one Kitty mentioned earlier."

Karl raised an eyebrow. "Well, we certainly have people in our circle who could use that sort of service." He chuckled and stood, then elbowed his son. "Your mother lacks a green thumb, wouldn't you say, Max?"

Max gave his father a mild smile, but his posture remained stiff and closed off.

If I wanted to be a business owner someday, I couldn't let intimidation by Max's cold demeanor or my station in life hold me back. "I'd love to help in any way I can." I pulled out several business cards. They were new, with watercolor olive leaves and my name printed in script, and I was more than a little excited to share them. "Please pass my name along. Warming up a space with the right plants is what I love to do. The design shop I work for is full service, so we have specialists who come out to care for the plants as well."

Karl tucked the cards in his stone-blue sports jacket. "You're more ambitious than the last gal who rented from Jack, I'll say that much. Though I don't know why Max has strangers living in the building." He sent his son an apologetic look. "No offense."

I wasn't sure that was a raving endorsement of my person, but it seemed to be a compliment in Karl's eyes. What did I expect from the people in these upper echelons?

Max tipped his beer and took a sip, still looking out at the others. "There are many choices I make that you and Mom don't understand."

"True," Karl said, a note of censure in his tone. He glanced past Max. "Don't forget to spend time with Gwenny. She misses you, you know."

Max finally met his father's gaze. "I'd rather you not push that."

Karl held up his hands. "Just calling it like I see it. You two fit together."

I glanced over at Gwen. Karl was right—she was stunning, with dark-blonde hair that glimmered in the sun like a medallion. Max's dark to her light was a golden couple made in heaven.

If I stood next to Max—not that I ever would, but if I did—I'd look like his frumpy sidekick.

The best I could hope for in life was to work for a family like Max's. Which wasn't a bad thing. I wasn't interested in social climbing. I was interested in paying my rent and supporting my family. And if I could do that while working my dream job, all the better. My goal was to grow my clientele, and this was a good lead. Though the tension between Max and his dad said now might not be the best time to continue my pitch.

"Maybe I should let you two chat?" I said.

"No," Karl said. "I'll rescue Gwenny and Sue Getty from Kitty's party planning." He winked. "She doesn't stop once she gets going. It was nice to meet you, Sophia."

Karl strode to the group of men and women I hadn't yet met, and my body stiffened. Because now it was only me and Max. And I'd planned to avoid him. Instead, I'd somehow ended up spending my time with him and his parents.

After a prolonged pause, I glanced over to where he was standing, the silence killing me. "Well, this is awkward."

"I heard what you told my mom about Jack."

Max's comment was so sharp and abrupt that I had to rewind the conversation.

There was only one thing he could have objected to—the one thing I'd feared he might have overheard and misinterpreted.

He turned a steely gaze on me. "You told my mother how attractive you find Jack. He just got out of a toxic relationship, Sophia. Don't even think about using him or you'll regret it."

My jaw dropped, and I stared after him as he stormed away and joined the others.

Gwen maneuvered to his side and immediately looped her slim arm through his and glanced back. She shot me a cutting look before returning her attention to Max. Meanwhile his mother smiled beatifically at the two of them.

The Golden Couple.

My hands shook. Even if Max had given me a chance to

explain, it wouldn't have mattered. He *hated* me. To him and his parents, I was nothing but a ladder climber, just like the last girl who'd sublet from Jack.

Humiliation roiled through my gut right as the Blue Angel fighter jets shot by overhead at an impossibly low elevation, the boom of sound making my heart race.

Everyone at the party watched the jets do their formations in awe, but not Max. He turned and stared at me with murder in his eyes.

He didn't trust me around his family and friends, that much was clear. And that kind of mistrust hit a raw spot. I'd spent my life trying to please. This kind of censure was impossible for me to ignore. I wanted to crawl in a hole and hibernate for a year or two.

This living arrangement was never going to work. I couldn't share an apartment with Jack if Max was going to show up every other day, spewing venom my way. I wanted to love it here, and Jack was amazing. But Max and his family and circle of friends were something else.

My insides twisted, and my head grew woozy. For years I'd worked to build a better life for me and my sister, and even my mom when she would allow the help. But it didn't matter how hard I worked; it was never enough because *I* was never enough.

Even among people who didn't know my past, I was damaged goods.

Chapter Six

Sophia

THE NEXT AFTERNOON, MY SISTER ENTERED GREEN Aesthetic hauling a tote full of books over her shoulder. She was wearing jeans and an oversized UCSF sweatshirt, and her wavy brown hair was unbound.

Elise's hair defied nature and always looked like she'd just returned from a blowout. No one should have a good hair day *every* day. It was probably her most annoying quality, aside from the corn chip addiction that kept her slim and trim. I'd grow a second inner tube on a diet like that.

She looked toward the rear of the shop where I was working, and I waved her over.

Hugging her giant bag to her chest like a baby, she edged her way back, maneuvering around the plants and fancy containers on display.

She sank into the chair across from my desk and huffed out a heavy sigh, her tote slipping dramatically to the floor with a loud *thump*.

"Your day going that good?" I said, heavy on the irony.

43

She sat forward and rubbed her shoulder. "I spent the last two hours creating the mathematical formulas for regression analysis. My brain hurts. But forget about that. What's this about you moving?" Elise's critical look said she was totally on to me. "It took you months to find that place. Why would you give it up?"

I'd texted Elise last night that I was moving, but I'd done it right before bed so I wouldn't have to justify my reasoning, at least not right away. But now my time was up.

She leaned closer, probably reading the uncertainty in my expression. "Can I take your apartment now that you don't want it? Say the word and I'll move in tonight."

She was testing me. We both knew I'd confess the true reason I was moving, because I caved under heavy scrutiny.

I looked at the drawing in front of me and shaded in a tree, ignoring her for as long as possible. My designs were created with software, but I hand-drew mocks. "You can't afford it," I said, my lips twisting as I considered plant spacing and generally tried to not think about leaving Jack's apartment and returning to my mom's place.

Now that I'd had a night to sleep on it, I realized that no part of me wanted to move back home. Then I remembered how frequently I would be forced to see Landlord Devil and his first family friends if I stayed at Jack's.

Nope. Couldn't do it. I couldn't handle that kind of condemnation on a regular basis.

I smiled at Elise, trying to distract her. "How's the rest of school going?"

She rolled her eyes. "Brutal. And I'm referring to your comment about my finances, because that was harsh. True, but harsh. And school is painful right now. Not sure I'll be able to do this nursing gig. I'll never get through the math. Why does a nurse need statistics, anyway?"

I looked up and rattled off: "Mortality rates, infection rates, disease rates by population density—"

"How do you even know these things? You're an artist."

"There was a lot of math in business school." I twisted my mouth to the side. "Though I always seem to struggle with converting miles into kilometers, which is annoying as hell, since I have to do it every week."

Elise snorted. "We're not European. Why would you need to use kilometers?"

"Most countries use kilometers, Elise, and I work with international clients."

"When do you deal with foreigners?"

I shook my head in exasperation. "Only on a weekly basis. Do you ever pay attention when I tell you about my job?"

My criticism rolled right off her. "I zone out from time to time. You can blame it on the five hours of sleep I get during exams, which seems to be every other week."

I pulled out my bag and started packing up my work materials. I was going to be late if I didn't get a move on. "Well, the large events I plan are with people from all over the world, and it trips me up when they talk about kilometers and getting around the city." I held up my drawing before tucking it in a folder. "What do you think?"

Elise leaned in because she was farsighted and wasn't wearing her glasses. Her lips puckered. "What kind of shop is that?"

"A high-end beauty salon. They're going for a nature theme." My sister usually praised everything I worked on, but she was taking forever to give me her opinion on this one. Which had me wondering if it was crap.

I was about to reassess when she finally nodded. "If

that's a design for a salon, it's going to be the nicest one in town."

"Are you sure?" I scanned my work one last time. I couldn't add additional plants, but I could reposition them and put in more height in certain areas.

"I'm certain. They giving you gift certificates for all your hard work? Because I could use a facial."

I rolled my eyes. "It'll be nice when you're no longer a starving student. No, my clients aren't giving me gift certificates. They're doing this thing called payment for services rendered. Also known as capitalism."

Her rose-hued lips pulled into a straight line as though she disapproved. "What about tips for good work?"

"No tips. Quality is expected, or people hire someone else."

She threw up her hands. "And this is why I'm not studying business." She pulled off the hair band that was perpetually on her wrist and swept her hair into a low ponytail.

Elise's hair was a couple shades darker than mine, though my skin tone more closely resembled our father's Mediterranean heritage. So, essentially, my hair coloring was light brown next to tan skin—not much contrast there. I'd take Elise's blowout goddess hair in a heartbeat, but my pale-green eyes weren't so bad.

I glanced at my phone and tucked away the design. "I've got to go." There was just enough time for me to swing by my client's shop before it closed for the day. "I want to get this approved before I start on the digital renderings." I paused and watched Elise hoist her heavy tote onto her shoulder. "Regarding the apartment, my landlord—*owner*, whatever—is a dealbreaker. It won't work." Best to leave Elise with the short explanation and make a fast getaway.

Her expression was pure disbelief. "Are you kidding me? *That* is the reason you're moving? Because you think the hot landlord sucks?"

I stepped into a pair of heels I'd tucked under my desk and rooted around for some cash in my purse. "Don't give me a hard time. Landlords can make a place a living hell."

Her eyes narrowed. "Is he making it a living hell? Or are his hellish good looks distracting you?"

I squinted in disbelief. "What is wrong with you? Not everyone obsesses over looks." I had exactly one minute to catch a ride to my client's store if I wanted to make it there by closing. So I opted for blunt, knowing I'd pay for it later. "Landlord Devil doesn't trust me, and he's made that very clear. Not to mention he's rude and arrogant, and he gets on my nerves."

Elise tipped her head back and groaned, and her tote slid down her arm like an anchor. "You are so exhausting sometimes, you know that? Who cares what he thinks? I can understand why it wouldn't make sense for me to come over as often as we'd planned, but to move out? Have you lost your mind, Sophia?"

Possibly. All I knew was that the animosity I felt around Max was too much to bear. "He lives above me. I can feel his negative energy seeping through the drywall and down into my bedroom." I shivered. "And he has uptight friends and family—except for my roommate, who is awesome. But the rest of them stress me out too." I tried to shove cash into her hands, but she swatted me away. I let out a sigh and looked her in the eye. "The pressure to please uptight people will kill me. Now, take this cash so you can get yourself a proper book bag."

A touch of anger flared in her eyes. "I don't need a new

book bag. And have you ever considered *not* trying to please everyone?"

I shook my head dramatically. "Does not compute." I was a sad case, but my sister knew this, and she still loved me. "I'm going to start looking for an apartment tonight."

Elise slammed her hand on my desk, and I jumped.

I glanced around and said, "What the hell, Elise! We're at my work."

"Forget the landlord. Why do you do this, Sophia? Do you remember when Mom started collecting newspapers? You threw up for a month due to stress."

"That was a special situation," I said. "Mom had blocked the windows. I had vitamin D deficiency." I tried to shove the cash into my sister's bag, but she darted athletically to the side.

"You know that's not why you were ill," she pointed out. "You took it upon yourself to prevent wayward newspapers from reaching Mom's hands so she couldn't add to the piles. Good thing people stopped getting delivery around that time." Her expression softened, and she touched my arm. "The point is, I've had to deal with Mom's neuroses too, and you don't see me overcompensating."

"Because you have me to take care of everything." I regretted the words as soon as they left my mouth.

I never wanted my sister to feel bad that I'd taken on an adult role at a young age when it came to finances and other responsibilities around the house. It wasn't Elise's fault. And if our mother could have been different, she would have.

Elise blinked, then looked away. "I depended on you when I couldn't depend on Mom because I was young." She looked me squarely in the eye. "But I'm a grown woman now."

She was right. I knew this, and yet it was hard to let go without worrying everything would fall apart. "You're a *young* grown woman."

"Twenty-three, to be exact. Four years younger than you, Sophia, and you've been caring for me the last twelve years, so what does that say about you? *You* are young, and you should be taking it easy and not carrying all the responsibility. I don't have much money, but there's something called student loans. Not sure if you've heard of them?"

I straightened my skirt and sighed, agitated at the direction this conversation was going. "So you can live with debt for the rest of your life? No."

"You graduated with debt. *And* pay Mom's mortgage plus what you owe for school. You can't afford my expenses on top of your own, which is why you're sharing an apartment with a guy you just met, and why I've taken out student loans."

There went the knot tightening in my stomach. "I never wanted you to take out those loans to begin with. At the very least, don't take out any more. I'm moving home, and you won't need loans because I can use the rent money I'll be saving for your tuition."

Elise shook her head slowly and stared. "You're super annoying. You missed the entire point."

I did see her point; I really did. But it went against everything inside me to not protect my sister.

I glanced at my phone. "Let's talk later. I really do have to go."

Elise roped the thirty-pound tote onto her shoulder. "I don't need your money, so don't move back home for me." She leaned over and kissed me on the cheek. "Okay?"

I glared at the bag. "What about a backpack?"

"Oh my God!" she said as she hurried out of the shop. "You're doing it again. Stop mothering me!"

I raced out behind Elise and punched in a request for a ride from the app. But it wasn't until later that I thought more about our conversation.

Elise *was* a grown woman, but I was used to taking care of her and didn't know how to stop.

Maybe I should learn.

Either way, moving home served two purposes: I could pay Elise's tuition, so she'd stop threatening to take on a second job or more loans, and it would relieve me of the stress of being around Landlord Devil.

I hated the idea of moving home. But living beneath the devil's roof was worse. My mom's house was a lot to handle, but at least she meant well, and she loved me.

A person could put up with a lot when there was love involved.

Finding Jack's place had been a stroke of luck, but like most things that came easily, it had been too good to be true.

Chapter Seven

Sophia

I HELD THE RED BLOUSE TO MY CHEST, THEN SWITCHED it for the blue and huffed out a breath. What was I thinking, agreeing to this? I had no time for dating. I should be packing. Instead, I was going out with a stranger.

My boss, Victor, whom I'd grown close to these last several months, had been so excited to set me up with his son's friend that I couldn't say no. I mean, I could have said no, but I'd been wanting to meet new people and start dating again. At least now I could say my shallow ex-boyfriend wasn't the last guy I'd been out with.

After jamming my bare feet into fluffy slippers, I tucked my hair turban more securely on my head and shuffled down the hallway, holding up both blouses. "Which one?" I shook the offending tops in front of Jack, who was sitting on the couch.

He looked up from the soccer game and squinted. "What? Oh, um, the blue. No—red. Go with the red."

"Are you sure?"

"Hell no, but you needed someone to make a decision."

True fact. I'd turned to race back to my bedroom when a knock sounded at the front door, and I froze.

I looked over at Jack. "Crap!"

He set the remote on the coffee table and stood. "Your date picking you up?" he said, heading for the front door.

"No." And thank goodness. I'd told my boss I would meet this guy at the restaurant. But his showing up here wasn't what had me panicked. I was experiencing flashbacks of Landlord Devil showing up unannounced. I had that kind of timing when it came to him: my house in disarray, running into him punishing his ex, you get the picture. I'd avoided him over the last couple of days, and I wanted it to stay that way until I was gone.

I hid inside the hallway, and Jack opened the front door.

"Hi, I'm Elise," I heard my sister say.

She entered the house, smiling cheerily. Her hair was swept forward over one shoulder like a dark curtain, and her chest rose and fell as though she'd run up the stairs to our apartment. She dumped her book bag by the entry.

Jack tracked her movements with a steely, non-brotherly stare, which I did not appreciate. "You're the sister?"

"The one and only." She winked. "I'm sure Sophia's mentioned how awesome I am."

That girl had zero arrogance. None.

Jack scratched his jaw, seemingly perplexed. "Not exactly."

When the silence drew out, I called, "Back here."

Jack looked over, and I widened my eyes, lips compressed, sending him what I hoped was an eyeball death threat, because he was a little too focused on my pretty baby sister.

He held up his hands, acknowledging my unspoken words, and headed for the couch.

I liked Jack. He was a good guy. But he was fresh out of a bad relationship and still licking his wounds. People in pain didn't make the best partners.

Elise crossed to the hallway where I was huddled. "You look ready," she said dryly.

I tore off the towel turban and raced into my bedroom. "I'm going to be late. Why are you here?"

"Because you texted me and told me you had a blind date." She followed me into the bedroom and closed the door behind us. "You're probably seconds away from calling and canceling."

"Rude," I said and tossed the blue blouse on my bed before slipping on the red. I wasn't about to share how I'd thought about it multiple times. "I might have forgotten how to date. Or talk to men. This is going to be a disaster."

Elise gave me a sharp look. "You can't back out. And not because Victor set you up. He adores you and wouldn't hold it against you. You can't back out because I think you need a conversation with a man who isn't a client or your boss."

"I have a male roommate. We converse. He even helped me choose this top tonight."

She nodded in appreciation. "Baby steps."

I hopped on one leg and pulled on a pair of slim black pants. "I don't know why I'm even bothering to date. It will end up exactly how things did with Paul." I was being a Debbie Downer after I'd convinced myself this was the right thing to do, but when you know, you know.

Elise shook her head. "Very fatalistic of you. Paul was an ass. I could see his insecurities from a mile away."

I reached for a pair of nude heels on the top shelf of my

closet. "Well, I couldn't. Which means I shouldn't date until I can spot the bad apples."

Elise picked up the relaxation candle I'd bought off Polk Street this week and sniffed. She scrunched her nose and set it down, elucidating my ass-poor taste in—well, everything, apparently. "You doubt yourself, and that's why you can't figure out men's motives."

I threw up my hands. "I shouldn't need to figure out their motives. It should be apparent. And anyway, Paul didn't have any hidden interests when we met. He liked me; he was just shallow and scared of his parents."

Elise made a sound of disgust. "A man who can't speak for himself is extremely unattractive. You're better off without him."

"That's what people always say when you get dumped," I pointed out.

I'd cared about Paul, but when I looked back, there had been red flags, especially when it came to his family. He'd taken me out and I'd met his friends, but never his parents. I should have seen the signs. Now it was hard for me to trust anyone, including myself.

Elise sat on the bed and patted the mattress. "I'll do your makeup. You don't play up your eyes enough."

I sat obediently and blindly transferred essential items to a small black purse while my sister worked on my eyes. Deep down, I desired a relationship. And going on a blind date through a trusted source was better than giving my number to a stranger at a bar or connecting through a dating app.

She squeezed my cheeks, holding my head in place. "Quit moving. Unless you want winged eyeliner?" She quirked her brow suggestively.

"I'll stick with the natural look, thank you." I waited patiently while she beautified me.

"Almost done?" I asked after a few minutes. But when I opened my eyes, she was staring, a light smile on her face.

"I'm proud of you," she said and tucked the eyeliner pencil back into the makeup bag. "I know you're scared to date, but it can't hurt to have more friends in your life, right?" She considered me thoughtfully for a beat. "At the very least, this guy could become a friend."

I'd had casual friends over the years, but no one who was a constant. My sister was my best friend. "Sure."

"Now, where's your pepper spray?" Elise said, swiveling her head dramatically and looking around my room.

I dropped my jaw. "You just told me tonight would be fine!"

Elise laughed. "I'm teasing. Victor is more protective than I am. He wouldn't send you into the arms of a psycho."

"As if you can tell by just looking whether or not someone is a psycho." I glanced in the mirror across from my bed and frowned. "I said *natural*. This is more makeup than I normally wear."

"You normally wear almost no makeup, so yes, this would be more. Your eyes are beautiful, and you don't play them up enough. You should wear makeup like this every day."

I stood and grabbed my purse. "That would require an extra five minutes of getting ready time in the morning, and you know I need my sleep." I checked my phone. "I better go, or this guy will be waiting."

Elise shot me a look of frustration as we made our way down the hallway. "It's okay to be late, Soph. Part of your problem with Paul was that you took on the burden of everything, including making sure he was never put out. It's okay for a man to be put out. The ones who stick around despite it are the ones you keep."

Sometimes Elise was wiser than her years. "I'm working on it, okay?"

Elise and I looked up at the same time the faint sound of voices came from the living room.

A sinking feeling came over me as my heels clacked on the hardwood floor, with Elise walking quietly beside me in sneakers. The sound of the voices grew louder. More distinct, male, and familiar.

Jack stood abruptly from his place on the couch the moment Elise and I entered the room, his gaze on her before moving sharply away.

I caught that look of interest, but it wasn't enough to distract me from the other person taking up the space.

Jack muted the TV and made his way to the kitchen. "Max, this is Elise, Sophia's sister."

Elise smiled and greeted Max while the tension in my belly grew. Why did my roommate have to be best friends with this man? If Max were only the landlord, I might be able to avoid him. There'd be no reason to move.

Somehow, I knew Max Burrows would show up tonight —the first time I'd been out on a date in a year. As though he sensed my vulnerability and sought to capitalize on the moment.

Max nodded a greeting at Elise, then slowly swept his gaze over me and my outfit. "Going somewhere?"

"She has a date," Elise said brightly, and nudged me with her elbow.

My face heated. Why the hell was I embarrassed? I was twenty-seven years old, almost twenty-eight. I should be going on dates every weekend. It was only because I was a workaholic wounded animal after my last relationship that I'd failed to master that twenty-something rule. "I should get going." I glanced at Elise.

"Oh, yeah, me too," she said.

"You sure?" Jack said, carrying beers from the fridge. "You're welcome to join us. We're about to stream a movie."

Elise gave a noncommittal shrug. "I don't have any plans, but I don't want to interfere in your man time."

In answer, Jack handed her a massive bowl of popcorn and the beer he'd brought over for himself, and then walked into the kitchen and grabbed another.

Elise sank onto the light-beige feather and down sofa, the kind you can't get up from. Not only because it was super soft, but also, why leave a cloud?

She started munching popcorn. "What are we streaming?"

What was going on? My sister was hanging out with my roommate and Landlord Devil, the man I was trying to escape? And why was it only me Max hated?

"Your date picking you up?" Max's low voice skated over my skin like a sensual touch.

Damn this man and his beauty. Even though he loathed me, his words sounded like a caress, causing butterflies to riot in my belly against my will.

I pulled my purse higher on my shoulder. "No, I'm meeting him. I'll see you all later," I said to the room.

"Have fun!" Elise called, beer and popcorn in hand, sitting in what would have been the space between Max and Jack on the couch. If Max were seated.

Instead, Max just stood there, watching me with a steady gaze, his expression the tiniest bit nervous.

I scurried out the front door and paused to catch my breath. Nerves and something I couldn't identify thrummed through my veins. This night was weird. Why wasn't Max making rude comments? Because his friend was there to hear? Because he couldn't come up with anything cutting?

I pinched my brow. And why was I thinking about Max Burrows when I had a date to meet?

Chapter Eight

Sophia

I RETURNED TO MY APARTMENT LATER THAT NIGHT, expecting the house to be quiet, as it was nearing midnight. Instead, my sister, Jack, and Max were still sitting in the living room, and the atmosphere was tense. And this time, the tension wasn't coming from Landlord Devil.

At first, no one seemed to pay me any attention, and that worked, because I was disappointed in myself and how the date went. But then I caught the dynamic going on in the living room, and I stilled.

Elise was sitting with her back to Max, facing Jack, her jaw shifting back and forth like she was an inch away from exploding, and it took me aback. She wasn't the type to get riled up unless it was with me. "How can you defend him!" she said. "He was such a jerk."

Jack scratched the back of his head and stood, his mouth parting in a wide yawn. "The guy had been cheated on and dumped by his fiancée. He had reasons."

Max caught my eye as I stood near the entrance and

scanned me as though to make sure I was all in one piece. He rose and said, "I'm taking off."

Had he been waiting for me?

I gave my head a mental shake. Max hated me; of course he hadn't been waiting. He was probably hoping someone would take over babysitting duties for my sister and his best friend.

I set my purse on the counter and watched Max stride to the front door and shoot me one last lingering glance before slipping out like a thief in the night.

"Elise?" I approached the living room. "You okay?"

My sister didn't acknowledge me. In the next instant, anger filled her expression and she grabbed a pillow from the couch and threw it, nearly hitting Jack in the face. My jaw dropped.

Jack tilted his head to the side. "Did you just hit me?"

Elise glared. "If I had wanted to hit you, I would have."

I stepped between the two of them. "What's going on?"

Elise glanced up. "When did you get here?"

"Just now. I said your name, but you were too busy hating on Jack to hear me."

Elise blinked, then stood. "We're not fighting."

Jack snorted, then picked up the dishes and empty beer bottles from the coffee table. He made his way into the kitchen.

I stared at my sister. "What do you mean, you're not fighting? You just threw something at my roommate. How is that not fighting?"

Elise walked around me toward the front door, avoiding my eyes. "I should get going."

"Elise Marie, don't you dare leave without talking to me."

She grabbed her book bag from next to the door and then paused. "How was your date?"

That was a smart move, turning the focus on me. "It was fine."

Jack stopped what he was doing and leaned against the counter. "Define fine."

I was tired, and it was two against one. Tomorrow, I'd force Elise into telling me what the hell was going on between her and my roommate. "He was a nice guy," I said and reached for the nearest tea mug I'd left out. This one said, *It's too peopley outside*. I took a sip and winced. The tea was ice cold, of course, but I needed a distraction. Why the hell had I thought I was ready to start dating?

Jack looked at Elise, and they exchanged some sort of silent communication. Which was super annoying. Hadn't they just been yelling at each other?

I walked into the kitchen and hunted for the chocolate truffles I kept on hand in times of duress. Like when I went on a blind date and didn't know how I felt about it. Only the chocolate wasn't where I'd left it, in the cupboard above the cutlery. And neither was the craft chocolate I'd bought in Noe Valley last week.

What the hell?

Jack was a salty guy, hence his pilfering of popcorn when he had the munchies. And my sister had never understood my chocolate obsession, so she wasn't likely to have cleaned me out. "Have you guys seen my chocolate? I swear I put it here."

Jack set the bottles in the recycling bin. "Not a chocolate person. But Max was rooting around in the cabinets earlier. He might have grabbed some."

My face heated and my molars clamped together so

hard they made an audible *clack*. Chocolate was my one freaking indulgence...and *that asshat* took it?

Did he have a death wish?

"That man has a death wish," Elise muttered, reading my face. She opened the front door. "I'm taking off. I'll call you tomorrow for date details, Soph."

I cringed. "Do we need to have that conversation?"

"Yes," she said pointedly, and closed the door behind her.

Jack stopped what he was doing, his eyes widening. "Oh, wow. Sorry about the chocolate. What kind was it?" He pulled out his phone. "I'll order you more right now."

"No." I waved him off. "It's no big deal."

Lies. It was a big freaking deal! Those truffles were exported from a French chocolatier in Vancouver and cost the equivalent of a venti mocha apiece, hence the reason I saved them for special occasions only. And it grated that Max, of all people, had eaten not just one, not two, but all six.

The low hum in my head was taking on jackhammer decibels. *I will not kill Max Burrows. I will not kill Max Burrows.*

Jack grabbed a handful of cashews from a bowl he'd brought into the kitchen and tossed one in the air, catching it in his mouth. "Max is used to helping himself to my food." His expression turned abashed. "Sorry about that. I didn't know the chocolate was off-limits. I'll reimburse you. Actually, I'm headed to Trader Joe's this week and can grab some more."

I swallowed and tried not to gag. "Trader Joe's? For chocolate?

"It's not the same?"

"No," I said. "But don't worry. I was getting low on my

stash. I'll pick up more tomorrow." I wouldn't be living here much longer anyway. There was no reason to put Jack out because of Landlord Devil's rude, chocolate-grubbing thievery.

"Here." He fished into his navy sweatpants, pulled out a leather wallet, and handed me a twenty-dollar bill. "Is that enough?"

Not at all, I thought. But no way was I going to admit how much I spent on chocolate.

Some women loved shoes. Gourmet chocolate was my vice and where my extra paycheck went. Along with the fancy anxiety candles, expensive chocolates were by far the most luxurious thing I allowed myself. "Don't worry about it." It wasn't Jack's fault his best friend had no respect for food property.

I heated some water, grabbed a chamomile tea bag, and was about to go sulk in my room when Jack touched my shoulder and handed me the twenty.

"For when you go shopping again. Also, you never finished telling how your date went. You think you'll go out with the guy again?"

I stepped out of my heels and picked them up, considering how to keep it vague. "He was nice and kind of cute, but I'm not a good judge of character."

Jack shrugged. "No one is until they get to know someone, and you just met him. Give it time."

My date really had been nice. And he was cute. He worked in the Financial District, which I didn't hold against him. And he'd dressed in slacks and a sports coat for our date, so he'd put effort into it. He'd also pulled out my chair for me at the restaurant and paid for dinner even though I'd offered to split. We'd talked about our respective jobs, and he didn't look at me like I was crazy for spending my time arranging plants, which earned him bonus points. All in all, the evening had been pleasant, and if the guy asked me out again, I wouldn't mind.

But that wasn't the problem.

The problem was I'd found myself comparing him to Max Burrows—more than once!—and that had me wanting to bash my head against the wall.

Why Max? Why?

When my date smiled, there'd been no smirk, and somehow that seemed suspicious, like he wasn't revealing his true self. Because I'd grown used to an honest smirk, or better yet, a full frown from a man. Then later, when my date stood to walk me out of the restaurant, he hadn't tucked his hands in his slacks like a certain rich asshole, and somehow that was another strike against him. Because hands in pockets meant... I didn't even know!

Had I lost my mind? Was I attracted to jerks now? What the hell? And to make matters worse, the jerk in question had stolen my most prized possession while I was on my date.

I was livid. And needed to see a therapist. Or maybe I needed a swift knock to the head.

I let out a slow breath. I hadn't been on a date in over a year. It made sense that I was comparing the new person to the only male who'd occupied my thoughts lately, even if said thoughts were filled with rage.

Except that wasn't entirely true, because I'd been around Jack more than Max.

I bit my lip and closed my eyes. I had convinced myself to move out of Jack's because of this asshole. So why the hell was I comparing other men to him?

Chapter Nine

Max

THE DINNER PARTY MY PARENTS WERE HOSTING WAS packed with people I'd grown up around. All wealthy, and most fairly entitled, though some were cognizant of how the rest of the world lived.

I greeted familiar faces as I made my way to my mother, who did not fall in the *aware* category. But I loved her despite her shortcomings.

"Max," she said and squeezed my arm while peering across the room. "Doesn't Elizabeth look stunning?" A woman I'd known most of my life was walking toward us. I used to steal candy from the front pocket of her backpack when we were kids.

Lizzie looked a little different these days. She'd lightened her red hair to reddish blonde, and she'd replaced her glasses with contacts. Or maybe she'd gotten eye surgery? Either way, she was more polished now compared to our school days, but she still possessed the same mischievous smile I'd come to appreciate.

"Kitty," Lizzie said, and leaned in to peck my mother on the cheek. "How are you? And Max. I haven't seen you a decade. You almost look handsome now that you've grown into your ears."

I grinned. Lizzie had never cared that my family was rich. Perhaps because her own was filthy rich too. Instead, she ribbed me at every opportunity. "How are you doing, Lizzie? The East Coast treating you well?"

"I don't live on the East Coast anymore, Maxwell, and you would know that if you bothered to return my calls."

I chuckled. "Apologies. I'm not a good phone person."

"Or a good text person, or an email person." She shook her head. "You're a tremendously annoying friend, you know that?"

"In fact, I do. Jack tells me on a regular basis."

My mother sent Lizzie a look of approval. "I'm glad you're here, Elizabeth. Someone needs to put my son in his place. You two catch up." She gave Lizzie's shoulder a squeeze. "Don't be a stranger," she said and walked off, waving to someone across the large foyer.

My parents' foyer was one of the grandest in town, with a four-story domed ceiling painted by the artist William Hahn in a one-of-a-kind San Francisco street scene. Most of the parties began and stayed in here until dinner was served.

I glanced around to see if my father's investors had shown.

Lizzie sent me a side-eye. "You don't deserve Jack for a best friend," she said thoughtfully.

"This is true." I lifted my champagne glass in a mock toast. "I'll be better about keeping in touch. I've missed you. Forgive me?"

She rolled her eyes. "I'm immune to your charm, Burrows. Just pick up my calls, dammit."

Lizzie was the only female who gave me a hard time, and I always deserved it.

But maybe not the only person. These days, Jack's new roommate was especially triggering.

Something about Sophia had set me off from the beginning, and I couldn't explain it. My adrenaline kicked in when she entered the room, her pert little mouth taunting me. I'd initially thought Sophia had designs on Jack, which had my hackles up. My best friend had been screwed over by his last roommate/girlfriend. Then Sophia went on a date with another man last night and shredded every theory I had about her.

Sophia wasn't interested in Jack—it only took me a week or more to figure that one out. Instead, there seemed to be something going on between Jack and Sophia's sister.

I'd been wrong all around, and now I was mentally cringing, thinking back to the occasions I'd been an ass to Sophia, believing her to be someone she was not.

What could I say? I was protective of the people I cared about.

But that wasn't the worst part. Normally, Sophia's deplorable wardrobe and frazzled hair did nothing to recommend her. Offhand, I'd say she wasn't my type. Particularly in the beginning, when I thought I'd seen beneath the veneer of a beautiful smile and suspected her of a secret interest in my friend. Then later, of trying to grow her business by using my family and friend connections.

Only she hadn't looked frazzled last night. She'd been composed and beautiful, and it nearly sent me into a panic. Watching her walk out the door to meet another man made my skin itch and my heart race.

I'd been wrong about her when it came to Jack, and I might have overreacted to her conversation with my father.

I might have also underestimated my interest in her.

Lizzie nudged me in the rib. "Am I already boring you?"

I sent her a reassuring smile. "Never." I was spending far too much time thinking about the woman who shared Jack's apartment. "It's just been a busy week."

"Well, I might be able to help with the workload," Lizzie said. "I returned to San Francisco for a partner position at Johnson and Robe."

I nodded in appreciation. "The lawyers who handled the Emerson deal? Congratulations. They're a good group."

"I'm glad you think so, because I want you to hire us on retainer."

I looked over with mild surprise. "My company has had its legal battles, but a retainer isn't necessary."

"There's more to an attorney than lawsuits, and you know it. Contracts are numerous in real estate, and you need experts who have your back."

"Jack loves contracts. I usually throw anything unusual his way."

Her mouth twisted to the side in mock disappointment. "Abusing your best friend again, I see."

"He enjoys the abuse. Never seen anyone get more excited over legalese than Jack."

"Well, if Jack ever tires of doing pro bono work for his best friend, and you find you need an excellent team on your side, give me a call."

I wrapped my arm around her shoulders and squeezed. "It's good to have you back, Lizzie. And it's good to have a moral law firm at hand. Not that morality and lawyers go together."

She wiggled out of my grip and laughed. "You're the

worst, Maxwell. Call me when you need me. Or to hang out. I could use a Max-and-Jack beer fest."

And then she pulled a true Lizzie and caught me off guard with her next comment. Narrowing her gaze, she said, "I heard you broke things off with Gwen. How'd that go?"

I set my glass on the tray of a passing waiter instead of smashing it into a thousand pieces on the marbled floor. Gwen had always been determined, but she'd taken things too far. We weren't together anymore, not that she cared. "Gwen and I broke up several months ago. She's in denial."

Guests had started moving into the formal dining room, but a few of us were still milling about in the foyer. My head was beginning to pound. I was beyond frustrated with my parents' attempts at getting me and Gwen back together, and I'd stayed up way too late last night thinking about why Sophia had looked distraught when she returned from her date. Essentially, other than Lizzie moving home, the women in my life were a problem.

Lizzie's mouth twisted, and she looked off in the distance as though pondering. "We grew up together, but I never did like Gwen. You're too nice for someone so cold."

"I thought I was cold and didn't return calls?"

She nodded. "You're terrible at returning calls, but you're nothing like the ice maiden. She'd sell her firstborn child for a membership to Villa Taverna. Speaking of exclusive clubs, doesn't your mom have a membership there?"

That was a harsh characterization of Gwen, though after my parents' financial crisis and Gwen's reaction to it, Lizzie wasn't entirely wrong.

Not many people knew about my parents' money troubles, but I'd shared them with Gwen, and her response had been enlightening. She'd told me we should put our relationship on hold until we knew how society would react. I'd never shared the reason we broke up with my parents; they were paranoid about their financial losses as it was.

"My mother has a membership to Villa Taverna," I said to Lizzie, "but the roster is tight-knit. It's been decades since Gwen's family set down roots in San Francisco, but apparently that's not long enough, even with my mother's support." I tipped up my chin at an acquaintance across the foyer. "I suspect Gwen hasn't told her friends about the breakup because for now being tied to my parents is a boon. Her family are still considered newcomers, whereas my parents are at the top of the pecking order."

Lizzie shook her head. "This city is full of assholes. And of course Gwen didn't tell anyone you broke up. Why would she let go of Maxwell Burrows?"

I lifted an eyebrow. "You say that as though dating me is a good thing."

Lizzie made a disgusted sound in the back of her throat. "If you're into pain-in-the ass rich guys, then yes, it could be a good thing. However, not all of us are masochists." She shot me a comical look to show she was only half serious.

If I ever needed an ego lashing, I could pick up one of Lizzie's calls.

Her expression grew serious. "You weren't a good fit with Gwen, and I never understood why you were dating her to begin with."

"Not a good fit..." I considered that a moment. "You're the first person to think so."

My mother, and everyone else hobnobbing in the mansion tonight, had thought Gwen and I would get married, and they supported it.

As though her ears were burning, Kitty took that moment to look up. I loved my mom, but she was partially responsible for the reason this town believed Gwen and I were still together. Even my own mother wouldn't acknowledge it was over.

Never underestimate the influence of a mother hellbent on making a good match for her son.

With the moves of a linebacker, in her Jimmy Choo pumps and silver embroidered cocktail dress, my petite mother shouldered past Mr. and Mrs. Drake on her way to intercept me and Lizzie. "What are you two whispering about?"

"Just telling Lizzie here how much happier I am now that I'm single."

My mother frowned. "Said like a man who has everything. One day you'll wish you had the support of a good woman."

Gwen wasn't a bad person. But she was too caught up in appearances to genuinely love anyone. It was a casualty of wealth and power. "I don't plan to be single forever."

I'd thought I could spot a schemer from a mile away after my breakup with Gwen and Jack's horrendous relationship with his last roommate.

Now I wasn't so sure.

I'd been wrong about Sophia. And a part of me was uncharacteristically pleased about that.

Chapter Ten

Sophia

Elise opened the semi-walk-in closet inside my bedroom and studied the space. It was bigger than a reach in, but small in the sense than only one person could step inside at a time. Then again, any walk-in closet in San Francisco, where space was a rare commodity, was unheard of. "Did the white dresser come with the closet?"

"No," I said, puffing up my chest. "I bought it and put it together."

She looked over her shoulder. "You built this?"

"Don't act so shocked."

"Well, I am. You suck at building things." She eyed the dresser. "How long did it take you?"

I crossed my fingers behind my back. "An hour."

I may have taken care of things back home, but not without help. I had a phone and knew how to call in the professionals.

Elise sent me a disbelieving look.

"Fine," I said. "It might have taken closer to two hours to build."

She looked at me pityingly. "You realize that when you move, you won't be able to bring this with you, right?"

I glanced at the closet. "It'll fit through the doorway. Especially with the help of my loving sister."

"That's not what I'm talking about. It won't fit *at home*."

The breath whooshed from my lungs, and I stilled. I'd been so focused on moving forward, I'd forgotten what it would mean to move back.

My new furniture wouldn't fit at Mom's. Nothing would fit inside my family home, not even me.

I squeezed the top of my head, forcing back a headache. Moving backward didn't matter. And it didn't matter if the darn dresser fit. My aversion to hostile people who disapproved of me surpassed my reluctance to move into my mother's house. Mostly.

Part of this was my fault for caring so much what people thought, and part of this was Landlord Devil's fault for his attitude and subtle threats.

I joined my sister at the closet and started pulling the jeans and pants I'd carefully hung not long ago off the hangers and setting them in one of the boxes I hadn't gotten rid of. "I have no choice. Max has made it clear I'm not wanted here."

"He seemed fine last night. He even stuck around until you got home."

That *had* been a surprise. Though it likely had nothing to do with me. "To be your and Jack's referee! What was up with you two?"

Elise waved off my comment. "We disagreed about a reality show and men's motives. It was no big deal."

"No big deal? Elise, for a moment there, I thought you might come to blows."

She sank onto the bed, her gaze focused on the wall. "Maybe it's not such a bad idea for you to leave this apartment."

I sat beside Elise, shocked. She had been urging me to move out of Mom's for years. She was the last person to support my neurotic reason for moving back home.

She turned to me. "That Jack character is a massive jerk."

Now we were getting to the real issue. Enough of this relaxed attitude about me moving out.

Elise's face turned a reddish shade, and her hands clenched in her lap. "He had the balls to say that women are to blame for why men flip out."

My head jerked back. "Wait, what? That doesn't sound like Jack."

"And then he went on to praise some guy on the reality show for lashing out at a woman in order to protect his fragile male ego," she said, her voice rising.

I glanced at the door. "Keep it down. Jack is home, and he can hear you if you yell like that." My nose scrunched. "Are you sure you understood his meaning?"

She looked off, her lips pursed. "In so many words."

Which could mean anything. I waggled my head. "Okay, well, Jack is fragile right now. His last girlfriend did some pretty awful stuff."

Elise's face snapped up to mine. "Did you just defend him?"

I held up my hands. "Hell no. I hate it when women are blamed for men's bad behavior. But I understand why Jack might be sensitive right now."

"Doesn't justify his defense of a man being an asshole," she muttered.

"True. But there are reasons men behave the way they do, even if they're wrong."

Elise's eyes narrowed, and she studied my face. "What about the landlord? You willing to excuse his bad behavior because of life experiences?"

Fair point. "That's different. Max Burrows is a jerk, and Jack is a sweet guy."

"Jack is not sweet!"

I clamped my hand over her mouth, and we toppled onto the mattress. "What did I say? Stop yelling before I kick you out."

Elise sat up and smoothed her already flawless blowout hair. "You can't kick me out. You need me to help you move."

True fact. "Well, don't get me kicked out before I leave this place. I need it for a few more days. I won't be able to finish packing before the end of the weekend."

She eyed me critically. "You had all day and yesterday. It's your own fault for dragging it out. Unless you *wanted* to drag it out..."

"Excuse me for not being a machine. I was forced to go on a blind date—"

"No one forced you."

"—and now I'm behind."

The sound of the front door closing drifted back. Then came the sound of a familiar male voice.

My eye started twitching. "What the...?"

Elise perched her chin on her hand and grinned. "Hmm, sounds like your nemesis has returned to see his bestie." Her face twisted as though she'd eaten something bitter. "Are Max and Jack really best friends? Max is so tailored, and Jack is...unkempt."

"They're best friends," I said and stood, agitation making my body vibrate. "And Jack is a clean guy; he just dresses casually." I shot her a glare. "Not sure why you're pointing fingers, miss queen of sweatshirts."

Elise's mouth parted. "I'm a grad student and poor," she said, but I was already fading her out mentally.

Why was Max here?

How often did those two hang out? I was so right to break the lease.

Shit. *Breaking my lease.*

Would Jack and Max give me a hard time about leaving? They couldn't fault me for an emergency move-out, could they? Because getting out of Landlord Devil's orbit was an emergency. The way my brain had malfunctioned on my date, it wasn't healthy to have Max in my life.

I took a deep breath. "Come on. I'm going to ask Jack to break my lease, and for Max to give me my deposit back."

Elise winked, and the corner of her mouth turned up. "Ballsy. And not like you at all. Are you sure you'll survive a confrontation?"

I grabbed her arm and pulled her up. "Support me for once, will you?"

She moved to the door in front of me and glanced over her shoulder. "As your buffer, you mean? I will, but I'm telling you, if that Jack character says anything the least bit misogynistic, I'm not holding back."

I tilted my head to the side. There was something seriously weird going on between Jack and Elise, but I couldn't worry about it right now. I had my own drama to deal with. "Just don't say anything that will make the situation worse."

Not that I trusted Elise with her hotheadedness, but she

was my only resource at the moment. And she was correct—I sucked at confrontation, so I wanted her there as a buffer.

We walked down the hallway, and the voices in the kitchen grew louder. The sound of the fridge opening and closing floated back. Along with cupboards closing. Jack was an eating machine. Then again, Max had been the one to deplete my chocolate stash, so both were a nuisance in the food department.

Thankfully, I'd had time this afternoon to run by my favorite Noe Valley chocolate shop. I used the twenty bucks Jack had given me and added another twenty to splurge on six more chocolate ganache truffles with gold filigree. Because I was worth it.

At the end of the hallway, Elise stopped abruptly, and I nearly ran into her back. "What's up?" I said, but she didn't answer.

I looked over her shoulder and into the kitchen—and started to hyperventilate.

Max was leaning against a cabinet, dressed in a navy-blue cashmere crew sweater and tan pants, his thick shoulders stretching the knit. His hair was combed back, with a natural wave in his dark locks, and his face looked clean-shaven. He was a damned magazine model. But that wasn't why my temperature rose and my heart sped up. Well, not the only reason. Not the important reason.

Maxwell Burrows reached back and popped another one of my new truffles into his mouth before licking his fingers in an altogether sexy and infuriating manner.

"I'm going to kill him," I said.

Something pushed me back. It took me a second to realize my sister was trying to shove me in the direction of my bedroom.

But I didn't care why I'd come out here, or what I

needed from Max regarding the lease. How dare that egocentric jerk eat my chocolate. Again!

Max looked up, caught sight of me pushing past my sister, and lifted one eyebrow. He watched me intently as I made my way toward the kitchen. Then he slowly reached back, grabbed another chocolate truffle, and popped it in his mouth, chewing it with a glint in his eyes.

He knows the chocolate is mine?

He was dead.

I stormed into the kitchen and pointed my finger in his face. "What kind of rich guy can't buy his own chocolate?"

Jack's head snapped up from inside the fridge. He looked at his friend, eyes narrowing on the open gourmet chocolate box. "Dammit, Max, those are Sophia's. Learn some manners." He closed the fridge and walked over, shaking his head. "Max is a rich guy who forgets he's wealthy. Sorry, Sophia. It's an old habit for him. He's been raiding my cupboards since middle school."

Ignoring Jack, I inched closer to Max until we were toe to toe.

Max, sorry? He didn't look sorry. His smirk had dropped, but his eyes were defiant cobalt orbs I wanted to jab with my finger.

"Can I help you?" Max said, as Jack wisely eased back and closer to my sister.

Elise snickered behind us, and I shot her a glare over my shoulder. She motioned zipping her mouth.

I turned back to the man who was about to become a eunuch. "What do you think you're doing?"

Landlord Devil extended his hand, holding the last truffle—he'd eaten all of them! "Want one?"

I breathed in, then slowly out, closing my eyes to

concentrate on my breathing and not strangling the six-foot-plus man in front of me.

While I attempted to calm myself, Max said, "I better get going, Jack. Catch you later."

My eyes popped open as Landlord Devil swiftly eased past me and sauntered to the front door, walking out while my mouth still hung open.

Elise approached. "Wow. I like him. He's good for you."

I squint-glared. "Have you lost your mind?"

"No," she said smugly. "It looks like you have this under control." Was she giggling? "I'll come by in a couple of days."

That jarred me from my anger stupor. "But I need your help now!"

"Bye!" she called as she ran out the door behind Max.

What in the hell was happening?

I turned to Jack, who was rummaging in his wallet. "I'm so sorry, Sophia. I should have warned him as soon as he came over. Here," he said, and shoved another twenty at me —fifty percent of the cost of the chocolates that the devil had consumed. "I promise to remind Max about the candy. I keep forgetting what a chocolate hog he is." He chuckled. "You guys are so much alike."

I nearly choked on my spit. Were Jack and Elise living in some alternate reality? "Alike?"

"He'll have to bring his own chocolate next time," Jack said, as though this were the solution to all my problems.

"Next time," I mumbled like a madwoman. "There won't be a next time," I said and stormed after Landlord Devil.

Chapter Eleven

Sophia

Before I could take the time to contemplate what I was doing, I marched to the top floor of the building and knocked on Maxwell Burrows' door. I also did more breathing exercises, because I was ready to kill him with my bare hands.

After a long pause, I heard the bolt shifting, and he answered the door, his eyes widening as though he were surprised to see me.

My mouth went dry, and my thoughts scattered. Max had changed out of his sweater and into jeans and a ratty T-shirt, and he'd done it in a hurry. His hair was sticking up in the back, as though he'd pulled the sweater over his head and hadn't time to smooth it into place. The T-shirt he now wore was so thin it hugged the muscles in his shoulders and chest, and the jeans hung low on his narrow hips. All of this combined to blow a fuse in my brain, because Max didn't look like his normal self.

He looked like the easygoing hot cousin.

His brow pinched, but it wasn't a scowl. More like a look of guarded perplexity. "For your information, my office already has a plant person."

My jaw clenched. In one fell swoop, he'd insulted my profession and accused me of soliciting. And nearly made me forget why I'd come.

Ignoring the hair sticking up that had him looking almost human, I said, "I'm not here to sell you something. I want out of my sublease, and I want my deposit back."

He leaned a shoulder against the doorjamb—and there was the scowl I'd expected. "Why?"

For some annoying reason, my face heated. "You take every opportunity to insult me, like now with the plant dig, and"—I paused, calming my breathing—"you're stealing my chocolate. The chocolate is the last straw. I work hard to afford those chocolates, and they don't belong in your grubby hands."

He blinked as though shocked. As though we hadn't been at each other's throats the last two weeks. Then his expression turned to ice, and he studied my face for a long heartbeat. "Jack could charge you for breaking the lease."

"He wouldn't do that." I didn't know Jack wouldn't do that, but I was banking on his being a decent guy.

Max's gaze narrowed. "I warned you not to use Jack just because he's a nice person."

"Yet not so nice last night with my sister, was he?" I imagined Jack was like any person licking their wounds after a breakup. But that didn't excuse the sexist crap toward Elise.

Max's gaze was hard and unfeeling for a long beat. "Fine. Consider the lease broken," he said and shut the door in my face.

———

A DAY after my lovely encounter with Max, he sent a brief message via Jack that my deposit check would arrive in a day or two since he "trusted me to move out by the weekend."

As easy as it had been for Max to usher me out, Jack wasn't so happy. "What is Max talking about? You just moved in."

I watered the outdoor plants I'd bought from my boss at a discount for the apartment niche between our two bedrooms. It was too small for a courtyard but let in light and was the perfect spot for greenery. I'd never had space at Mom's for plants. It had been a pure luxury to have it here.

I'd questioned myself multiple times this morning about what the hell I thought I was doing moving out of this apartment. Then I remembered Max slamming the door in my face, and my hesitation evaporated. "It has nothing to do with you," I told Jack.

I'd been putting off telling him about the move because of how much I liked him. But my time was up.

"Is it because of Max?" he asked.

I tested the soil moisture of one of the plants with my finger, avoiding the question.

"Because if so," Jack said, "give him a chance. He comes across wound up at first, but he'll calm down. He really is a great guy."

I snipped off a dead leaf a little too violently. "I'll have to take your word for that." I felt bad doing this to Jack last minute, but it was the right thing.

He sighed. "Sophia, I'll leave the lease available for the next couple of weeks. Please take some time to reconsider.

If you do, I promise I'll put a lock and bolt on your chocolate so Max can't get to it." He scrubbed a hand down the back of his head and mumbled, "Max and his sweet tooth."

But it wasn't just the chocolate. It was every word Max uttered, every accusation.

I stood and gave Jack a light smile. "That's very kind, but you don't need to hold the lease. Let's grab a drink after I get resettled. I'll be your wing woman the next time you go out."

He chuckled. "I probably could use that. Speaking of progress in the romance department, have you heard from your date?"

I slammed the heel of my palm to my forehead. "Shit. I forgot to return his call."

I'd been so distraught over the idea of moving out that I hadn't thought about the guy Victor had set me up with, even though he'd called for a second date. I couldn't get over the fact I'd compared him to the devil upstairs, and now whenever I thought of my date, I thought of Max Burrows. It wasn't helping my mental state.

Jack laid a brotherly hand on my shoulder. "Either way, I'm available for wingman duties too." His gaze wandered off. "I could use the distraction."

That was cryptic, but it wasn't like I was making sense these days either. It was insane to move from this place, but I couldn't get over the strain of living beneath Max.

I swung by Mom's the next afternoon after work to assess the situation at home, taking in the two-story Mediterranean revival. It stood out even though the houses in our neighborhood were nearly identical.

Right before my father died, he'd hired workers to repaint the exterior a pale tangerine my mom had chosen.

The old place had been this warm shade of sunset, but now the chips and cracks in the orange revealed a gray subsurface and discoloration from dust and dirt. And then there was the white garage door that had never quite hung right—or really, ever been white. The color was a sallow yellow now, and mud-splotched. But my mom refused to repaint the house. She refused a lot of things, and Elise and I had stopped asking.

A shiver ran up my spine. It felt like a year had passed since I'd been home, not less than a month. I was backsliding, and the only way I could justify it was to tell myself it was temporary.

I knocked so as not to surprise Mom, then pulled out my key and opened the front door. My leaving had caused a massive anxiety crisis for my mom that lasted a solid week. After I moved in with Jack, she'd often sounded agitated over the phone. I wasn't sure what I was in for, and sometimes diving in was easier than dragging it out with a preemptive phone call.

The first thing that hit me when I stepped over the threshold was the smell. Familiar and unwanted, a mixture of dust, mold, and something sweet I could never quite identify. Elise and I had gone to great pains to wash our clothes every week (especially the items hanging in the closet), so the fabric wouldn't absorb the odor and make us smell when we went out. Whatever nostalgia I'd had for this place had faded a decade ago. Now the smell was like a gut punch that caused an immediate spike of adrenaline and my instinct to flee.

The space that made up the living room and dining area looked exactly the same. I wasn't sure why I'd hoped my moving out would make a difference. As though fewer people in the house might change things. But if I'd taken a picture the day I left and compared it to now, there'd be no difference. The same newspaper, with an image of a New Year's Day parade from twelve years ago, dangled precariously at the top of a ceiling-high pile of papers, magazines, and more newspapers. I was terrified to move too close to that particular stack for fear of being buried beneath it.

Several other tall stacks of mail and paper covered an ancient couch I hadn't sat on in about fifteen years. There were cardboard boxes, an ugly old table lamp with a brown stain on the once-cream shade, and anything and everything you could imagine creating mountains of junk in the living and dining rooms.

Thank God Mom threw out food waste. Some hoarders didn't.

My mother walked out of the kitchen, holding a ratty towel but looking neat as a pin in an outdated skirt and top she'd been wearing for as long as I could remember.

Her face lit up. "Sophia! What are you doing here? You didn't tell me you were coming. I would have straightened up." She looked nervously in the direction of my bedroom.

Other than the tea mugs I sometimes misplaced, I needed things orderly, or it gave me anxiety. I'd made a deal with Mom when I was in high school that my bedroom was off-limits. Other than taking up half my closet with clothes she never wore but refused to get rid of, she'd kept up her part of the bargain. But all bets were off once I moved out. I'd been gone less than three weeks, but it seemed that was enough time for my mom to have taken over my bedroom, given the look she'd just sent me.

"Is it okay if I move back?" The words came out sluggish, as though stuck to the roof of my mouth. This wasn't what I wanted, but I had no other option at the moment.

"The place I found isn't working out, and I need somewhere to sleep while I search for something new."

Her eyes widened in either excitement or surprise—it was unclear what went through my mom's head when it came to her house. And then her forehead smoothed. "Of course, honey. This will always be your home. Though"—she looked behind her again—"your room might need tidying."

I stepped closer and gave my mom a hug. "I know, Mom. Is there anything I can box up?" I'd stopped asking to get rid of things a long time ago, because it stressed Mom out and made her angry any time Elise and I brought up the notion.

Skimming her eyes over the living room and past an old exercise bike precariously holding clothing that had never been worn—the tags still on them—she seemed to search for something. A second later, she moved off the narrow path of bare rug and climbed on top of a pile of clothes—the only way to enter the living room.

My mom leaned down and lifted a half-full plastic container she'd magically spotted amongst the clutter. "This one still has space," she said happily, and maneuvered her way back. "Go ahead and put anything you want out of your room inside here."

Meaning I could place items she'd recently stashed in my old bedroom inside the plastic box, but she wasn't getting rid of them. She hadn't been able to get rid of anything since Dad died over fifteen years ago, and she routinely collected more, much to my and Elise's dismay. "Sure, Mom."

My mom returned to the kitchen with her dishrag, and I made my way down the narrow, darkened hallway, with books and clothes and plastic knickknacks shoved up against the walls, to my bedroom.

Before I opened the door, I mentally prepared myself. It had been spotless when I left, but that wouldn't be the case now.

At first, the door wouldn't budge. I shoved a little harder to get it to open and then stepped inside, but really that meant climbing over the top of a low mountain of clothes.

I was numb. I always felt hopeful that things would be different and then straight numb when they weren't. The floor was covered not only with clothes but also boxes and papers. An old toaster peeked out of one of the boxes in the corner, and travel toiletries and plastic pill containers spilled out of another. Two dozen cheap vases were stacked against a wall, and a scratched-up wooden hope chest I'd never seen was covered with lamps and other items.

Tears burned my eyes, and I set the plastic container on top of a clothing pile, hitching my workbag higher on my shoulder. My mom picked up things off the street and through social media, but it boggled the mind the sheer volume she could collect in a short time. Was she getting worse?

Every time I saw evidence of my sweet mother's mental illness, it was like being swamped by an ocean wave, powerful and impossible to fight.

There was no point in trying to pack today. I needed at least twenty boxes to clear everything out, not a half-full plastic container.

Absently, I heard the doorbell ring.

"I'll get it," my mom called, her voice carrying over the din of noise echoing inside my head.

Still pondering my dilemma, I thought nothing of

someone coming to the house—until I heard the deep, liquid voice of a man.

I stumbled over clothes, knocked into a box, and nearly sprained my neck as I swung my head around the corner of my bedroom doorway to peer down the hall, giving myself a moment of vertigo.

Max Burrows...was inside my mother's hoarder house?

Chapter Twelve

Sophia

GROWING UP, I RARELY INVITED FRIENDS TO MY HOUSE. On the few occasions I did, before I knew better, those kids either said horrible things about me at school or ghosted me, or both. Either way, I lost whatever connections I had outside the home.

Max Burrows wasn't like the friends who discovered my secret. He wasn't a part of the middle class, so even if I'd grown up in a typical middle-income home, that wouldn't have been normal to him because he mingled among the elite. He hadn't liked my pink panties dangling off the couch or my mugs—or pretty much anything about me, and that was before he'd seen the worst of it.

I kicked a blown-up exercise ball in the hall out of the way and scurried to where Max stood, my heart racing. "What are you doing here?"

I attempted to shove him back out the door, but the darn man wouldn't budge, not even when I was inches away and glaring at him.

He smiled at my mother, then spared me a glance. And that was when I realized how close I was and that I still had my hands on him.

Leave it to Landlord Devil to have a firm body beneath the buttoned-up exterior. I dropped my hands and stepped back.

"I came to give you this," he said, and handed me an envelope. He was wearing a suit, per usual, this one a subtle gray plaid with a zippy charcoal tie, and he appeared polite, revealing nothing of his thoughts.

Which I had to give him credit for, because my childhood friends had never waited until they were out the door before they said exactly what they thought about the house.

"This is the address on your lease application," he said. "I was on my way to an appointment and thought I'd drop off your deposit check."

———

Max

"Can I get you something to drink?" the older woman, presumably Sophia's mother, asked. She'd also been the one to answer the door.

"No, Mom." Sophia grabbed my arm with a firm grip for someone so small. "Max was just leaving."

"I'd love a glass of water." I smiled, and Sophia frowned. She was cute when she was angry. Cute at other times too, but especially when I'd riled her up. She didn't seem the type to anger easily, and I took special pleasure in arousing it in her.

"I'll be just a moment," her mother said and hurried off into what looked like a kitchen. Difficult to tell, as the room was full of disparate items. Was that a dog kennel on the counter? I hadn't seen any dogs or cats. Though I'd seen a lot of other things wrong with the picture.

The home Sophia's mother lived in was extremely cluttered, to put it mildly. There was very little space in which to walk and a distinctly unpleasant odor.

I glanced at the small hand on my arm, tightened in a death grip and attempting to tug me back the way I'd come. "You need to leave," Sophia said in a low voice. "My mom isn't well."

It was clear there was an issue with the house, quite possibly from a habit of the mother's, but Sophia's mom seemed like a warm person and in possession of her faculties. "I'm good."

Sophia's lips compressed, and her fair eyes glowed with anger.

If looks could kill, I'd be dead right now.

Her mom reappeared a second later, carefully holding a glass with sunflower decals along the top edge. "Here you go," she said, handing me the glass. "Sophia mentioned your name was Max?" Sophia promptly dropped her hand from my arm, her body taut and vibrating with frustration beside me. "She doesn't bring many people around," her mother said, looking up in thought. "It's been, what, a year, Sophia, since your friend Paul visited?"

Sophia's face paled, and her green eyes grew haunted.

A hollow sensation swept through my gut. It was all fun and games when Sophia was feisty, but not when she was upset.

I gulped down the water and handed the glass to her mother. "Thank you. I didn't realize how thirsty I was until you offered. I should head out." I touched the underside of Sophia's elbow. "Can I give you a ride? I'm headed back to the apartment." I wasn't, actually. I'd been on my way to an appointment, but I'd decided to reschedule it because this was more important.

She peered up as though confused.

"Go, go!" her mother said and ushered us toward the door. "Don't worry about a thing, Soph. I'll have that room cleared out in no time."

Sophia winced, but she reached back and gave her mom a tight hug that had my chest constricting.

She might be ashamed of the house, but not the mother.

I was envious. Appearances were everything where I came from, the downside of growing up in a place that was rigidly controlled. The warmth and overt caring between Sophia and her mother was the opposite of what I'd experienced.

We walked down the steps to the concrete sidewalk, and I maintained a light touch on her arm the entire way. Sophia seemed out of it, and I worried she'd trip and hurt herself if I let her go.

I guided her to my car and opened the passenger-side door, regretting my decision to come here more by the second. Had I known it would be this distressing for Sophia, I wouldn't have done it.

She shook her head as though finally realizing where we were standing. "I can catch a ride."

"I'm going home anyway. I don't mind taking you."

She hesitated a moment, but she must have been too exhausted to argue, because she stepped inside the car and settled in the front seat, setting her workbag on the floorboard.

I let out a heavy sigh of relief as I rounded the rear bumper. Sophia was upset, and I did not feel good about letting her find her way to the apartment. I would have, in fact, turned into the stalker I wasn't and followed her to make sure she got there safely.

As soon as Sophia fastened her seatbelt, I started the car and pulled onto the street. Her silence was worrisome. "Are you okay?"

Her voice was soft and faint when she replied, "Why did you come today?"

Why *had* I come? It suddenly seemed less about the deposit and more about understanding this woman. Only now I was regretting my decision. I hadn't wanted to hurt her, and that seemed exactly what I'd done. "I already told you."

Her glare on the side of my face was weighted with anger. "You gave me an excuse about the deposit, but no rich landlord personally delivers a check. Especially not before a tenant has moved out."

My office could have mailed the check, and typically that was done after a tenant moved out, but there was another reason for my visit. "I'd like you to reconsider breaking your lease."

She pinched the bridge of her nose and closed her eyes. "Why?" she said with a look of exhaustion. "Or you'll sue me for breach of contract?"

Okay, I deserved that. I'd been surprised and then annoyed when she told me she was moving. But it wasn't because of money. "Jack wants you to stay, and he believes I'm the reason you're leaving." That was the truth. Just not the whole truth.

There was a chance I'd pushed an innocent woman to flee. I wasn't proud of it.

I also didn't want to see her go.

Her eyes met mine briefly, filled with equal measures of anger and hurt. "And if I don't stay?"

I gentled my tone. "You are free to break the lease without repercussions."

She shook her head. "Are you doing this out of pity? Offering me my room back after you saw my mom's place?"

I looked over, brow furrowed, before returning my gaze to the road ahead. "There's nothing wrong with a humble home."

She made a derisive sound in the back of her throat. "Humble... That guy my mom mentioned—Paul? He was my last serious boyfriend. He dumped me as soon as he saw where I lived, after we'd been dating a year and were considering marriage. He told me he didn't want my mom to be a part of his future family. It's more than just the home."

My hands gripped the steering wheel. On the outside, I had the ideal family, but it was all smoke and mirrors. "That guy you dated was a shallow excuse for a human being."

"Agreed," she said, then seemed to catch herself. She looked as though she hadn't expected my response.

Imagining Sophia hurt by others for things out of her control... It bothered me. And I was the dickhead who'd added to her pain on the rooftop, and probably a few other times because of my trust issues.

"No pity," I finally said. Because I didn't pity her. What I felt was admiration. "My best friend's happiness is important, and he says you're a good roommate. And that I have been...rude."

She snorted, and I took that for agreement.

I wasn't a total ass, just occasionally when my protective instincts fired in the wrong direction. "You asked for the deposit, and it caught me off guard. Jack passes on the reduced rent to whoever sublets. I'm not used to someone giving up a thing of value. Especially not when it comes to the opposite sex. That's the world I live in, and people rarely sway from their roles."

"So what you're saying is, women don't turn down your money." Her expression was pure annoyance, and relief flooded my chest. The distress she'd exhibited at her mom's had me antsy and prepared to bust down buildings to protect her. "Maybe those women actually liked you?" she said.

I sent her a look.

She smiled. "Right. I can see why women wouldn't like you for who you are on the inside, what with your handsome looks and fancy sports car blocking the view."

"Do I sense sarcasm?"

"You realize you can be rich, good-looking, and genuinely liked? Though that last one could be a struggle."

Swinging briefly into oncoming traffic, I dodged a double-parked car. "I deserved that."

"I'm just saying," she continued, rubbing salt in the wound, "that if you were a kind person, which I question, there might be people who could tolerate your presence." She shifted toward me, and the side of my body lit up. "For the record, I'm not one of them. I have a particular distaste for arrogant, rich men. No amount of money can compensate for a chocolate-stealing thief who shows off his wealth with his suits and expensive sports car."

I rubbed my chest in mock pain. "Ouch."

Her lips twitched in what looked like a smile. She didn't hate me. I hadn't won her over yet, but she didn't hate me.

There was a Machiavellian side of me that enjoyed riling up Sophia. She didn't back down when I was being an ass, and I respected that. But I was even more pleased to make her smile.

We drove the rest of the way in relative silence, except

for the erotic tension that filled the air—possibly entirely on my end.

I let out a sigh. I was attracted to a woman who hated me. Because of course I was.

Back at the apartment, I followed Sophia up the stairs, trying hard not to stare. I'd been on dates since Gwen and I separated, but you'd think I'd been locked up in a monastery. Now that I'd mentally admitted my attraction to Sophia, the floodgates had opened, and my gaze snagged and held on a pert little rear. I had issues.

She stopped on the landing and swung around. "I'll stay at Jack's as long as you don't pity me."

I didn't dare breathe, worried she'd take it back. Which solidified my ruination when it came to this woman.

"No pity." There was something undeniably appealing about her holding to her convictions.

"And one more thing," she said, one curvy hip cocked. "My sister will be staying now and then, so don't give me a hard time about it."

"Whatever you and Jack work out is fine with me."

She turned for her apartment, and I was about to head up to mine, forcing myself to remain cool and not look back, when I heard her say, "Oh, I forgot..."

I looked back, and the view was worth it.

"Touch my chocolate again," she said, fire in her eyes, "and you'll lose a digit."

A vision of a jerry-rigged finger guillotine inside her chocolate cupboard flashed before my eyes, and I smiled.

I liked this girl.

Chapter Thirteen

Sophia

If there was one person I didn't trust to witness my mother's house, it was Max Burrows. But not only had my rich, arrogant landlord seen the place, he hadn't run away in horror.

Which was shocking.

Max had been polite to my mom and even escorted me home. It was more than I could say for Paul, or anyone else, for that matter.

My sister was my best friend, and that was because no one else had stuck around once they saw where I lived.

So Max wasn't a total ass. A mild ass, an incremental ass, but not a total ass. Time would tell if the rest of his critical, food-stealing behavior improved.

"Elise, you can come over," I told my sister over the phone, as I tended the small plants on my bedroom windowsill.

"Landlord Devil gone?"

"No, but he's got virtual reality goggles on, and he and

Jack are oblivious to everything going on around them. They're bumping into furniture and shouting at the TV, being nuisances. Anyway, I'm not worried about you staying the night, because Max and I came to a weird truce."

My sister made a loud hoot, and I pulled the phone away from my ear. "Soph, I'm so happy you're staying there and that you worked things out."

"Me too." And I really was. Returning home would have been traumatic. Even my mom had sounded relieved when I told her my new place was going to work out after all. It probably had more to do with her not needing to remove items from my old bedroom, but still. She was happy, and I was even happier.

"You sure you're okay with me living at the apartment?" I asked. "What about your issues with my roommate?"

"I've decided to rise above," she said. "I won't let your roommate get to me."

Famous last words, I thought, but kept it to myself. Elise wasn't known for her self-control. "Bring your school stuff. I've got work to do as well."

An hour later, I opened the front door for my sister. Her hair was down, and she was wearing shorts that showed off her toned legs, with a long-sleeved shirt tucked in the front. "What's with the lipstick?" I asked.

Her eyes darted to the side as she set her book tote next to the kitchen peninsula. "What? I always wear lipstick. You're the one who shuns makeup."

Okay, that was true. But her lipstick looked freshly applied, and she never put on makeup to hang out with me. My Elise radar went off.

We headed into the kitchen, and I handed her an

orange-flavored soda water before we grazed on chips, salsa, and tiny Oreos she'd pulled from her bag.

Elise leaned on the counter, studying the guys in the living room. They were standing, wearing VR goggles and headphones, and staring in the direction of the TV, moving around jerkily like they were fending off monsters. "They really can't hear us?"

I tossed a bite-size Oreo in my mouth. "Nope."

Jack waved his arms in the air, and then he made a parkour move that nearly knocked over a lamp on the end table. He scrambled to his feet.

Max gripped his shoulder, as if to say, "Great job," and I shook my head slowly. These knuckleheads were going to break something.

Elise waved a chip in their direction. "You're going to need new furniture after they're done. How old did you say these specimens of masculinity are?"

I looked up, mentally calculating. "I think Jack is twenty-nine. Max is the same age."

Elise nodded. "So, old enough to not destroy furniture."

Max nearly fell over the couch, and I winced. "Apparently not."

Elise nodded. "Good, good. At least we agree."

We headed into my room, where Elise proceeded to lounge on my bed while visually going through my closet and picking apart ninety percent of my wardrobe over the next hour. "Those side-zip trousers have to go." She eyed them critically. "They're way too big on you now."

"I realize that," I said, making space in one of the closet dresser drawers for Elise to leave some things at my place, "but I need work clothes. I can't afford to replace my entire closet." I stood and looked down my body. "Apparently, I was eating my emotions while living with Mom. As soon as

I knew I was moving, I started shedding pounds without even trying. And that's on a steady chocolate diet."

"You weren't overweight when you lived with us, but I know what you mean. You shrank."

"Thanks for the lovely description."

She pursed her lips in thought. "You must have been carrying around water weight, because you look exactly the same, just a bit smaller."

It was a strange thing to drop ten pounds in what felt like overnight, but I had more energy these days, so that was a bonus. Stress was no joke.

"Speaking of attire," I said, "I'm not sure why you're critiquing mine. You live in athleisure."

She sat up, affronted. "Hey, I'm on a budget."

"So am I!" I argued. I couldn't remember a time I wasn't on a budget, planning for my schooling or Elise's.

She rose from my bed and stretched her arms over her head. "I should probably get going."

"Why? You just got here. Stay and study, and I'll work. That's the beauty of me having my own place; you're not confined to Mom's anymore."

"You sure it's okay?"

I wasn't certain Max would accept Elise spending as much time here as I wanted her to, but considering how often he came by the apartment, it would be hypocritical of him to complain. "It should be. Not like anyone even noticed you enter."

"Guys are weird when it comes to their video games," she said. "I'll grab my book bag. But let's get more food. I'm famished. I ran out of corn chips this afternoon, and I've been hungry ever since."

Clearly, Elise's corn chip diet was still in full effect.

On our way to the kitchen, Max and Jack took off their

goggles, and their skin was lined from the headgear they'd been wearing for hours.

Max high-fived Jack. "It's pretty intense, man."

"Told you." Jack sank onto the couch and rubbed his face.

"What's intense?" Elise pulled out bread, meat, and cheese, and proceeded to make herself a sandwich.

Max looked over, finally noticing us. He lifted his chin in Jack's direction. "Jack built a VR world that's going to change the way people game."

Elise slathered mayo on a slice of bread. "Really? Can I see?"

Max held out the goggles, and she shoved her unfinished sandwich at me and walked over.

Jack's face twisted. "I don't know. It's not out yet, and the software is proprietary."

Elise rolled her eyes. "I'm a nursing student. Who would I tell? Besides, you need a woman's viewpoint. I doubt you've even thought of how female gamers will perceive your new toy."

Jack sighed. "Fine, but just for a minute. I want to make the fixes Max pointed out."

Elise grinned and put on the headgear, adjusting it to fit her smaller head. And immediately started walking around and bumping into furniture.

Jack gently lifted the headset from her face, and she blinked up at him. "Stay put, will you? You can't move more than a foot or two. Remember, we're in my living room."

"Yeah, yeah." Elise reaffixed the VR goggles.

They had a bickery dynamic, those two, but who was I to judge? Not like Max and I always got along.

Speaking of the Landlord Devil, Max walked into the kitchen, comfortable as could be, and helped himself to one of Jack's sparkling waters while I finished making Elise's sandwich. He proceeded to scour the cabinets, lifting a cracker from this box, a granola cluster from another. All of which he shoved into his sensual mouth.

He was better looking now that I knew he wasn't a total asshole.

I grabbed my mug from this morning (I was trying to get better about not automatically reaching for new ones), made myself tea, and tried to ignore Max and his sexy mouth. It wasn't hard with Elise squealing every few seconds in the living room and dodging imaginary objects. Jack and Elise were pretty entertaining, though different than watching Max and Jack.

Elise hopped around like she didn't know what in the hell she was doing, while Jack both maneuvered invisible objects and seemed to periodically rescue Elise.

"Can they see each other inside there?" I asked. "Like virtual avatars?"

Max looked up from his rummaging and walked over to where I stood. Then he tossed something into his mouth that sent a rush of heat up my neck.

He wouldn't...

I leaned closer and sniffed—and received an unsettling dose of hot-guy clean scent and *chocolate*.

My gaze shot to his face. "Did you just eat my chocolate?"

Jack didn't buy chocolate. There was only one addict in the house, and that was me.

Max looked down and raised an eyebrow. "It was in Jack's section."

I pressed my lips together. It was either that or I would spew molten lava from my mouth.

I let out a strained breath. "Jack doesn't eat chocolate,

and you know that. Not to mention, the cupboard hasn't been cordoned off by roommate."

"Which is why this roommate situation is perfect," he said, licking his elegant fingers. No hairy digits for pretty-boy Burrows. "You eat chocolate, as do I, and I enjoy the stuff you buy."

The nerve! "You enjoy it because I pay a small fortune for quality."

He extended a hand to my chocolate stash, which he'd pulled out without me knowing, and popped a black forest truffle into his mouth. "You should watch how much you spend on incidentals."

Heat inflamed my chest. Pretty sure smoke spewed from my nostrils. That was it. I didn't care if he was my landlord or rich and hot. *He was going to die.*

I squared off in front of him and poked his chest, stepping forward until I had him pressed up against the stove. He wasn't built huge like a bodybuilder, but he had athletic pecs that resisted my angry, poky finger. "You are not allowed to touch my chocolate. What did I say about your fingers and losing one?"

Max had eased back with each step forward I made, but he'd been smiling the entire time and seemed to be holding back a laugh. His expression softened into a look of innocence. "How was I supposed to know Jack didn't buy that chocolate for me? He knows I like it."

I reached up and wrapped my fingers around his muscular neck. "Do you have a death wish?" I wasn't squeezing hard, but this pretty little rich boy had no shame. He needed to know I meant business.

His gaze dropped to my mouth. A second later, I felt the weight of his hands on my hips.

To hold me back? But it didn't feel like he was pushing

me away. His hands were hot and wide, gripping just a little, and shooting sparks down my lower belly.

I was all bluster. And without real intent, coupled with the slushy feeling taking over my limbs from his hands on my hips, I slid my palms to his collarbone and couldn't catch my breath.

We stood like that, gravitating closer. His warm breath grazed my face, and my heartbeat grew erratic...until Elise let out a loud yelp.

I jumped back and knocked my elbow on the counter at the same time I caught sight of Elise on Jack's back.

Only she'd missed landing squarely and was dangling partially off the side.

Jack tried to grab her, but they were off balance. And then they were falling.

"Shit," I said, rubbing my elbow and running into the living room.

Jack was flat on his back with Elise straddling his waist, her mass of thick hair covering his head as she struggled to push herself upright.

"Elise, are you okay?" I asked.

Max must have been right behind me, because he lifted Elise's goggles off her head.

She looked up, then down at Jack, and scrambled off him.

Jack sat up and jerked off his own headgear. "What the hell was that?" He glared at my sister.

Elise's lips parted. "That thing was coming after me, and you have all the swords."

Jack pinched his eyes closed and seemed to grind his teeth. "Which I can't use against the monster if you've pinned my arms to my body."

"How was I supposed to know that? This is why you

need a woman to help you design the game. I should have had swords too!"

Jack groaned and rose to his feet. "You have to earn them in the game." He looked at me pleadingly. "Sophia, help me out here?"

"Time to study, Elise," I said and grabbed the crappy tote of books she'd left near the kitchen.

Elise rolled her eyes, but she followed me to the kitchen and swept up the sandwich I'd finished making for her. "Fine, alienate half your audience," she said to Jack. "Just know, women aren't going to like your little game." She sauntered down the hallway, shoulders squared. "And what's with the giant breasts on my female avatar?" she shouted behind her.

I shook my head. It wasn't easy keeping Elise out of trouble.

But when I looked toward the living room, Jack wasn't the one making eye contact with me, Max was. And he looked dazed.

The same way I felt.

Because what the hell happened in the kitchen?

Chapter Fourteen

Max

I shoved my phone in the inner pocket of my suit jacket and pressed the intercom. "I'm leaving," I told my assistant. "I'll check email later for the contract on the updated landscape specs for Cityscape."

"You got it," Derek, my assistant, said.

"What is Cityscape?"

My dad was leaning against the doorframe to my office.

"When did you arrive?" I asked.

"Just a moment ago. I couldn't help but overhear."

Dread filled my chest. I'd been putting off this conversation for weeks, but it seemed I couldn't avoid it any longer. "It's our next big project," I told him.

Karl Burrows blinked twice in a deliberate way I'd come to interpret as *I'm not happy with you, but I'll give you a moment to correct yourself.* "Your company has the capacity for another project along with the Starlight building?"

I maintained an even expression. "My company decided to pass on Starlight."

My dad straightened, and this time there was no blinking. Only rage shone in his eyes. "What are you talking about, Max?"

I tucked my hand into my suit pants pocket. "I investigated Starlight at your request. There aren't enough investors, and city planners are pushing for quality, multi-residential buildings, not high-end condos that only the top one percent can afford."

He laughed. "There's no limit to the luxury this city can handle. Let someone else do affordable housing."

I moved to the entrance of my office, pausing a few feet from my father. "That's not the way I run my business. Profit is important, but it's not the only factor. Besides, the Starlight project is cost-prohibitive, and frankly, more of a spec project."

Color rose in my father's cheeks. "We agreed Starlight was the way out for our family. This is about more than one of your pet projects."

"You and Mom agreed this was the way out after the investment sank your finances—"

"Without which, you'd have none of this!" He waved his arm at the floor of cubicles and offices behind us.

I glanced at the executives who supported my real estate development company and noted their attention on us. I pulled my father into the office and closed the door.

"The last thing I want is for you and Mom to be destitute, but that isn't the situation. You lost a fortune, there's no doubt. But you're still wealthy, and you will be for the rest of your lives. You made a poor investment choice and lost a jet, a luxury yacht, and a few vacation homes. But you have money in the bank and a mansion in the city. I won't base my development choices on making you richer."

My father threw up his hands. "Is this another one of your 'help the people' speeches?"

My parents had been on edge ever since my father placed an unfortunate bet on a hedge fund a college buddy of his had pushed. I understood where the stress and lack of empathy came from, but I refused to support it.

My jaw shifted and anger made its way up my chest. "I considered the business proposal for Starlight and decided my company's time and resources were better spent helping a larger portion of San Franciscans—at a profit for my company, of course. Starlight might have earned back some of the money you and Mom lost, but not close to all of it. And that's if we managed to keep costs down and find the right buyers. The biggest advantage in moving forward would be to your reputation. The gossip around Starlight would outshine rumors about the losses you incurred."

My dad stepped forward confrontationally. "It wasn't only our money."

Karl Burrows might come across as a happy-go-lucky rich donor, but he could be ruthless. "You talked others into investing," I said. "But that's on you, Dad. Don't pull me into this."

"It's on you too! Why do you insist on distancing yourself from your family?"

I let out a strained breath. "I have nothing against our family, and I would like for us to be close. But that doesn't mean I'll make the same choices you and Mom have."

My dad shook his head and put his hands on his hips. "You wouldn't have a fortune if it weren't for us."

I nodded. "This is true. You paid for my education, and friends of the family provided seed money for my early developments. Which made me lucky and more fortunate than most. But I'm in a position now to continue doing what I love while helping others. That's what drives me."

My father laughed. "Max, we've always given to charity. Why sacrifice your fortune for others? This is nonsense. Do the Starlight project, and make me and your mother proud."

I closed my eyes briefly. "I had hoped that the choices I've made and what I'm doing already make you proud."

My father hesitated for a moment before he spoke. "Don't you think some of those things are a waste of time and effort? You could be earning so much more with Starlight. No need to sacrifice the bottom line for people who will land on their feet without companies catering to them."

This conversation was pointless. My father was wrong. Starlight wasn't a sure thing, and impoverished people didn't pull themselves out of poverty by sheer will.

I'd lived an entitled life. But some people, like my dad, saw that as their due. I credited spending so much time with Jack's family that I never had.

I checked my phone. "I need to be somewhere. Starlight is off the table, but feel free to pitch it to another company."

I moved to pass him, but my father blocked the way. "You know you're our only chance at getting Starlight off the ground. Are you really going to do this to your mother?"

I moved around him. "Like you said about those who have far less—you'll land on your feet."

My phone vibrated on my way to the parking garage, and I checked the screen.

Jack: Meet us at O'Malley's in the inner Sunset.

THE CONVERSATION with my dad about Starlight left a sour taste in my mouth. I rarely saw eye to eye with my parents, but I cared about them and wanted them to be happy. I just wished their happiness didn't hinge on my doing their bidding. Hanging out with Jack would be a welcome distraction, and I was glad to see him getting out again.

Max: Be there in 20.

IT WASN'T until I made it to O'Malley's that a sinking suspicion replaced thoughts of Starlight and my parents. Jack had said "us" in his text message.

I scanned the room and caught sight of a familiar dark-haired woman with baggy slacks and white sneakers standing at the bar. Sophia was here, and suddenly my pulse kicked up a notch.

She was more interesting than I'd imagined, and I'd been fighting imagining her since the day she moved in with Jack. That near kiss in the kitchen last night had been less of an impulse and more a result of the attraction that had been building since we met.

Sophia stood near the bar, squeezed between a man in a dark button-down and a barstool. She was attempting to gain the attention of the bartender while seemingly fielding the man's questions.

The urge to walk over and shove the guy away from Sophia was as intense as it was disturbing. Fighting for a woman's attention had never been a consideration. Not until I met her.

I angled for Jack's table and made my way across the busy pub. The place was old, with smooth, wide-plank wooden floors and tables with a thick, shiny finish over old-growth redwood. Some people looked like they'd come from the Financial District, while others were dressed casually.

Jack looked up. "You made it." He was wearing jeans and an untucked button-down. I hadn't seen Jack this cleaned up in months. Sophia's sister was also there, drinking a beer and laughing at something on her phone.

I tipped my head toward the bar. "What's going on?"

Jack's gaze landed on Sophia. "She went to grab another beer. Guess she got distracted. This is our night to be each other's wingman."

A prickly heat filled my chest, and I looked her way. "I'll head over. I could use a beer."

"Bad day?" Jack asked.

I gripped the back of my neck. "I told my father I wouldn't be doing Starlight."

"Ahh," Jack said and nodded. "He wasn't happy."

My parents and Jack had always gotten along because Jack was an exceptional person. He'd been among the few students clever enough to gain entrance on scholarship to the prestigious San Francisco private school I attended. Later, he received more scholarships to attend an Ivy League school. He also understood Kitty and Karl and their limited ability to put themselves in other people's shoes, and he never judged them for it. "It's the only life they've known, Max," he'd tell me.

I turned to the bar, but Jack grabbed my shoulder before I could go anywhere. "Dude, don't interfere in whatever Sophia has going on." The woman in question was smiling at something the man next to her had said, and I almost heeded Jack's advice. Almost.

"Me? Interfere? Never." My words were casual—and didn't hold an ounce of truth.

Jack's look said he knew exactly what I was up to. "That kid is skittish with the male population. You saw her the night she went on the blind date." He glanced at Sophia worriedly. "I should be over there helping her."

Elise set her phone on the tabletop and placed her chin on her hand. "What are you two talking about?"

"Nothing," I said at the same time that Jack said, "Sophia."

Elise twisted around and looked at her sister. "Ooh, she's hooked one. Nice!"

"Not particularly," I murmured under my breath, and headed for the bar.

I heard Jack calling my name, but I ignored it, my hand in the pocket of my suit pants. I lifted my chin at the bartender, and she caught my gaze. I held up two fingers and said, "Guinness."

The bartender nodded, and that was when Sophia looked up, her beautiful eyes widening ever so slightly. Her gaze flashed to the man beside her, then back at me.

I pulled up behind her and sent the man a direct message. It went something like this: *Back the fuck off.*

"Could have just said she's taken," the guy murmured and turned his back on Sophia.

She spun around in surprise. "What just happened? I was talking to him."

The bartender slid two pints my way.

"Is there a problem?" I said innocently, and passed her a pint.

"Thank you," she said, gripping the beer. "How did you get your order so quickly? I've been waiting for forever."

"You sure you didn't miss the bartender while talking to your friend?"

Her gaze narrowed. "Were you eavesdropping?"

"I would never do that." Of course I would.

Her delicate jaw shifted. "I'm trying to date more—or really, at all—and you're not helping. Jack is a much better wingman."

I caught the guy she'd been talking to weaving his way across the bar. "Shall I bring him back?"

Eyes narrowing again, she sipped the dark malt. "Did you scare him away on purpose, Max?"

I'd never considered myself a territorial man. My ex-girlfriends would have been thrilled if I had exhibited this kind of caveman behavior with them. But I'd never felt possessive when it came to anyone else, only for the woman who was subletting a room from my best friend and spent an unusual amount of money on chocolate. Her animosity toward my dickish behavior coupled with her cute rear in baggy pants and fiery green eyes called to me. And I didn't feel the least bit like fighting it anymore.

I slid a large tip to the bartender and casually inched closer to Sophia. "Now, why would I scare him away?"

She seemed to chew on that a moment. "Who can say? You also eat my chocolate even though I've threated to maim you for it, but at least that I understand. I have good taste in chocolate."

"This is true."

A flash of dark hair crossed my vision before Sophia was shoved into my chest and beer splashed between us. The sticky malt was the least of my concerns, because all my senses homed in on Sophia's soft frame and light scent.

"Whoa!" Elise said, and reached for napkins from the bar.

Sophia swiveled her head and glared over her shoulder at her sister. "What the hell, Elise?" She was still holding on to my arm, and I didn't feel it necessary to point it out.

Elise thrust napkins at the two of us. "Sorry about that. This place is crowded. I overshot the bar when I beelined past the pub-crawlers. Let's go back to the table." She looked over to where Jack was sitting. "Your friend is avoiding me, and it's getting boring."

Jack avoiding an attractive woman was...unusual. Come to think of it, he'd been acting strange around Sophia's sister from the start. I'd assumed he was steering clear of women for a while, but seeing him out tonight, I wasn't so sure.

Sophia straightened, putting a bit of space between us, which I reluctantly allowed. We headed to the table, and the look on Jack's face was one of relief.

"What took you so long?" He shifted in his seat, angling his body away from Elise as we sat down.

"I'm assisting Sophia with her dating life," I said. "It seems her taste in suitors is lacking."

Sophia shot me a furious look that got all my senses firing. "Excuse me? My taste is excellent."

Elise choked on what looked like a half-full gin and tonic. "Your taste in men sucks."

"Not anymore it doesn't," Sophia said, pushing her light-brown hair over her shoulder confidently. "I've turned over a new leaf, and Jack is helping me."

I needed to have a talk with my best friend. His loyalty could use fine-tuning.

"Exactly," Jack said, missing my cutting glare. "Speaking of which..." He turned to a group of men at the table beside us. "This is my friend Sophia I was telling you about."

Four average-looking guys proceeded to check out Sophia.

I hated them instantly, as well as Jack. Had he not received my subliminal messages?

Sophia's body stiffened at the attention, and she sank her head into her hands. "Oh my God."

"Smooth," I told Jack.

"What?" He leaned forward. "These guys are okay," he said in hushed tones. "We've been talking while you all were at the bar."

Sophia lifted her head. "Hi," she said shyly—adorably—and started a conversation with one of them.

My blood pressure rose, and my chest felt uncomfortably tight. I should take off, let her do her thing. Being around Sophia while she was trying to meet other men wasn't good for my health. But that wasn't what I did.

"What do you do for a living?" I overheard the man ask her. An investment banker, by the look of his suit and dress shirt with no tie.

"I'm an interior designer by training."

"She arranges plants," I said, and sipped my beer. No need for this guy to realize how amazing Sophia was.

Sophia shifted until her back was to me. "I design interior greenspace," she clarified.

"Huh," the guy said, tilting his head as though confused. "That's different."

"Well, it is, actually," she said hurriedly. "Most people don't realize how important plants are for the flow and vibe of our indoor spaces. It's—it's, you know—vital that we feel good, and it can actually make the rooms feel less cluttered."

Interesting that she used the word "cluttered." It

wouldn't surprise me if her mother's home had influenced her career.

Sophia tucked her hair behind her ear and cleared her throat. She was nervous, and it showed, but I wasn't generous enough to help. Not when it came to another man pursuing the woman I was interested in. Because I was smart enough to realize I had a serious interest in Sophia, who should be off-limits, since she was technically my tenant. She also harbored feelings of loathing for me, so there was that too.

"Sophia here leaves her mugs all over the house and has frizzy hair when she gets off work," I said. "She needs good greenspace to keep up the appearance of a decluttered room and person."

Her back popped upright at the sound of my voice.

"So she's messy?" the man said. "Messy can be fun." He cast her a licentious smile I wanted to rip off his face.

Her head swiveled in my direction. "I am not messy, Maxwell!" Darts shot from her eyes, but at least she was looking at me.

"Oh, I get it," the guy said. "You two live together." His thick brow furrowed. "But your friend said you're single."

He was sharp, this one. Which made my confidence soar. As awkward as she came across with the opposite sex, Sophia was a bright woman. She wouldn't date a moron.

"I *am* single," Sophia said.

The man looked at me, then back at Sophia. "Right, well, it was nice meeting you," he said, and turned toward the others at his table.

Sophia swiveled in her chair and faced me squarely. "Did you just cockblock?"

I checked my phone. "He was a creep, and you're better off without him."

She leaned forward, eyes hot with anger, and a waft of her soft-scented shampoo drifted my way, reminding me of the bar when she was pressed against me. The scent was some sort of coconut-vanilla fusion, tempting me to run my nose along her neck and breathe in. "That is for me to decide, Max. What is wrong with you?"

Good question. I tipped my chin at the bartender, who miraculously caught my eye and flagged the only waitress in the place. "I need another drink."

Chapter Fifteen

SOPHIA

We made our way home from the Irish pub, and Elise waved her arms drunkenly while Jack carried her on his back into our apartment.

"Giddy up!" Elise said, and kicked his butt with her heels.

Jack stopped abruptly, his face dark red. "Elise, I swear to God, if you do that one more time, I'm dropping you."

Elise had said "giddy up" about five times, and Jack had threatened to drop her just as many. I wasn't worried he'd follow through, but I was confident Elise would regret this night in the morning.

"Plop her on the couch," I told him. "I need to get some water into her." I shook my head and stared at my sister. "Why did you drink so much?"

She drunkenly pointed toward the door where Max stood. "I'm a poor graduate student who doesn't get out much, and Max was buying. His card has no limit."

Max appeared amused by the whole scenario.

"This is all your fault," I said.

He shrugged unapologetically.

Jack squatted, his rear turned to the couch, but Elise was clinging to him like a barnacle.

I leaned down in her face. "Elise, let go of Jack."

She released her arms and fell onto the couch, then curled into the fetal position. "Night, night."

Jack raised his arms above his head and twisted at the waist, stretching his back. He'd carried Elise from the Uber and up the long flight of stairs to our apartment, and she'd been damned unruly. I seriously owed him.

"I should head out," Max said, checking his phone.

"Not just yet." I'd finally mustered the nerve to talk to a couple of men, and Max had come along and ruined it, along with my confidence.

I was not messy! Only my mugs were scattered, not the rest of me. I couldn't help it that I had a lot on my plate.

I followed Max to the cement landing in front of our apartment and closed the door for privacy. "What was up with you tonight? I thought we cleared the air after my mom's house. Why were you telling that man my worst habits? That's just rude. I keep that stuff well hidden until months into dating."

His lips twitched, but I was being serious!

"Is that what you were doing tonight? Hiding?" He moved closer, crowding me against the door, and pressed his hand to the wall beside my head. It was an extremely intimate pose, and my belly tightened.

I glanced at the hand and tried not look at his mouth a few inches away. The clean scent of his aftershave wasn't helping me focus. Damn Landlord Devil and his good looks. He was using the old lean-in-and-smolder technique to distract me, and it was working. "No, I wasn't hiding, but you know how it is. It's hard to let people in. You saw how awkward I am with someone new."

He chuckled. "It was a sad showing."

My mouth twisted. "You don't have to agree with me."

He leaned closer, which forced me to tip my head against the door or risk contact. "I could spare you all this awkward effort," he said casually.

His blue eyes were crazy beautiful this close. "What do you mean?" I said dazedly.

"You don't need to date other men."

"I don't?" I said absently, hypnotized by the blue Burrows orbs of seduction.

"Not if you're dating me."

Before I could process his words, Max's lips pressed against mine...

I experienced a moment of vertigo, my first thought being that he'd accidentally bumped into me. Until his lips started moving, seducing me in a sensual glide.

Max Burrows tasted like cherry ChapStick—a hint of the sweetness hidden by the devil exterior.

My stomach dropped, and heat flared up my spine. There was no awkward knocking of teeth, just smooth, pillowy lips and a hint of tongue dragging me under.

Uptight, arrogant Landlord Devil was a good kisser.

Instinctively, I clung to his suit jacket and pulled him closer.

One of his hands gripped my hip, sending flutters south to vital pressure points...

I leaned back, breaking contact. "Uhhh," I said, a flash of panic taking over. As good as it felt to kiss Max, my brain wasn't prepared.

"Yes?" His gaze slid back to my mouth, and for a moment there, I wondered why I'd pulled away.

Until I gave myself a swift mental knock upside the head. "What's going on? You don't want to date me."

Did I really need to point out the obvious?

He tucked a lock of my hair behind my ear. "I don't?"

If only my body would sync with my mind, because right now my body was all, *Yes, yes, he's the one I've wanted,* while my brain was like, *Max Burrows is a cocky asshole!*

"Wait, you do?" I said. "I mean, you don't. You can't."

"Can't I?" I swear he leaned in to kiss me again.

But the old brainbox finally kicked in, and I darted out from under his arm. "See you later," I said and ran inside the apartment like a coward.

As I pressed my back to the door, my chest rose and fell as though I'd done a dozen laps up the stairs. I muttered, "Oh, no."

"Why 'Oh, no'?" When I looked up, Jack was surfing his phone from the living room couch, and Elise was nowhere in sight. She must have gone to bed.

"Nothing!" I said a little too loudly.

In some strange turn of events, I'd made out with Jack's best friend—the man I'd spent the last few weeks hating.

And I'd liked it far too much.

———

THE NEXT MORNING, I woke with an exhaustion headache and my heart racing from anxiety. I'd stayed up late last night, with Elise snoring softly beside me in bed, thinking of all my encounters with Landlord Devil: the pink panties, his annoyance at my admitting Jack was handsome to his mother, his stealing my chocolate repeatedly to annoy me.

I covered my face with my pillow. Sometimes sexual

attraction and hate looked an awful lot alike. Especially if you weren't prepared for it.

What was I doing? Max was sophisticated, and I... wasn't. He was rich and I was poor. He had classy friends and family, and I had Elise, my drunken sister/best friend. I wasn't ashamed of any of it, but it didn't change the fact that Max and I didn't go together.

I rolled onto my stomach and pressed my face into the mattress. Why did the kiss have to be so good? Couldn't he have had a lizard tongue? He could have committed any number of acts men did that turned women off, but every little touch from him had, unfortunately, had the opposite effect.

I threw my pillow across the room and swung my legs over the side of the bed. Blurry-eyed, I stumbled into the bathroom and showered. I couldn't waste the day away thinking about Max. I had things to take care of for work, and my boss wanted to meet up, even though it was a Saturday.

I reached for a blush-hued blouse from the closet and did the best I could, pairing it with light wool slacks that were a size too big. Elise was right. I needed to suck it up and buy clothes that actually fit...

Elise?

I spun around and stared at the mattress. When did she leave? She'd definitely been in bed when I returned from talking to Max last night, because I'd made her drink a giant glass of water, and she nearly choked on it while bitching me out for mothering her. We'd bickered for a few minutes —the usual—and then she'd starfished out on the mattress and was snoring within seconds.

But she hadn't been in bed when I woke, I realized. Had I slept longer than I thought and missed her leaving?

After throwing on my clothes, I grabbed my workbag and left my bedroom for food and to find Elise. And froze just outside my bedroom door.

I observed several things all at once: Elise sneaking out of Jack's room, a glimpse of Jack's naked back as he sat on the edge of the bed facing away, and my sister's eyes flashing wide as though she'd been caught.

I pointed at the door she was slowly closing. "Why were you in his room?"

She slapped a hand over my mouth and shoved me into my bedroom, nearly mowing me down in the process. "Be quiet!" She shut the door and tiptoed to the window, where she glanced out, worrying her lip with her teeth.

"You're the one whisper-shouting," I pointed out.

Elise paced back and forth, her hand on her forehead. She was wearing a man's T-shirt, and most definitely not the sleepshirt I'd supplied her with the night before.

I blinked several times. "Elise Marie, what did you do last night?"

She stomped her foot and glared. "If you try to mother me in this moment, I will cut you."

I glanced down her body. "With what? Jack's T-shirt?"

Wrong thing to say, because Elise really did look ready to kill me.

I feigned zipping my lips. "Are you going to explain why I saw you leaving my roommate's bedroom? And think before you answer, because I know you weren't in my bed when I woke this morning."

She sat on the edge of the mattress, in shock. "I slept with him," she said, her voice high and panicked.

Okay, okay, no need to jump to conclusions. She couldn't mean it the way it sounded. "Did you get up in the middle of the night and go to the wrong bed?"

She dropped her head into her hands. "I think that's what happened. Originally."

"Originally?"

Elise rose and started pacing again in her bare feet. "I don't remember walking in there, but I must have, after getting up to use your bathroom." She spun on me. "You strong-armed me into drinking way too much water last night. This is all your fault!"

"That you passed out in Jack's bed?"

"That I slept with him!" she whisper-yelled.

I grabbed her hand and made her sit. She was making me dizzy. "Jack knew you were drunk. It's awkward, but he won't hold it against you that you crashed in his bed."

She hunched over. "I wouldn't call it drunk." Her gaze slid to me nervously. "More like I was slightly intoxicated and enjoying making Jack do things for me."

My jaw dropped. Some of her behavior last night had been an act?

"Either way," she said, "when I woke up to use the bathroom a few hours later, I was sober but groggy, and I must have walked out of your bedroom and into his. I'm not used to the bathroom being connected to the bedroom."

Elise was a master sleepwalker, so this made sense. "Just tell him you sleepwalk and that you made a mistake."

She straightened and wrung her hands. "It's not just the sleepwalking. I talked in my sleep after I was in his room."

Ah, got it. I'd had entire conversations with Elise while she was asleep when we were kids. No wonder she was embarrassed. "Jack is an adult. He won't hold whatever you said against you."

Was her face paler than normal? "You don't think he'll hold it against me that I moaned his name and sexually attacked him?"

124

I flinched. "Wait, what?"

She glanced at the door as though Jack might barge in at any moment. "That's what I'm trying to tell you!" Then she was up and scavenging for the clothes she'd thrown on the floor last night and pulling them on over Jack's T-shirt.

I attempted to process what she was saying. "You... kissed him?"

She stopped what she was doing and glared. "A little more than that, Soph. Stop being such a prude. I told you I slept with him."

For some reason, I couldn't utter the S-word in relation to my sister and my roommate. Jack was more like a brother. That was why I figured he and Elise bickered. Like they had their own sister-brother thing going on—though now that I thought about it, that didn't seem right either. Jack had always been a little too focused when it came to Elise.

And then I was furious. "Wait, you'd been drinking. Did that asshole take advantage?"

Funny how my roommate could go from a good guy to a total jerk in the span of a heartbeat. But if he'd taken advantage of her, he was about to lose his favorite appendage.

Elise pulled the bag she'd been carrying last night onto her shoulder and closed her eyes, letting out a slow breath. "Simmer down. I was stone-cold sober by the time I dream-moaned his name. I'd had a very dirty dream about your roommate, for some unfortunate reason, and it woke me. And then I saw him sleeping beside me, and..."

I held up my hands in anticipation. "And?"

"I sort of—attacked him. Or really, I rolled on top of him and kissed him lightly on the lips." She touched her mouth. "Sexiest peck of my life. He seemed taken by surprise for all of a hot second, and then he was kissing me back, and—we

125

slept together. And it was ridiculously hot, but now... Nope. Can't face him."

"Ohhh, shit. Shit, *shit*." I looked around, suddenly understanding her distress, because holy hell. Jack and Elise? Max was insanely protective of Jack. I could only imagine what he'd think if he found out Elise had snuck into Jack's room. Jack was in a vulnerable state after his last relationship. Max was going to kill me!

She glanced past me to the window. "How high up are we? You have a fire escape, right?"

"I think so," I murmured, distracted. "Wait, Elise. You can't climb out of my window to avoid Jack. Have you lost your mind? Go talk to him."

"Can't," she said and unlatched the window. She perched on the ledge and fumbled with the escape ladder. "There's no way I can face your roommate ever again." She lifted her leg over the ledge, then looked back. "Sorry, Soph. Guess I won't be seeing you until you move out of this place."

I scrambled after her. "I'm not moving, remember? I could be here for years. Be an adult!"

She shook her head. "He knows I had a crush on him now. I can never face him again."

I tugged her back toward the room, but she resisted. "You have a crush on Jack?" I asked.

Her face contorted, and she batted at my hand, dislodging it. "Lower your voice! Had—I *had* one. My crush is gone. Now I need to get out of here. Close this behind me, will you?" she said as she descended the metal steps.

Elise was doing it. She was actually risking her life to avoid Jack.

I leaned over the ledge and watched nervously as she made it to the pavement from what looked like a sturdy escape ladder—freaking Landlord Devil and his attention to detail.

Elise peered around, then ran away like a cat burglar.

Where was she going? That wasn't even the direction of the closest bus stop.

Running from a one-night stand via the fire escape had to be the worst walk of shame in history.

By the time I got myself together and entered the kitchen, Jack had left our apartment. His bedroom door was wide open, the bed made, and there was no sign of him.

What was wrong with these two? Jack was a late-night working hermit, and now he was leaving by seven in the morning? You'd think they were sixteen, not in their late twenties. Then again, I'd run for my life after Max kissed me, so fleeing romantic situations had apparently become an epidemic in the building.

Max would probably blame me for what happened last night. Or maybe not. I didn't know. I wasn't used to amorous, kissing Max. I was used to the Max who chewed me out, and this seemed like something he'd blame me for.

Unable to stomach anything heavy, I made a fruit smoothie and took off for work, hoping the distraction would do me some good.

Chapter Sixteen

Sophia

This Saturday, Green Aesthetic had a few events to coordinate, and considering the trucks lined up in front, every vendor in town had shown up on our doorstep.

"No, not the Presidio," Victor said into his cell phone, his back to me. He pointed feverishly at a man with a stack of boxes on a hand dolly and gestured for the guy to move out of the way. "The white miniature rose plants," Victor continued, "are going to the 40 Under 40 Awards at the Fairmont." His long-sleeved, tucked-in button-down was wrinkled in the back, and his short blond-and-gray hair was sticking up at odd ends.

I stepped aside for the guy with the dolly, and Victor caught sight of me, his shoulders sinking as relief flooded his features.

He covered the phone. "You came at just the right time to save my sanity."

"What's going on?" I said, as a crew of workers loaded

parlor palms onto a truck at the curb. "Why are the plants here and not at the venues?"

Victor let out a long breath, closing his eyes briefly. "Because James quit, and I haven't had time to hire another coordinator."

On the plus side, Victor was good at his job, and everyone wanted to work with him. On the downside, Green Aesthetic didn't have enough coordinators to handle the load, and it looked like my boss was ready to crack. "Why didn't you call me?"

If James had quit suddenly, and Victor was running all four venues, this was bad. Victor was a genius at design, but he was terrible with running the daily ins and outs.

We moved out of the way of more workers taking product from the back of the store to the street, and Victor said, "I screwed up. But I'll fix it. That's not why I wanted you here today."

Glancing around, I wasn't so sure he could get things running smoothly. This would be a tough one for me to untangle, but I loved this sort of challenge. "I don't mind helping."

Victor gestured for me to enter the shop and followed behind me. "Forget all this. I have something more important to talk to you about. Do you remember when I hired you that I told you I'd retire soon?" Yeah, and I'd hoped he hadn't been serious. Working for Victor had been a dream, and I wanted it to continue. I wasn't ready to find another job. "I said I would give you as much experience as possible, remember? Well, time's up. I'm retiring."

"Now?" My voice came out in a squeak.

This was too soon. No one would hire me with less than a year of managerial experience. And there were only a couple shops like Victor's in the city to begin with. But

Victor had worked his ass off for decades; who was I to begrudge him his retirement?

"I understand," I said, my heart sinking.

The plans I'd laid were once again not going well, although this time it wasn't due to my neurosis. I'd have to find another job immediately if I wanted to hold on to my apartment and continue helping Elise with tuition and Mom with her bills. I pressed my fingers to my forehead at the pressure building behind my eyes.

Victor touched my shoulder and smiled gently. "Sophia," he said. "I'm not laying you off. A couple years ago, I couldn't have imagined being able to hand off the business to someone else. But everything changed the day you walked through the door. You have the passion and talent I was looking for in a design manager, and you've even grown the business in the short time you've been here. I'm offering for you to take it over."

This was the second time in the last twenty-four hours that my brain couldn't catch up to reality. First with Max and that naughty kiss, and now with Victor. "Wait, what? Are you serious?"

He laughed. "There's no one I feel more comfortable entrusting the business to than you, not even my son."

I swallowed, holding back a well of emotion. From the moment we met, Victor had felt more like a father figure than a boss. And now he was offering me something I'd only dreamed of having sometime in the distant future. It felt too good to be true.

"You're the best boss I've ever had," was all I could come up with, blinking back tears. "When I finally managed to branch off on my own, I thought I'd be building from scratch. I never dreamed of anything like this."

Victor rubbed his jaw and looked around. "Not from

scratch, but things don't look too good at the moment, do they?" He chuckled. "Today's chaos is my fault. In all honesty, I don't have the energy anymore, and I want to retire."

Regardless of how incredible this opportunity seemed, the truth was I'd only just moved out of my mother's house and was barely keeping my finances in check. "I'm honored that you would consider entrusting the business with me, but I don't think I can afford it."

His face brightened, a twinkle in his eye. "I already thought of that. From what I've gathered, you're the sole provider for your family, and that's a big responsibility. If you run the place, I'll maintain the capital so you don't have to. I have no doubt you'll build the business in ways I never could, and in turn, I'll take a portion of the profit. We'll set up a contract so that you can buy me out over time. It would be an investment for me and a career for you."

He looked around the storefront. "I love this place, but I just can't do it anymore, doll. I'm in my fifties, but physically I might as well be fifteen years older. Tim is threatening to leave me if I don't step back and reduce my hours."

Tim was Victor's boyfriend of twenty years. Victor had come out later in life after a rocky adolescence of trying to fit in. He'd had a son with his one high school girlfriend when he was just eighteen—talk about surprise and confusion mixed together. But Victor had always said that raising his son was the best blessing he'd ever been given. He'd also stayed close with his son's mother, regularly checking in on her.

"Tim would never leave you," I said. "He adores you."

Victor smiled. "Maybe, but we'd like to live out our golden years together, and he deserves more of me. You've already brought in new clients with your unique twist to green design, and our customers are beginning to associate the place with you. It's as much yours moving forward as it is mine."

"But I haven't even been here a year," I said, still unable to believe his words. Was I the only one thinking logically?

"And every client we have asks for you," he pointed out.

He was flattering me. Maybe. I wasn't sure. All I knew was that he was offering me a golden opportunity. "I love the idea. I'm just not confident I can do it."

"I know it's a lot, but think about it, okay?" He looked down at his phone, which had begun to ring nonstop. "I'll have my lawyer draft a business proposal. There's no rush. If today hadn't been so chaotic, I would have taken you out to lunch to discuss it. But"—he crossed his eyes comically —"things didn't go according to plan."

I chuckled. "I will consider it. And no matter what I decide, thank you, Victor. It's a huge honor that you'd think of me."

He grinned. "If I'd had a daughter, I would have wanted her to be as smart and tenderhearted as you, Sophia. Instead, I have an incredible son, who sadly works as an engineer." He shook his head. "How did an artist produce an engineer?"

No one was more committed to their son than Victor, no matter how much he poked fun. He talked lovingly of his son and his son's long-term girlfriend nearly every day, and I was fortunate to have Victor rooting for me too.

I never had time to think about how much I missed my dad. I'd hit the ground running to help my mom, and I never stopped. But times like this killed me in all the best ways, reminding me how much I missed having a father and how lucky I was to have people like Victor in my life.

I reached over and hugged him.

He gave me a tight squeeze before pulling back and shouting at workers near the front door, "Hey, hey, not there!"

He shook his head, holding up his phone and showing me six phone calls he'd missed during the few minutes we'd spoken. "These knuckleheads. I better do a better job of taking over James's coordinating. In the meantime, would you be able to run one errand? I wouldn't normally ask on your day off, but this is a top-tier client who reached out. Can't say no when influential people come a-calling."

"Gosh, no," I said. "Half of the business I've brought in has been through word of mouth from large clients I've acquired. Word of mouth is everything. What's the address?"

Max

MY MOTHER rarely called me to the house, but today she had insisted.

I let myself into the mansion on Franklin Street and made my way to her private salon. Dozens of priceless paintings covered the paneled wood-and-fabric walls, and there had to be an equal amount of art spread over the furniture in the large room. Every table held marble and fine-jeweled curios, along with silver and crystal serving wear. The furniture was upholstered in bright shades and patterns, with pillows to match. Some might call it high style; I called it blinding.

Expecting a pitch to invest in my father's development project, I searched the room for my mother. But she wasn't the only person here today.

My mother didn't immediately catch sight of me—not with my entrance on the far end. And not with all the commotion.

A woman, bent at the waist, was dragging a plant twice her size slowly across the floor, scraping the pot noisily against the hardwood. "Over here?" she asked in a lightly winded but familiar voice.

I looked sharply at my mother standing in front of floor-to-ceiling paned windows, heat spiraling up my neck

"I changed my mind," my mother said, tapping her lip, focused on the circus she'd created and not my presence. "I'd like it on the other side of the room."

Unable to stand it any longer, I said, "What is going on?"

My mother spun her head in my direction, her face brightening at the same time Sophia's head snapped up and her lips parted in surprise.

Sophia's light-pink blouse featured a dirt smudge down the front, and my blood boiled. No telling how long my mother had enslaved her with a half-dead sixty-pound plant inside the ancestral home.

Had my mother sniffed out my interest in Jack's room-mate? I wouldn't be surprised if Kitty had hired a private investigator to look into my personal life. She was a wily one, and she wanted me to marry a society woman.

"Maxwell, you've arrived," my mother said, her gaze sliding to the far corner of the room—where Gwen was sitting primly on a robin's-egg-blue velvet couch, sipping coffee from hundred-year-old china.

"Max," Gwen said and set her drink on the mahogany table that had been in this room since I was a toddler. My mother wasn't a hoarder, per se, like Sophia's mom, but she had her share of clutter. Just really expensive clutter.

Gwen glanced at Sophia, who quickly brushed soil from her hands, avoiding my eyes. "Josie Gates hired Green Aesthetic, and she raved about their design," Gwen said. "I forwarded the tip to your mother." She smiled at my mom. "Aren't they just fabulous, Kitty? They even move plants during a consult."

Sophia turned away as though ashamed.

Disgust and rage coursed through me. Gwen's actions were somewhat surprising, but not entirely. My mother's, however, were more so, and I'd never been more ashamed.

Moving plants was not a part of Sophia's job duties. But my mother never thought about things like that, and neither did Gwen, which I'd realized too late in our relationship.

Head held high, Sophia brushed back a few strands of hair that had fallen in her face and grabbed a worn leather bag next to the floral couch with a weird bamboo base I never could figure out. She gave my mother a stiff smile. "I'll draw up some design suggestions and get them to you later." She hurried toward the door.

I subtly reached for her arm as she passed. "Are you okay?"

She shook off my touch and kept walking, her face flushed.

I wanted to run after her and apologize, but I got the sense she wouldn't welcome it. Not right now.

I leveled a look at my mother. "What do you think you're doing?"

"My, my!" Kitty said. "Don't be so dramatic, Maxwell. I'm hiring a designer. I met Sophia at your rooftop party, and then Gwen recommended her."

Gwen glanced between us nervously, but she didn't say anything, and she didn't get up to leave.

I crossed my arms. It was possible my mother knew

nothing about my interest in Sophia, but she'd humiliated a friend. "Sophia is a highly educated, skilled designer. Ordering her to move heavy objects is not a part of her job. Not to mention it's insulting."

My mother rolled her eyes. "Pish. I was nice, wasn't I, Gwenny?"

Gwen delivered a charming smile to my mother. "Of course."

Bullshit. I could only imagine how Sophia had felt being bossed around by a rich client. She probably hadn't believed she could say no. And then there was Gwen, coddling my mother's ego. "I'm leaving," I said.

My mother's forehead wrinkled. "But we haven't discussed the reason I asked you here today."

I turned my back on her and walked to the exit of the stuffy salon no amount of light and air could break through. "You have a phone. Use it next time."

Chapter Seventeen

Sophia

"WHAT'S WRONG?" MY SISTER SANK INTO THE BOOTH at Bay Café after I'd called her over for an emergency meetup. She was looking showered and rather put together after her undignified early morning getaway.

I took a bite of my croissant, barely tasting it. "How long do you plan on refusing to come to my apartment? Because meeting here every time we want to get together is going to become a nuisance."

Elise had refused to meet at my place, and after running into Max at his mother's, all I wanted was to return to my bedroom for the next six to seven years and stream *Gilmore Girls* from my laptop.

"Forever," Elise said flatly.

I threw down the croissant. "This is ridiculous. Talk to Jack and work things out."

Elise reached across the table, stole the croissant, and jammed it into her mouth. "Not happening," she mumbled, croissant flakes falling from her lips.

I could be stubborn, but Elise was a donkey.

"So what's up?" she said, poking me in the arm after she'd finished chewing my food. "Why aren't you eating?"

"I'm eating," I said and sipped my water. In truth, I didn't have much of an appetite. I was embarrassed, confused, excited, and worried all at the same time. "My boss offered for me to buy Green Aesthetic."

Her eyes widened. "Are you kidding? That's incredible."

"It is," I agreed as the waitress dropped off two plates: a sandwich for Elise and a salad for me. I picked at the roasted beet and apple salad. "Victor's putting together a business proposal. It's exciting, but I'm worried I'll be getting in over my head."

Elise studied me as she took a bite of her BLT, which I'd preordered because she'd texted me that she was "ravenous." This I translated to *get food stat* or there'd be a hangry situation.

"You might be getting in over your head," she said, "but if anyone can take on the responsibility and succeed, it's you."

Somehow, I managed swimming through uncharted waters well. But there was always a first time to sink. "It's a risk."

"But a good risk. It's what you've always dreamed about, so why the sad face?"

I brushed Elise's croissant crumbs from the table. "Victor asked me to meet a new client today for a consult." I looked up and caught her eye. "It was Max's mother."

I explained how I'd met Max's mother at the rooftop party, along with his ex-girlfriend.

Elise's mouth twisted. "That's a weird coincidence."

"Or not." I pinched the bridge of my nose.

Being called over to Kitty Burrows' house had felt like a setup. She'd been expecting me personally, and then there was Max's ex sitting there, cozy as could be. But there was no way Victor would have done something like that. He didn't know Max and his family; not to mention, he was the kindest man alive. The one time I'd dared look Max in the eye in his mother's fancy drawing room, he'd seemed surprised to see me. He couldn't have set it up either.

"I didn't know it was Max's parents' home until a man opened the door and led me to the back of the house, overlooking a garden." I set my fork on the table, giving up on the salad. "A garden, Elise. A freaking garden in the middle of San Francisco. And not some small patch of grass. Oh no, Max's family lives in a Victorian mansion I've ridden the bus past a million times and assumed was a museum. His family is so rich they have a man who answers the front door—"

"A butler."

"—and a spiral staircase the size of Coit Tower."

"That sounds like an exaggeration." She continued munching on her sandwich. "However, Max paid for our drinks the other night, and he owns the building you live in. Are you really surprised he's wealthy?"

"No," I said, grudgingly. "What was surprising was the kiss he gave me the night before his mother ordered me around like a servant."

Elise stopped chewing. *What?* She set her sandwich on her plate. I'd finally said something that won the battle for attention with her appetite. "You kissed Landlord Devil?"

I avoided her eyes. "He kissed me, but I...reciprocated."

"Damn straight you did." She leaned back, hand on her head as though excited or shocked or both. "I'm missing how this is a bad thing, Soph. Max has his shit together, and he isn't hard on the eyes. Please tell me you aren't considering ditching him in favor of another of the Paul variety?"

"Did you miss the part about his mother? And if 'rich' is your only criterion, Paul's family was extremely wealthy. Not that I want a repeat of Paul. If anything, I learned a valuable lesson about dating a guy who comes from a wealthy family. As in, think twice."

Elise shrugged and picked up her sandwich. "Rich people are raised different. Everyone is probably a servant in Max's mother's eyes. Don't take it personally."

"How can I not?" I said and picked my fork back up. I pushed salad around on my plate to distract myself. "We're not equal. I can't kiss Max anymore. Down that path lies destruction."

Elise let out a light sigh. "It was just a kiss. Go out with the guy and see if you like him."

That was the problem and the reason I'd spent most of my waking hours today thinking about him. I didn't want to like Max. He stole my chocolate, and generally drove me nuts, but I didn't need to go on a date with him to know if I liked him. I already knew that I did. The kiss had sealed the deal.

I'd hated Max up until he flipped the switch on me and showed me that he wasn't as shallow as I'd imagined. He'd been kind to my mother the day he met her, and then he'd escorted me home. In contrast, Paul's reaction to meeting my mother had led to our breakup.

Max had kissed me *after* meeting my mother. And with kissing skills no man should possess. Not if a woman was supposed to remain upright and not melt into a puddle of drool and dirty thoughts.

"What if it was only a kiss to him?" I said. Max might

very well be toying with me, but I could easily see myself falling for a classy man with kissing skills. My lips were not immune, and neither was my heart. I pointed my fork at Elise. "Besides, you act like dating Max would be no big deal. If it's no big deal to put your heart out there, what about you and Jack? Because clearly there's an attract—"

"La, la, la—anyway," Elise said, cutting me off and sticking her fingers in her ears. "As I was saying, did you like kissing Max?"

I glared. "Kissing Max was like the stupid mansion—I couldn't comprehend the indulgence before I experienced it."

Elise paused a beat, then said, "That was poetic." She tilted her head and tapped the side of her chin. "I did not see this coming. I should have, with my talent for sniffing out your love life."

I shot her a disbelieving look. "Since when have you been a bloodhound in the romance department?"

"Since I predicted Paul would leave you."

Ouch.

Elise had told me to throw my ex back the very first night she met him. Then I proceeded to date him for a year. So, she had me there. "Well, apparently, you were too busy sniffing out my roommate to notice the sparks flying in the other section of the apartment."

Elise's face turned bright red. "We will not discuss that other individual. Back to LD. What happened after he kissed you?"

"LD?"

"Landlord Devil."

I took a sip of water. "I ran away, of course. I'm not capable of mixing hate and love."

"But is it hate?" she said in an annoying, squeaky, high

voice. "Maybe he's been eating your chocolates to get your attention."

"Like a ten-year-old boy?"

"I'm just saying, never overestimate the emotional maturity of men. They resort to caveman tendencies when faced with perplexing situations. Like, say, having feelings for a woman they weren't planning to like."

I blinked several times. Some of what she was said made sense. "How can you dish wisdom like this one moment, then slither down a fire escape the next?"

"It's a talent," she said, and picked the tomato off her BLT, leaving her with the *L* and the *B*. "As far as cave brain goes," she said, chewing another bite of her sandwich, "women have their own fight-or-flight instincts."

I swirled the ice cubes in my glass. "I can't date Max, no matter what that kiss did to me. His mother treated me like the help. That's a power struggle I want no part of. Even so..." I gave her a tentative look. "What if he doesn't have plans to date me, Elise? What if I was just a booty call?"

"Did you give him booty? Because if you did, I'm impressed. You typically make your boyfriends wait months before you put out."

"No, I didn't give him booty! But what if that's all he wants, and I'm his cheap sidepiece?"

Elise touched my arm with a reassuring grip. "There is no way he thinks of you as a sidepiece. You're way too uptight for that." I glowered. "Besides," she said, "I think the technical definition of a sidepiece is a man or woman who dates someone already in a relationship."

My mind flashed to Gwen. But even Jack had said Max and Gwen weren't together anymore.

"But seriously," Elise said, "don't give up on Max just yet. I have a feeling about him..."

"Your Spidey-senses are misfiring after your one-night stand."

She reached across the table and pinched me on the arm. Hard.

I cackled and rubbed the area. I'd never let her live down the fire escape for as long as I lived.

"I'm serious, Soph," she said. "Don't give up on LD."

But what was there to hold on to? Max and I didn't fit. He came from San Francisco royalty, and I was the lowly commoner. A financially strapped lowly commoner to boot.

"Let's be real," I said. "Our family would be a stain on the Burrows line."

Elise rolled her eyes. "I see you're still watching Korean dramas."

"Hell yes, I am. Paul introducing me to K-dramas was the only good thing that came out of our relationship. Getting back to my point—this happens all the time in the Korean chaebol families. The oldest son of a business conglomerate falls in love with a poor girl, and the family pays off the unworthy sap to keep her away. It's all about money marrying money."

Elise polished off the last of her sandwich. "I mean, you're probably right. In a lot of cases, I imagine wealthy parents want their children to marry someone in their same socioeconomic sphere. But look at the building Max owns and where he lives. It's nice, but it's not billionaire nice. And consider his best friend, Jack, who's about as normal as they come. Whatever Max is doing, he's not flaunting his wealth."

"You have a point." Max dressed well and owned what I would consider a very nice Victorian building, but he didn't live in the mega mansion on Franklin Street. I hadn't even been aware people lived in those places, hence my belief it was a museum until I met with his mother. And Max stole other people's food, which was just uncivilized. I bet the chaebols didn't steal chocolate.

"Besides," she said, sending me a skeptical look, "are you planning to marry Max or date him?"

"Stop harassing me. You know I'm a newbie back on the dating scene and have no idea what I'm doing. I'm in way over my head."

Elise wiped her bacony fingers on a thick paper napkin. "You're jumping the gun and ditching a guy before you know his motives."

"There's nothing for me to ditch," I said. "I doubt Max is thinking anything serious. He's probably forgotten all about the kiss. And anyway, I have a business to run if I'm to take over Green Aesthetic."

Elise's mouth twisted to the side. "You're seriously considering it?" At my nod, she said, "It sounds like a great opportunity, but don't forget to take care of yourself. I worry that you'll take care of everything and everyone except for number one."

"No worries there." Forgetting about Max Burrows and his kiss *was* taking caring of myself. Nothing good could come from dating him.

Chapter Eighteen

Sophia

Elise called a couple days later, and she was losing her shit. "We have rats. Big, fat, greasy rats like you'd find in a New York City gutter. I called an exterminator, but Mom won't let the guy in! I have a midterm in thirty minutes, Soph. Do something!"

So much for taking care of myself and not everyone around me. In truth, I'd just wrapped up with a client and didn't have another appointment that day. At least, not one I couldn't easily reschedule. "I'm on it," I said.

Victor had given me the formal business proposal this morning, and I hadn't taken the time to look at it yet, but that could wait too. I raced across town to my mom's house.

She answered the door, her expression harried, wearing what Elise and I called her muumuu, an oversized, billowy dress she'd owned since Elise was born. Quite possibly a maternity dress she'd never let go of. "Why aren't you at work?" she asked, as though there weren't an emergency brewing in the house.

I scanned the floor for rodents before stepping inside. "Elise says we have rats."

My mom's gaze skittered to the side. "Maybe one."

I rubbed my forehead and looked around. Were the stacks of newspapers and magazines taller today? Had things gotten worse? "The last time this happened, the exterminators couldn't get to everything, Mom. This is a problem because of the condition of the house."

"Rats are cute, don't you think?"

My jaw dropped. "No, I don't think they're cute. These aren't domestic pets. They're rats coming in off the street because our home is a perfect breeding ground for rodents."

My mother pouted, but I saw the worry in her eyes. "I pick up. There's never any food left out."

I rubbed my forehead and let out a strained breath. What was her rock bottom? Was she going to start cohabitating with rats now? "We have to pack up the extra stuff in the house and clean the place."

Elise and I had managed to get my mom to "consider" packing up the house and garage and moving boxes to a storage facility once or twice before, but we'd never gotten her to commit. The timing was always bad, or she wasn't feeling well. Getting rid of anything was out of the question, as that resulted in severe panic attacks and crying, but even she understood the house was a safety hazard. Elise and I worried that if we didn't declutter and clean the place, Mom would get sick or hurt. Or Elise would get sick or hurt.

My mom paced the narrow track of carpet between the entry and the hallway. "Not now, Sophia."

"Yes now, Mom. Not today, because I have to get back to work, but soon. And you're letting the exterminator in. Elise said you refused."

"He'll spray toxic gas to kill the rats and poison us."

Rats. At least she'd admitted there were more than one. "My understanding is that the place Elise called uses humane methods to get rid of the problem. Traps and such. Either way, the workers need access, but that won't be enough. With the house in this condition, the traps won't solve the problem long-term. Rats will keep coming back unless we do something major."

She got a hopeful glint in her eye. "Then there's no point in letting pest control in today. There's no time to pack, as you said."

I groaned. She had a mental illness, likely unresolved trauma from losing my dad. I understood that, but the situation drove me batshit crazy. My initial instinct was to lure my mom out of the house, toss everything in a dumpster, and set fire to it. But then I took a deep breath and calmed the hell down.

This was my mother's house. Her things. Taking away her control in that manner could result in a worse mental state than the one she was in. I had no solutions, but I knew that much.

"Mom, you can't live with wild rodents. What if they have rabies? Pest control will set traps today and return later to remove the animals they catch. But they'll need to return once we clear everything out. They can't manage the problem with all this stuff around." Were other women forced to convince their moms to get rid of indoor rats, or was I just special?

"Oh, great!" my mother shouted. "Why not throw me out of my own house!"

Frustration burned so hot, tears welled behind my eyes. She never meant it when she said stuff like that. It was desperation. "Moving your possessions somewhere safe is not throwing you out. You'll still have furniture and your daily household items. We'd only move the things you don't regularly use, and we'd place them in storage. Where you can visit your stuff any time you like."

She'd never visit the storage facility, and it would cost an arm and a leg in monthly fees, but it was the only thing my mom had ever considered. Her attachment to possessions was indescribable.

She glanced around, twisting her hands nervously. "I'm not agreeing to moving anything. And I'm going to my bedroom while those men are here."

I wrapped my arm around her shoulders and walked her back. "I'll take care of everything. They'll be gone before you know it."

———

THE EXTERMINATOR TOOK LONGER than expected. By the time I returned to the shop, Victor was yawning and had cleaned off his desk for the day. "Everything okay?"

No. Not at all.

Victor knew some things about my family, but I never shared the trouble we had at home with anyone.

I turned toward my design desk. "You head home, and I'll take care of any last calls that come in."

He gave me a soft smile. "Why don't we both leave early? The projects will hold until tomorrow, and I want you to take some time to consider the proposal. Can't consider it if you're working long hours and helping your mother."

Victor knew my mom had issues, but he'd never asked for specifics. He was supportive without knowing the details, and I'd always appreciated that. "I don't mind staying."

He shook his head. "Nope. Go home. Have a good meal and a glass of wine. You deserve it."

Okay, when he put it like that...

I often worked late, especially when we were short-staffed, but if Victor wasn't worried about closing early, why should I be? There'd be plenty of time to stress myself out running the business later. For now, I did as he suggested and closed the shop with no intention of working from home that night.

Chapter Nineteen

Max

THE LAST TWO DAYS HAD BEEN UNUSUALLY BUSY. IN addition to meetings with accountants, engineers, and architects, I'd met with city planners to go over the final schematics for Cityscape. Everyone was on board, very likely because my company would provide much-needed affordable housing—affordable by San Francisco standards, at any rate. Most of the units would be priced in the middle-income range, with a few exceptions for low-income families. Everything was going according to plan, and that made me nervous. Real estate developments rarely went according to plan.

The last item the planning department required was detailed schematics for landscaping, which was to be expected. The building was in a high-traffic area, and city planners wanted more greenspace with each new project they approved. But all that greenspace talk had me thinking of Sophia.

Technically, I had never stopped thinking about her.

Sophia had stolen my attention from the moment she carelessly discarded pink panties on my best friend's couch. I'd brushed off the attraction and told myself it was just another woman looking for a rich boyfriend. But that was an excuse. I'd liked her. I just hadn't been ready to admit it.

A part of me had been tempted to kiss Sophia sooner than I cared to admit, and I'd finally given in to the temptation the other night in front of her door.

Bad move. I didn't know how Sophia had felt in that moment, but that kiss was the best damn thing I'd experienced in my life. It was luxury and comfort and arousal all in one, and I was hooked.

If tonight went as planned, I'd catch Sophia on her way home. I had it on good authority (Jack) that she returned around six after her shop closed. Jack said she sometimes worked late, but typically from home.

Visiting my best friend at his apartment after his roommate came home from work wasn't stalking. I wanted to see Jack, and if Sophia was there too, that couldn't be helped.

The delusions I told myself were colorful.

After parking two blocks away, I headed on foot to the apartment and rounded the corner to my street, but the vision in front of me wasn't what I had expected. A pulse thrummed in my eyelid, and I let out a sigh.

My mother was stepping out of a town car, a driver holding the door open for her. She wore a pale gray pantsuit, which meant she was all business today. She caught sight of me as I approached, her lips compressed as though someone had tried to hand her a pair of knockoff Stuart Weitzmans. "Still parking on the street, I see."

My parents had been horrified to learn I'd converted the garage of my building into a studio and parked my car on the street. "What can I do for you, Mom?"

"You don't answer my calls."

I was still irritated with her antics regarding Sophia and the green design of her parlor, but my mother wasn't a bad person. She was simply unaware at times.

I leaned down and kissed her cheek. "Not when you insist on bending me to your will."

"When has anyone managed that?"

She had a point. Burrows tenacity ran deep. "I'm assuming this visit is about Starlight?"

"Not here." She moved in the direction of the stairwell. "Let's talk upstairs. It will give you a chance to show me what you've done with the apartment. Jack mentioned you remodeled yours at the same time you repaired the damage to his rental."

"It made sense," I said as we walked up two flights of stairs. "The studio was vacant then as well, and updating the electrical and plumbing for the entire building was more economical than one unit at a time."

We reached the top floor, and my mother leaned a heavy hand to the wall, panting dramatically. "And you didn't think to add an elevator?"

There was no sense arguing. My mother didn't believe in economizing.

I punched in the code to my unit and let her inside.

She looked over the updated kitchen with a critical eye. "It's very modern."

Anything newer than 1900s design aesthetic was too modern for Kitty Burrows, formerly Kitty Haas. The late 1800s and early 1900s, when her grandfather had made a fortune as a gold rush supplier, were her family's heyday. "My designer calls it urban modern with warmth." I gestured to the kitchen. "Espresso?"

She frowned. "It's five thirty in the afternoon, Maxwell.

You'll stay up all night if you drink caffeine now." She took a sharp breath and looked away. "Pour me a decaf. And add half an espresso to that."

My mother fooled no one with her decaf bullshit. If she could attach a caffeine drip to her arm, she would. Besides, I didn't keep decaf in the house, and she knew it.

She frowned when I set down the espresso, and then proceeded to guzzle it with ladylike delicacy. Pushing aside the saucer and cup, she said, "Your father tells me you refused to see reason where Starlight is concerned."

"It's too expensive and benefits few, including the city." The same thing I'd told my dad, which bore repeating due to the stubbornness gene.

She looked at me sternly. "It benefits our dear friends, and your father and me."

"Precisely. Very few people, and extremely wealthy ones at that. I told Dad not to put his money into that hedge fund, and he didn't listen. He made a mistake, but I'm not responsible for cleaning it up."

She lowered her chin. "You've grown cold in your thirty years."

"If by cold you mean responsible and empathetic to the plight of those with less, then yes."

She rolled her eyes and stood, wandering to a window that overlooked the neighborhood. When she turned back to me, her expression was one of concern. "Your father and I want to leave you with what we had. Is it too much for us to want to rebuild?"

I set down my cup and joined her at the bay window. "I understand your nostalgia for holding on to what your great-grandfather built, but I won't live my life trying to recreate it. I have my own dreams and aspirations."

"To help others," she deadpanned.

"I'm not entirely altruistic." Sophia's comment about my car and clothing came to mind. Clearly, I had my own extravagances. "But yes, helping others is a part of it."

She shook her head in disbelief. "How did we raise such a conscientious child?"

"It's astonishing, isn't it?" I hadn't the heart to tell her Jack's family had more to do with it than she or my father.

She smacked my arm good-humoredly. "And with a smart mouth."

I checked the time. Sophia should be home by now. "Mom, was there anything else you needed? I have an appointment."

She continued to wander the apartment, looking inside rooms and frowning. "There's hardly enough space for you, Maxwell. What will you do once you marry? Don't you want children?"

And here was her other favorite topic. If it wasn't money, it was marriage and procreation. Though that last one had been at the forefront of my mind lately too. Specifically, with a certain feisty, chocolate-loving female.

"There's plenty of time for marriage and kids," I told my mom. "I can always buy a larger place if need be. I'm not financially crippled, like you and Dad."

Kitty glared comically. "I take back the smart mouth comment; you're a very rude son."

I laughed. "This is a three-bedroom, Mom. I'm sure I can squeeze a kid or two in here."

"Or you could return home to Franklin Street and live with me and your father. You could have an entire floor to yourself." She grinned innocently.

"We both know that's not happening."

"A mother can dream," she said, sighing and glancing inside one of the bedrooms. "Just make sure you get rid of

this metal contraption before you marry." She waved chop-
pily at the air. "It's not safe for young children."

"The in-home gym will have to go," I admitted. "I'll join
a gym if I want to maintain my six-pack abs."

She shook her head incredulously. "It's unfortunate you
got your father's sense of humor."

Winking, I said, "Fortunately, I didn't get his investment sense."

She attempted a frown, but I was wearing her down, I
could tell. "I'll be sure to share that with your father."

"He has my sense of humor, remember?"

Kitty rolled her eyes. "I'm leaving," she said and picked
up her purse from the kitchen counter on her way to the
front door.

With her palm on the handle, she stopped and turned to
me, her expression serious. "We'll be fine, your father and I.
Though I worry if others discover how much we lost, it
could hurt our standing in society." She glanced off, her
gaze strained before she looked back. "Promise you won't
share the extent of our misstep with anyone?"

"Gwen and Jack are aware, but you know how Jack is.
When I tried to tell him about our family history and
wealth when we were teenagers, his eyes glazed over. He
doesn't care about money. Gwen won't say anything
either."

My mother nodded. "Gwenny wouldn't say anything to
harm our family."

I wasn't so sure of that, but I wasn't about to tell my
mother why Gwen and I broke up. Chances were, Gwen
would never tell anyone about my parents' lost fortune,
because it would reflect poorly on her. She claimed to still
want to be together, and she couldn't have others knowing
my parents weren't at the top of the ladder any longer.

My mother looked slightly mollified, but the lines around her mouth remained.

"Mom, if you lose connections because of this, those people weren't worth your time."

She smiled sadly. "Connections are how fortunes are built, Max. Connections are everything."

Chapter Twenty

Sophia

For the first time in forever, I didn't bring work home. And it was a good thing too, because I couldn't get the lights to turn on in the kitchen or the living room, where I typically sprawled out my designs.

I walked up and down the hallway, flipping switches on and off to see what worked and what didn't. "Jack?"

No answer.

The guy was always home, eating my stash of snacks. Had he gone out to forage in the real world?

This was what I got for not orienting myself better to the new apartment; I had to rely on a guy to help me find the fuse box.

I was scrolling through my phone, searching for Jack's number, when a knock sounded at the front door.

The room was growing darker now that the sun had set, and I was still in my work clothes, only barefoot, as I'd kicked off my shoes the moment I got home. I was tired and cranky after the rat stress with my mom, but I padded over and looked through the peephole. And my heart raced.

Max Burrows had the worst timing.

I'd planned on avoiding him until the whole kissing incident blew over. But it was still vivid in my mind, and I wasn't ready for a post-kiss confrontation. I didn't know what the kiss had meant, and I was too scared to find out. Too scared it meant nothing and my hormones were overreacting, or that it meant something and I wasn't ready for that either. In short, I was an emotional hot mess.

Spinning around, I searched the room as though the answers were somewhere inside the couch cushions or the lampshade. Why the hell had Jack chosen today of all days to leave me on my own?

I smoothed down my pale blue shift dress, making sure it lay straight. I could do this, I thought, and opened the door.

And nearly fainted.

My chest locked up, and my head felt woozy. Max was in a tan suit this time, only he'd taken off his tie and unbuttoned the top button of his dress shirt.

Was it me, or had he gotten even better looking? He spoke, and my gaze rose from the patch of tan skin at his throat to his lips, and then I was having flashbacks to the kiss that had taken place in nearly this exact same location.

"Sophia?"

"Yes?" Why did I suddenly sound like a smoker of thirty years?

The corner of his mouth pulled up. "You okay?" He looked past me. "I'm trying to get a hold of Jack, and he's not answering his phone."

Right, *Jack*. "He's not here."

Max's head tilted as he glanced down to my bare feet and the room behind me. "You just getting home?"

"I got home a little while ago," I said, glancing back nervously.

He crossed his arms and tapped his finger on his biceps. "What's going on?"

This conversation would be a whole lot easier if I could look him in the eye and not at the small patch of flesh he was recklessly revealing. Had he no idea how hopped up my hormones were after that kiss? "Jack's not here, and the power is out in part of the house."

His arms dropped to his sides and he frowned, swiftly moving past me. "What do you mean, the power is out? Did you blow a fuse?"

I frowned at his immediate assumption that I'd done something wrong when I hadn't even been home. Some things never changed.

He headed down the bedroom hallway, and I followed close behind. "What are you doing?"

He looked over his shoulder. "I'm checking the circuit breaker." He stopped, hesitating, and looked back as though just realizing he might have overstepped. "Is that okay, or do you already know where it is?"

Of course I didn't know where it was. I'd only recently discovered my shallow orientation of the place. I knew none of the important things for an emergency. Did we even own a fire extinguisher?

I shook my head, and he rounded the corner to my room. *My room.* "Wait!"

Max had already entered the bedroom and nearly tripped over the tennis shoes I'd switched my heels for before going to my mom's this afternoon.

He frowned at the shoes and looked up. "Is there a problem?"

"You can't be in here," I told him.

He glanced around, his gaze landing on the cream bra I'd torn off as well.

I stiffened, heat blooming in my face. Apparently, I was a post-work clothes discarder. And this discarded apparel was dangling from the single chair in my room, reminiscent of the underwear that had marked the start of our relationship.

I forced my eyes to stare straight ahead and not down at my chest to see if it was obvious I wasn't wearing a bra.

Max lifted one eyebrow. "More unmentionables?"

I pointed my finger at the door. "Get out!"

"Sure. Though maybe you'd like me to show you the circuit breaker before I leave?"

He was so annoying, and that was a good thing, because I was no longer thinking about the kiss or the naked patch of chest taunting me. "Quickly."

He reached behind the bedroom door to a wall-colored panel I hadn't thought anything about because I wasn't used to electrical panels. When a fuse blew at home, my mom was the only person willing to climb the rodent-infested terrain of our garage to reach it. It was kind of her thing. Though now that I thought about it, probably not entirely safe.

The snapping of switches sounded, and then Max closed the panel. "Do you want to check and see if the lights are on? If not, something else could be the problem."

I gestured to myself. "You want me to go out there? Alone? While you stay in my bedroom?"

His eyes narrowed. "You're very protective of your room. I didn't even touch your silk bra."

"But you noticed it!"

His eyes crinkled at the corners. "As any man would."

"You go first," I said, shooing him out.

He gave me the half shrug of a confident man and walked out of my bedroom and down the hallway.

As we neared the living room and kitchen, I saw that the lights were on. Whatever switches Max flipped had done the trick.

He looked around, seemingly satisfied. "Don't worry about the fridge; it's on a different circuit, and I heard it running when I walked in."

I hadn't even considered the fridge. I swear I was the responsible one at home—dumpster-diving through the garage not included—but you wouldn't know it today. "Thank you," I said.

He scratched his jaw. Usually he was clean-shaven, but today he had a bit of stubble, and it made him look less refined, more rugged, and ridiculously hot. "About the other night..."

My body returned to its petrified state of a moment ago. He was bringing it up?

I wasn't prepared for my extremely hot, wealthy landlord to explain why he shouldn't have kissed me. "Totally forgotten," I said, feigning cheerfulness, and smiled for good measure.

He hesitated a beat, his brow pinched. A second later, he said, "I'd like to cook you dinner."

My smiled slipped. "What?"

"Dinner? Food? That thing we need to sustain ourselves?"

"You can cook?" I said lamely.

"Passably. You have plans later?"

"No," I said before thinking better of it. "But—"

"In an hour, then." He opened the front door to leave, but before he exited, he leaned into the doorjamb, raking his gaze over me, mouth curved up in a sensual smile. "It's casual. You don't even have to put your bra back on."

He knew! Heat flooded my face as Landlord Devil closed the door.

What was happening?

I liked food, and I wasn't a fan of cooking. It was the only reason I was considering ignoring Max's questionable behavior and having dinner with him. This would be payback for all the expensive chocolate he stole. It had nothing to do with the fact I couldn't stop looking at the slice of flesh he'd revealed, or the manly stubble next to those silky lips that had set my entire body on fire the other night.

I would not be seduced by Max Burrows.

Chapter Twenty-One

Sophia

AN HOUR LATER, I'D CHANGED INTO JEANS AND A T-shirt, along with my tennis shoes. Max had said it was casual, and I saw no reason to try to impress him. This was me foraging for a life-sustaining meal, and nothing more.

I checked my hair and makeup in my phone camera—I'm not a total savage; I'd applied lipstick—and knocked on his door.

Two minutes later, I was still waiting. What was taking him so long? I knocked a second time.

It wasn't a good sign that he was making me wait outside, reminding me that I needed to set mental ground rules.

There would be no kissing. I would eat Max's food because he owed me, and I was hungry. We could be friends —I'd allow that. But nothing more. The kiss had been a blip in what was to date my most confusing relationship with a man. Was he my landlord? Was he the asshole best friend of my roommate? Or something more? I didn't know. And because I didn't know, I was going to play it cool. I was business Sophia tonight—no more shenanigans.

Finally, Max opened the door, and he was out of breath, a grease stain splattered across a casual pale-blue button-down, the sleeves rolled up to his elbows. "Sorry. I almost burned the lasagna."

He rushed away and left me standing there with the door open. So I did what any sane person would do and stepped inside. And holy shit...

Max's house was nothing like Jack's and my apartment. Our place was nicer than most rentals in San Francisco, but Max's apartment was like a high-end showroom, only homier.

The hardwood floors were light, with herringbone zigzags, and a gas fireplace roared across the room, surrounded by dark espresso built-in bookcases. A patterned navy rug and an elegant sectional pulled the living room area together, while a ten-person polished wood dining table with upholstered chairs overlooked a stunning view of the neighborhood and trees. A separate hazelnut leather sitting area rested next to a corner window with a view of the Bay and Alcatraz. Everything was elegant yet comfortable looking, without appearing too masculine. And I needed to meet Max's designer because I was ready to marry her/him.

The ceilings were taller in Max's place than in my apartment, making Max's home feel massive. Though glancing around, I could tell it was indeed double the square footage of what Jack and I shared. But the kitchen was the real showstopper. With a built-in wall of hickory wood cabinets in a modern design, an espresso machine, and huge, expensive-looking professional appliances, the kitchen was the diamond centerpiece of the apartment. In the center stood a marble island with cabinets in the same nearly black espresso shade as the bookcases, and four modern, lighter wood barstools pushed up on either side for a bar-height table feel.

Max set a casserole dish on the island, the muscles on his bared forearm bulging distractingly. He nudged the Wolf oven door closed with his socked foot and pushed back a lock of hair that had fallen over his forehead. "Sorry, I thought it would be done by now. Then I realized it *was* done, and I'd nearly overcooked everything."

"Do you make food often?" It didn't seem like it, but who was I to say?

He scratched his jaw, clean-shaven now, and peered nervously at the casserole dish. "No, so I make no guarantees."

I walked over and checked the food. Hard to go wrong with noodles, marinara sauce, and cheese. "Smells good."

He glanced up, and I swore his gaze was nervous, which was incredibly strange coming from this man. "Don't say that until you try it."

This was a first, seeing Max out of his element. He'd put effort into tonight, and it was oddly charming. "I'm not a cook," I said, "so it doesn't take much to impress me."

"If all else fails," he said, "I have something else that should impress you."

"If you say it's in your bedroom, I'm leaving right now." I was half joking, but kind of not. Men never failed to surprise me.

A dark look crossed his eyes. "Has a man said that to you before?"

"No, but I've had other offers in a similar vein." I leaned closer and took another whiff of the lasagna, and my stomach rumbled. Between my mom's rodent woes and work, I'd forgotten to eat lunch.

Max mumbled something under his breath, then said, "I can't answer for others, but my only motive was a date and nothing more."

I caught the sincere look on his face. "So this *is* a date?"

He pulled down plates from a cupboard next to the oven and looked over. "That's typically what it means when a man asks a woman to dinner."

I sat in one of the barstools he set a plate in front of. "True, but you and I haven't always had the smoothest relationship. And you're my landlord. Don't you think it's taboo to date a tenant?"

He reached for one of the two wineglasses on the island and paused, catching my eye. "Only if you feel pressured to be here. Did you come because you felt you must, or because you wanted to?"

"I'm here because I'm hungry."

His lips twisted as though he were holding back a smile. "That's fair. I've given you a hard time in the past."

"And now?"

He slid the wineglass toward me and held up two bottles, one red and one white.

I pointed to the red.

"Now," he continued, "things are different."

They weren't really. I was still living paycheck to paycheck and had some interesting family issues, while Max was still the wealthy son of a San Francisco first family. The only thing that had changed was one sizzling kiss. Other than that, we were totally different.

"Nothing about us has changed," I said. "Not really. So why would you want to go out?" I hadn't expected Max to seriously want to date. I figured it was an impulse or a convenient booty call, but not a real first step to dating. Men like him didn't date women like me for the long haul.

"You have good taste in chocolate," he said without missing a beat.

Okay, he was funny now that he wasn't scowling. And kind of charming. But I was still on my guard. "This is true. But chocolate doesn't a relationship make. And your mother hates me."

He poured the red wine into my wineglass and then his own. "Chocolate *is* important. And regardless of how my mother may come across at times, I doubt very much that she hates you. She's kinder than she appears."

I tapped the side of my wineglass, studying him. "In that case, why should I date you?" A bank account didn't impress me—good character did. Though it seemed he might have that too.

He took a sip of wine and patted his stomach. "My rock-hard abs?"

I laughed. Abs *were* something my female brain couldn't ignore. "I do enjoy a nice landscape. What else?"

"I can promise mediocre meals from the comfort of my kitchen."

"No fine restaurants?" I teased. I really didn't care about expensive meals, but it was curious that he didn't try to woo me with it.

"If you wish, though we might run into my mother and her friends." His brow quirked. "I believe I ran into you at one of those before too."

My jaw dropped. *Nom Tea Parlor, the dim sum restaurant.* "You knew that was me?"

"Of course I knew." He swirled his wineglass and took a whiff of the vintage. His gaze flicked up to me. "Why do you think I gave up my reservation?"

My eyes widened, and he laughed at my expression. "But you didn't like me back then."

"Didn't I?" He walked around the island to a drawer and pulled out cutlery, setting a fork and knife next to our plates. "I might not have admitted my attraction, but I'd noticed you."

I shook my head. "Men are so weird. Why not just say you like me? Would have saved us a lot of back and forth."

He smiled. "The back and forth is the fun part. But I admit, men aren't the most direct where feelings are involved."

I tapped my finger on the table. So he'd known it was me all along at the restaurant. Something to dissect later. "No fancy restaurants, then, or we'll risk running into your mother and her friends. How about mediocre ones?"

"Always on the table."

I ticked off my fingers. "We've got rock-hard abs and mediocre food. Have I missed any other perks to dating Max Burrows?"

He walked around the island and stood in front of me, looking down in a way that shot lightning bolts through my belly. "I like you, Sophia. Will you give us a chance to get to know each other better?" He leaned down and kissed me. Nothing fancy, just a lingering peck, and *son of a bitch*, it was just like last time. My body vibrated with the pleasure of that touch, and a light dose of pleasant man scent engulfed me.

What was it with his kisses?

He tilted my head, one hand on my waist, the other lightly touching my jaw. He leaned down and explored my mouth with another soft yet firm kiss, and a little tongue that had me leaning into him.

He eased back, his eyes still on my mouth. "Are we dating?"

"Kissing. Kissing is another one of your strong suits," I said.

"I'm glad you think so, because I plan to kiss you a lot."

Chapter Twenty-Two

Sophia

MAX KISSED ME ONCE MORE AND SAID, "WE SHOULD probably eat. Unless you'd rather do other things?" His tone was pure suggestion.

My stomach fluttered. I was more tempted than I cared to admit, now that I'd gotten used to the idea I was actually dating this man.

Holy crap, *dating*. I wasn't just dating anyone, I was dating Max—the man I'd loathed for weeks.

"Food," I said shakily. "Probably best we eat."

"Pity," he said, staring at my lips before returning to his seat.

Max served us, and we didn't waste any time digging in. For me it had more to do with keeping my mouth busy and not focusing on his lips.

And then I realized something as I stared at my plate and chewed. "Hey, this is pretty good."

He chuckled, a low, rumbly sound that sent a frisson of awareness through my core. "You sound surprised."

I pointed my fork at him, ignoring my body's autonomic response to his deep, sexy tone. "You were the one who said you couldn't cook."

"I said I didn't cook *often*. But like anything I put my mind to, I'm good at it." He winked.

"Oh, wow." I shook my head. "Now I'm not sure we should date. Your ego might smother me."

He shoved a forkful of food in his mouth and chewed. "Too late. You signed on the dotted line with your lips."

I so had. "That was very sneaky of you."

"I will use whatever skills I have to spend time with you."

My gaze narrowed, and he grinned. But I was all bluster, because regardless of whether we fit or had anything in common, I was attracted to Max. And it wasn't only his beautiful appearance, though that was distracting. He had a sense of humor beneath that designer fabric, and it made him ten times more appealing.

When I thought back, Max had never been cruel. A cocky ass, yes. Misguided out of a protective instinct, which I could get behind. And now he was showing me the real man. A sometimes rumpled, occasionally silly, decent human being. And he kept bringing up those abs, which intrigued me. Did he really have a washboard under those suits?

I studied him as we polished off our plates. Apparently, I'd been ravenous, because mine was licked clean. "So how often do you cook for women?"

He glanced up as though calculating, then said, "Never." He scraped the last of his food into his mouth.

Part astonishment and part excitement rushed through me. "You've never cooked for a woman?"

Watching him chew was mesmerizing. Jaw muscles

flexing, tongue sensually sneaking out to lick juices from his lips...and the man wasn't even trying to seduce me! Not at the moment, anyway. He shook his head. "I've made espresso for my mother. Does that count?"

"Not even a little."

He nodded. "So, never."

I tilted my head. "But you had a girlfriend. You dumped her in front of our building."

He leveled me a look that said he might chase me around the island for such insolence and attack me with aggressive kisses. Or was that just my imagination?

A girl could dream.

"We broke up months ago," he said pointedly.

"Details," I said. "You never cooked for Gwen?"

"No."

"Interesting."

"Is it?" he asked.

"Kind of." I leaned on my forearms and tapped my lip. "I'm trying to figure out to what I owe such effort."

He sat back and took a sip of wine, looking at me over the rim of his glass. "I find myself wanting to do nice things for you."

I chuckled, but I was all squirmy on the inside. "Like steal my chocolate?"

"Funny you should mention that..." He stood and crossed the kitchen to a cupboard above the fancy espresso machine. He opened it, then faced me and leaned against the cabinet, legs crossed at the ankle, as though he were revealing a treasure.

And he was.

I blinked several times, making sure I was seeing correctly. Four three-inch by three-inch golden boxes rested on an empty shelf. Not actual gold—they were probably made of cardboard, with a patterned surface to make the boxes look like they'd been plated gold. But I recognized the emblem. "No way. Those aren't La Fleur au Truffe."

His eyes twinkled. "Aren't they?"

"They can't be," I said, half sitting, half standing in my excitement. "They cost two hundred and fifty dollars a chocolate."

He reached for two of the boxes and set them on the island in front of me, and I sank back into my seat. "I thought we should see what all the hype is about," he said.

My heart raced. I looked between him and the chocolates and touched the surface of the box in front of me. I was in the presence of La Fleur au Truffe—and it blew my mind. "Where did you find these?"

He opened one of the lids and pulled out a truffle. "My assistant put in an order a couple of weeks ago. They don't last long, so we better eat them. Say ah."

I opened my mouth, and he slowly placed the chocolate inside.

Rich ganache, vanilla, cream, and straight-up decadence, if decadence was a flavor, filled my senses. "Oh my God..." Mouth orgasm—that's what this was.

He notched his chin up. "Another?"

My eyes widened and I nearly choked. "Have you lost your mind?" I said, chewing and savoring. No way would I wash it down with wine and ruin the flavor. "I can't believe I just ate two hundred and fifty dollars. We can't eat two; that's too much."

Max opened the second box and tossed the truffle in his mouth. He chewed and nodded. "It's good. Not sure they're worth all the effort. Some of the chocolate I stole from your apartment was just as nice."

I pointed at him. "So you admit to stealing my chocolate!"

He lifted an eyebrow. "Was it ever in question?"

I thought back, trying to remember if he'd ever denied it. He'd certainly suggested Jack might have bought the chocolate for him, which was ridiculous. Jack didn't eat chocolate. "You played it like you didn't know it was mine."

He walked back to the cupboard and grabbed the last two boxes. "We better eat these before they go bad. Think of it as repayment for all the chocolate I stole and conservation of the planet. They don't last long, and we wouldn't want to have to throw them away."

This was madness. "I can't believe you bought La Fleur au Truffe for a date." Jack was right—Max and I had more in common than I thought, because reckless spending on chocolate was something I would do. "I can't believe it, but I respect it."

He shrugged, pleased with himself. "I owed you."

"You did, right?" I smiled, willing to justify this gift in any way possible. He owed me for all the emotional turmoil he'd caused with his early Max attitude and chocolate scavenging.

As though remembering something, Max said, "Why were you so jumpy earlier?"

It might be rude, but I didn't care; I blatantly ogled the last two boxes of chocolate. "When?"

"When I came looking for Jack."

My eyes narrowed because I'd just thought of something when he mentioned coming to find me. He said he'd ordered the chocolate weeks ago. Which meant the dinner date tonight had been pre-planned. "Were you really looking for Jack?"

"No, I came to ask you out. But why were you jumpy?"

Butterflies erupted in my belly. A girl could get used to this kind of attention.

Had I been jumpy earlier? I'd just gotten off work, and yeah, a lot had gone on today. "Well, first, because you showed up unannounced, and your presence has that effect on me. Second, because I have a big decision to make with work, and I was stressing about it."

Max knew about my mom's place, but no way would I admit how bad it was below the surface with a rodent infestation. I skipped to the other major distraction of Victor's offer.

"My boss offered to sell me his business." I glanced up nervously, hands clenched together. "I don't know that I can afford it, but I'm considering it anyway because I've always wanted to run my own shop." Max knew I came from humble beginnings—no point in sugarcoating it.

He topped off my wine, and I didn't fight it. Not like I had to drive home. "What are the conditions of the contract?"

Max was a businessman. He'd be the first to look for strings attached.

"Considering what I'd be gaining," I said, "there don't seem to be many. Victor, my boss, has asked for a small percentage of the profit each year, and he'll stick around until I'm up and running on my own. I've skimmed the proposal, but there's a lot of legalese, and I'm not a lawyer. Victor isn't the type of person to screw me over, but I need to know what I'm agreeing to. I guess when you showed up this afternoon, I was thinking about where to go for a second opinion."

He corked the wine and lifted his glass, clinking it

against my own. "Congratulations on the offer. Though I'd be leery of a contract stipulating a portion of the profits in perpetuity. You might be better off settling on a price and paying him off with interest over time."

"From what he said and what I saw in the contract, that's the idea. Though I need to look more closely."

"I can look it over, if you like," he offered. "Jack would be a good person to review it as well. He has a law degree and might catch a few things I don't."

I set my glass down abruptly. "Jack has a *law* degree? He builds video games."

"I'm assuming you know that Jack beat out hundreds of smart kids in San Francisco to attend a prestigious middle school on scholarship, yes?"

Jack had mentioned that. "But he's so laid-back. He doesn't look like a lawyer."

Max laughed. "What does a lawyer look like?"

I smiled and shook my head. "I guess saying someone in a power suit is cliché. Still, Jack doesn't give off the lawyer vibe."

"He doesn't, which is part of his charm. Aside from designing video games, he's passed the bar and is a savvy businessman."

I shook my head, mind blown. "I'm impressed, and yes, absolutely. I'd love for both of you to look at the contract. Like I said, I'm not sure I'm the best person for the job this early in my career. I have a lot of family financial obligations. But if it worked out, it would be incredible."

He nodded, his brow furrowing slightly. "If the business is profitable and has been for some time, you might not need much saved." He hesitated a moment as though just realizing something. "Sophia, you never mention your father. Is he still around?"

This was the question that, no matter how kindly asked, always made me sad. I'd probably miss my dad forever. "No, my father died a while ago."

He sighed and glanced down before looking back up. "I'm sorry."

The apology was sincere, unlike the automatic responses I received from most people, and it comforted me. "It happened when I was a teenager."

He studied my face. "That had to have been hard."

"It was," I said, thinking back. "It was brutal for me and Elise, but it mentally changed my mom. She never got over my dad. Honestly, neither have Elise and I, but my mom has been the most altered. You've seen our family home. You have some sense of what's going on there."

"The hoarding," he said, and my back stiffened.

Max spoke of hoarding as though it were no big deal and offered every sign of wanting to still date me, knowing how bad things were.

"Is it too sensitive a subject to ask how he passed?" Max said.

"It's not too sensitive, it's just kind of tragic. My mom had been asking my dad for years to paint the house. He'd just finished getting it done in her favorite color, and the workers left behind some paint cans. My dad loved our neighborhood because it was an easy walk to the restaurants and shops. He'd been on his way to the hardware store down the street to recycle the cans and was hit by a drunk driver in the middle of the day."

The same shaky feeling overcame me every time I told the story. I'd never get over how my dad was there one day and the next day gone.

I looked up and tried to smile. "The police said he died on impact, so that was one blessing."

I'd debated as a kid if it was better that my father hadn't suffered, or if I would have liked to say goodbye. Selfishly, I'd wanted one last moment with my father, but in the end, I was grateful he hadn't been in pain.

Max stood and walked around the island. A second later, I was engulfed in a warm, strong embrace. "I'm so sorry, Sophia."

I pressed my cheek into his chest, taking in the clean scent of him. Usually, Elise and I were comforting our mother, rather than the other way around. But in this moment, I was being comforted and cared for. In this moment, the weight of the world was lighter.

I could get used to it. Too used to it. Max wanted to date, but how long would it last? That was something to worry about later.

"My mom never forgave herself for what happened to my dad. She says that if she hadn't asked him to get the house painted, he would still be alive. She's been stuck in what-ifs ever since and unable to get rid of anything in our house out of fear it will shift the wind in some tragic direction—that whole butterfly effect. There's no logic to it, but that's the way her mind works now."

He looked down, his arms still holding me tight. "Do you believe that too?"

I shook my head and smiled sadly. "I don't believe my mom controlled what happened. If not the paint store, my dad would have been running some other errand. It could have happened at any time."

Max pulled away, and I pressed my lips together, holding back the urge to cling to him. I'd already grown used to his arms around me, and the absence was unsettling. "I think this sad story calls for more chocolate, don't you?"

Maybe my dad had sent Max to me, because a man who supplied excellent chocolate would be on my "ideal partner" list. "Is there a time when chocolate isn't called for?"

"A fair point," he said and reached for one of the golden boxes. He plucked out the truffle and ate it before I could blink.

I was a champ at wasting money on chocolate, but even I was having a hard time with this level of extravagance. "Don't you have anything else?"

"Unfortunately, no. There's a reason I wander into your apartment." His smile was mischievous.

"I thought it was to see me," I said, crossing my arms in mock anger.

"You and your chocolate."

That wasn't a satisfactory answer. "But which do you prefer?"

"Hmm," he said as though he needed to ponder it. "Shall we do a taste test?"

I gave him a skeptical look. This man was crafty with his kisses and expensive chocolate—not that I minded his tactics. "What kind of taste test?"

He pushed a lock of hair over my shoulder and stared at my lips, giving me a very good idea of what he had in mind. "I'm thinking of comparing chocolate-to-mouth versus mouth-to-mouth."

I shook my head. "Max Burrows, is this another excuse to use your kissing skills on me?"

"Is it working?"

"Yes," I said indignantly, when, in fact, I was eating it up. Both the chocolate and his kisses.

He opened the last box, pulled out the truffle, and placed it in my hand. "We're doing a public service, remember? These would go in the trash and become landfill without our hard work."

I laughed. "These wouldn't last two seconds in your home. I'm surprised you held out as long as you did."

He gave me a pitiable look. "I have no idea what you're talking about."

I ate the chocolate and gave him a peck. "You know exactly what I'm talking about."

He studied my lips. "It looks like you've got chocolate on you." He leaned down and kissed me, deepening the kiss while at the same time picking me up.

I let out a squeak of surprise as he carried me to the living room, where the kissing continued on the couch with me sitting on his lap, my legs hanging off one side.

I eased back. "You're a lot bigger from this vantage point." His thighs felt massive beneath my rear, his chest twice as wide as my own.

He grinned and pulled me toward him at the same time he slid down the back of the couch until he lay flat, and my body tumbled over the abs I wasn't brave enough yet to investigate. But I was doing a thorough investigation of his mouth.

He slid his hand up the nape of my neck and tangled it in my hair, holding me in place. "You're not an especially large person. More cute and compact." He kissed me softly.

I wasn't compact. I was average height and had a nice layer of fat on my belly from all the chocolate consumption, but I wasn't about to point it out.

The kissing and light stroking continued, leaving me lax with sexual brain fog. Max was the best kisser. There, I'd said it. But not to his face, because he was still LD, and that shit would go to his head.

He ran his hands up and down my sides, slipping his

palms beneath my top to the bare skin at my waist, but not any farther. He wasn't trying for more, and it was refreshing, if frustrating. Because the same couldn't be said for my gutter mind.

I sensed my hair mussed in some places, but his seductive, tender kisses left me feeling beautiful. "This wasn't what I'd planned to do tonight. I was supposed to be studying the proposal." I was still getting used to the idea of kissing Max and not killing him. Though the kissing part was becoming more natural by the second.

He slid his warm hand back and forth over my chocolate baby belly. "Would you rather get back to the proposal?" He shifted slightly, and I felt just how excited he was, even though his actions were slow and controlled.

Chills ran down my spine. He knew exactly what he was doing. "Not even a little, but I probably should. Today is the one night I gave myself to thoroughly review it."

Proposal or more kissing? Why was the universe putting these sorts of decisions in front of me? I was a weak, sexually frustrated woman who would like nothing more than to take this further. But I was also a breadwinner and supposedly responsible.

He sighed, mimicking my mental turmoil. "I suppose I should let you get to it. Unless you'd rather do other things?"

I laughed. "Stop encouraging me!"

"I would never do such a thing," he said and slid his hand around my waist to my ass, where it rested possessively.

I lifted my eyebrow.

"Just making sure you don't fall off the couch," he said with a smile that wasn't the least bit innocent.

His hands were large and warm, and they felt exactly right owning my rear.

"Why don't I walk you back?" he suggested.

"I live downstairs."

He sat up and adjusted me until I was square on his lap again and not using him like a lounge. "I wouldn't want you to fall after all that chocolate."

"Chocolate drunk—that would be a first. Though not improbable, considering my obsession." I felt high right now, but it had more to do with the kisses.

In the end, and after a few more lingering kisses, I got up and used the bathroom. And saw what I looked like in the mirror.

"Shit." I looked like I'd just had wild sex, with my face flushed, lips chapped, and my hair every which way, and we hadn't even gotten past first base.

I quickly smoothed down the locks, wishing for the thousandth time in my life I had Elise's hair, and returned to the kitchen where Max was waiting, composed and only slightly ruffled. Which made him look hot as hell and had me questioning my decision to leave.

I shook my head sharply and walked past him. "Better get going or I won't."

He snickered behind me, but he walked me to the apartment. The two of us snuck glances every now and then, and my face flushed every time. I was going to have to pinch myself once I got home.

At the door he leaned down and kissed me on the lips. "I'll call you tomorrow?"

"Okay," I said and reluctantly opened the door. I glanced back one last time and smiled before closing it behind me.

With my back to the entryway wall, I slid until my butt

hit the hardwood, my legs like jello. I breathed in and out and tried to calm my heart.

Max Burrows was my boyfriend. *My boyfriend.* He knew about my family, and he still wanted to date me. How was this reality?

Chapter Twenty-Three

Sophia

"What do you think?" Victor asked.

We'd just received a new shipment of designer plants for display, and I was logging in the fiddle-leaf figs. "Everyone wants these, so we'll have to fight to keep the display plants in the store."

Victor nodded. "That's my feeling too, which is why I have a distributor who's close and can deliver new plants within twenty-four hours. But I was referring to the business proposal. Have you had a chance to look it over?"

After the impromptu make-out session with Max, my brain had been mush. I'd lain on my bed for a moment and ended up falling asleep and not waking until the next morning. "Not yet, and I need to work on the Bane mansion design this evening."

Victor looked around the busy shop and frowned. "Should we hire another designer? It's not healthy to work every night, Sophia. That's not what I want for you if you take over the business."

I wanted to say I had it all under control, but Victor was right. Even though we'd caught up these last few months on backlog projects, new ones were coming in faster than we could handle. "I think we should consider it. Even if we only hire someone to take my mocks and put them into digital drawings."

"My son says there are a lot of people in the city with technical skills looking for freelance work," he said. "I'll reach out to him and see if he can point me in the right direction. I'll also put out feelers with a few architects I know. Find out if they ever outsource digital drawings."

I'd been so busy I hadn't thought of how to offload work that didn't require my expertise. If I was going to run a business now or later, I needed to learn how to delegate. "That would be wonderful."

He patted my shoulder. "Focus on the Bane design. I should be able to find the right person quickly, but I'd like you to interview them before we hire."

"Absolutely," I said.

He headed toward the back of the shop and stopped midway. "Speaking of my son, how did the date go with his friend?"

Between my mom stuff and Max changing the script on me, I'd totally forgotten about my date. I bit my lip nervously. "He was really nice, but I'm sort of seeing someone now."

Victor winked. "That's my girl. Glad you have someone in your life, Sophia. You deserve it."

He called out to a contractor standing by the entrance and motioned toward the back, where they disappeared.

I finally understood the meaning of having someone special in your life. When Max fed me or secretly bought me chocolates, it felt vital. He did thoughtful things to make my life easier and more enjoyable, and it made all the difference. I could easily get addicted to it.

My phone vibrated and I reached for it. Speak of the Landlord Devil...

Max: Dinner tonight? Chinese takeout okay?

MY MOUTH WATERED at the sound of takeout and the handsome deliveryman attached. But I really needed to get caught up.

Sophia: I have to work late. Tomorrow?

Max: Tomorrow it is. I'll meet you at your place at 6 with the food. Email me the proposal when you get a chance and I'll review it before I come over.

IF VICTOR HIRED someone soonish to help with digital designs, it would free up so much of my time. My brain worked best hand-to-paper, but clients needed formal drawings, and that was time I could spend hanging out with the new boyfriend I'd somehow acquired.

I texted Elise, who'd been ghosting me for days.

Sophia: Are you still alive? Do you want to stay the night tonight? I'll be working late, but you're welcome to crash and avoid the rats.

SHE TEXTED back a skull and crossbones. But hey, at least she responded.

I went to my *recents* and called her. "What's going on with you?"

"Nothing." Her voice sounded better than the last time I'd seen her, but she also sounded defensive.

"Elise, you can't avoid my place forever."

"There's no way I'm showing up at your apartment," she said. "I'd look desperate."

"It's not desperate to visit your sister. It's not like we can comfortably hang out at Mom's," I pointed out.

There was a pause, then, "But he doesn't know that, Soph. All he knows is that I made an ass of myself and then ran out."

I looked to the ceiling with impatience. "He's in his room most of the time. The point is, you might not even see him. You can use my room to study, out of the way of the common areas."

"Maybe," she said, but I could hear the doubt in her voice. "I crashed at a study partner's last night because the rat flat is not okay. Mom was taking tentative steps around the house when I came by to grab clothes, so she's not comfortable with the situation either."

We chatted a little longer about the unwanted rodent guests, and then I said, "Well, when you decide to come over, shoot me a text."

———

Max showed up the next night wearing jeans and a crew T-shirt and looking hot as hell.

I cleared my throat. "You clean up nicely."

He tilted his head curiously. "You typically see me in a suit. Jeans aren't usually considered an upgrade."

"I'm admiring the dressed-down version," I said.

He stepped closer, closing the front door behind him, and the heat from his body filled the space. "If this is what it takes to make you happy, I'll show up less dressed every time."

Visions of abs and muscles and all the things I'd felt the other night but hadn't checked out in the flesh flashed before my eyes, and my face heated.

He leaned in and kissed my burning cheek. "I'll take that as a yes," he said, grinning as I stumbled for words.

"You're terrible." Max knew his effect on the female population, and he was using it against me.

He moved into the kitchen, and a waft of Chinese food hit me as he passed. It was hard to think straight with him around, but my lusty thoughts were replaced temporarily with images of food.

"Did you get enough?" I hadn't eaten in hours, and now that I smelled delicious food, I was about to ravage the paper bag to get to it.

He set the bag on the counter. "I ordered three entrees and rice. That enough?" he said, no hint of sarcasm in his tone.

He'd just earned bonus points, because there was nothing worse than a man nitpicking how much a woman ate.

My mouth twisted as I considered. I was probably too

hungry to be rational. "That should be enough. Did you order extra rice?"

His expression was pure cockiness. "I'm not an amateur, Sophia."

Shit. No, he was not. "Good, good—just making sure." I hurried into the kitchen for plates and utensils.

We sat at the counter and dug into the food, casual style, like we had at his place, and a wave of comfort washed over me. Max wasn't as uptight as I'd originally thought, and I was giddy as I watched him eat. Giddy for the food, and giddy to be spending time with him. "Everything go okay at work today?"

He frowned slightly. "Work was all right, but..."

"But?"

He looked up and wiped the side of his mouth with a napkin. "My parents are going through something right now, and I'm not sure how to support them."

"Is it something you can talk about?"

"It's not something that's known by people on the outside. If it were known, it would be a big deal."

I held up my hands. "I don't want to intrude."

He smiled softly. "I want to share it with you. I want to share everything with you."

Oh, wow. This was not Max the uptight landlord. This was the Max he didn't show to everyone. And it made me feel special.

He set his fork on the side of his plate and then looked at me directly. "My parents lost quite a bit of money in a poor investment, and they're looking for ways to make it up."

"When you say 'quite a bit of money,' that equals destitute to me. But I somehow don't think that's what you meant."

He smiled sardonically. "They lost a large fortune, but they have enough left to live out their lives in comfort. This loss won't affect their lifestyle so much, but it will affect their standing in society if it comes out."

"Right, society." The foreign thing I knew nothing about. "What does it mean to lose your standing among rich people?"

He shrugged and bit into a fried wonton. "If their friends learn the truth, my parents will lose connections and business partners. Their name would be tarnished, and they likely wouldn't be invited to as many society events."

I pushed my plate away; I'd already eaten two platefuls of moo shu pork, orange chicken, and tofu vegetables. The food baby was at six weeks' gestation, and it was time to simmer down. After all, I'd restocked the chocolate, and there was no dinner without a nip of chocolate for dessert. "The friends they'd lose don't sound like good ones."

He smiled as if to himself. "My parents don't understand that. They've never had friends without strings attached."

If they never had genuine friends, being a San Francisco first family wasn't as much of a boon as I'd imagined. Maybe it was better to be one of the common folk.

"If their name is tarnished," I said, thinking things through, "does that mean your name will be too? Will it affect your company?"

He shook his head, scooping another heaping of rice onto his plate. "I'm not worried about things like that. I've built business relationships based on my work ethic. Some people do business with me because of the name, but the people I've been working with for years know better. I'm not interested in society standings. I have very few close friends, and the ones I do have wouldn't drop me over this."

So confusing. "If it won't affect you, and your parents will only lose superficial friendships while living out their lives in luxury, how is this a problem?"

He huffed out a breath. "It shouldn't be. But my parents care about things like social standing. It's how they were raised."

"Weren't you raised like that?"

"To some extent, yes. But I had something they didn't—I had Jack and his family. Jack lost his mom right after we became friends, and I saw how that loss affected him and his dad. They struggled with finances in the wake of her death, and that was a cruel twist of fate. His dad worked long hours and could barely make ends meet, all while grieving his wife."

He poked at the rice without eating it. "High society will tell you poor people are lazy, but that's not true. They just don't have the same connections, resources, and luck. I don't care much for society's opinions when it comes from a place of ignorance. Not to mention, wealthy people can be hypocrites." He looked up at me through his lashes. "You'd be surprised how many are in debt."

I held my hands up. "Wait, are you saying rich people aren't really rich?"

"Oh, they're wealthy, but not as wealthy as they claim. They keep up appearances and sometimes don't have as much money in the bank as it would seem. My parents now fall into the second category, and they want me to help them maintain the image. And help them rebuild their wealth."

"They want to be obscenely rich instead of only filthy rich?"

"Correct."

I shook my head. "This is so strange. I had no idea classism existed among the wealthy. And no offense, but I'm not sure I feel sorry for your parents."

"You absolutely shouldn't," he said. "My parents will be fine. They brought this on themselves because they were greedy and wanted more. So much more that they blindly listened to a sure thing that wasn't sure at all."

"So your parents are worried about losing their standing, thanks to a dumb investment, and they think you have the means to fix it?"

"They think I can help them regain what they lost."

I winced. "Can you? Isn't that a lot of money?"

"An obscene amount of money, remember?" He shook his head. "It would take me a lifetime to earn my parents back their fortune, and a good deal of luck. And I have no interest." He ran his fingers through his hair, his gaze distant. "If what I build impacts people negatively, I won't do it. And most of the time, that's what it takes to earn the kind of wealth my parents lost."

"You won't do it because of what you experienced with Jack?"

He glanced at me. "I can't look the other way. It's why I chose my next project instead of the Starlight project my parents wanted me to invest my time and money in. Starlight does nothing but make the extreme wealthy richer at the expense of the community."

"And you saying no made your parents unhappy," I said, catching on.

He closed the takeout cartons, which were mostly empty. Max had a nice appetite too. "I've told them where I stand, but my parents think I'm making a mistake. They see no reason not to use me to regain their financial standing before others discover the truth."

I shook my head. "That's messed up. You're their son."

He looked over and smiled. "I like the casual Sophia. She's not afraid to speak her mind."

"Was I ever?"

He chuckled. "You've always called me out when I was being an ass, and it's part of your charm."

This was a compliment, but it also meant he liked that I put him in his place. "You have a twisted mind, Maxwell Burrows."

I hadn't tried to put Max in his place. There were times when I cowered instead of speaking up to others. But Max had been so darn arrogant that I'd forgotten to be afraid and was too furious to back down.

"In any case," I continued, "I'm sorry you're feeling pressure from your parents." No matter how crazy parents were, no child wanted to let them down.

He scanned my face, then down my body, igniting heat where his gaze touched. "Enough about family. Why don't we go back to your room and look at that business proposal? I have a few ideas."

Was that innuendo?

Did I care?

Back to my bedroom it was.

Chapter Twenty-Four

Sophia

TRUE TO HIS WORD, MAX TALKED ABOUT THE BUSINESS proposal back in my bedroom and didn't try to kiss me.

What the hell? What happened to the sexy innuendo?

He lay sprawled on my bed, legs crossed at the ankles, with his weight on one elbow, providing a very nice view of his biceps stretching the fabric of his T-shirt as he looked over the proposal. He pulled something from his back pocket.

My mouth gaped. "You wear glasses?"

His faced turned the slightest bit pink. "If I want to read, I do."

I held up my hands. "You said nothing about glasses." This was straight-up librarian porn. How was I supposed to concentrate? "You have to take them off."

He looked perplexed. "Is there something wrong?"

"Extremely wrong. It's too hot." I fanned myself and glanced at the window. LD in sexy nerd glasses might require popping open a pane.

His mouth kicked up on one side, and he patted the bed. "Why don't you lie next to me?"

Could I safely lie next to him? Hell no! I'd jump his bones, proving to the world that mounting innocent men ran in the family. "I'm not sure that's wise if we're to get any work done."

He frowned. "How am I supposed to give you my thoughts on the proposal with you so far away?"

He was totally goading me, and I was biting, because I wanted to snuggle next to my hot new boyfriend *who wore glasses*. "Fine, but only so we can go over the proposal," I said, all proper like, when I was really trying to figure out how long it would be before we could move on to other things.

"Strictly business," he said, a twinkle in his eye.

At least we were on the same page.

I sank onto the bed beside him, inching closer and watching him closely, as though he might strike at any moment. Not afraid, but not trusting the casual façade of no-sexy-time Max. I leaned over his shoulder and glanced at the proposal. "What do you think?"

He flipped a page. "It's a fair offer. He stipulates an end to the percentage of the profits, given current valuation, though I'm not an expert on the value of this type of business. I can ask around."

I nodded. "I have a good idea of what it would cost to go into business on my own, and this is ready-made, with loyal customers. I'd be earning significantly more right off the bat, and he's not asking much in terms of payment."

"He's essentially offering you a low-interest loan," Max said and flipped another page. "You're also free to sell the business as long as the loan has been paid in full."

Max set the contract down and wrapped his arms around my waist, pulling me onto his chest.

Now we're talking. I lifted one eyebrow, feigning innocence. "Is this a part of the platonic business overview?"

He kissed my lips, and I snuggled in closer. "We're done with that part. This is the full-body portion of my services."

I laughed. "Just make sure you keep your glasses on."

His brow pinched. "Do you really like them?"

"Have you any idea of the attraction of Clark Kent? Yes, I like them. But you don't need the glasses. You're potent without them."

"Noted," he said and slid his hands to my waist and under the hem of my top. "But just so you know, they're going to get in the way when I kiss you and do other things."

I reached up, pulled off the glasses, and tossed them on the mattress.

Max laughed and rolled until he was on top, holding his weight above me and carefully setting the glasses on the nightstand.

"That was a smooth move," I said, staring at his lips only inches away.

He kissed me and ran a hand up my side and below my bra line, teasing me.

"Um, I think you missed a spot," I said and wiggled. "Your hand should be a little higher."

He grinned and covered my breast with his large palm. "Like this?" He pushed up my breast and kissed it through the fabric.

My breath hitched. "You found the spot." I ran my hands beneath the hem of his T-shirt, gliding my fingers over his stomach as we kissed, while crackles of electricity shot beneath my skin.

And then I felt it: the telltale undulation of defined abdominal muscles.

I pulled back and looked him in the eyes. "You really do have rock-hard abs!"

He laughed and resumed his efforts to push down the neck of my top and expose my cleavage, kissing every inch of my décolletage. "You doubted me?"

"Not doubted," I said, ruminating while I ran my fingers over his toned midsection. "But how do you maintain this with your chocolate addiction? I have a fine layer of padding thanks to mine."

He eased farther down and hiked my shirt beneath my breasts, kissing and running his hands over my belly and waist. "Your body looks perfect to me." He lifted his head and looked me in the eye. "Though you're wearing too much for a thorough investigation."

"I think the bigger issue is why you're still wearing your cumbersome T-shirt."

Without another word, Max reached back, jerked his shirt over his head, and tossed it over the side of the bed.

He slid my top up and over my head, and I barely registered it, I was so distracted by the view. "Crap."

He glanced at my face. "Problem?"

"Yes." I stared at his smooth skin and defined muscles. Because it wasn't just his abs that were perfect; his arms and shoulders were spectacular. "You're too pretty. I can't compete." Even so, I continued to feel him up.

"There is no competition," he said. "You're much too beautiful and sweet for me."

Before I knew it, he'd reached behind me and unhooked my bra.

"Hmm," he said, looking me in the eye. "Seems like

someone has been hiding a couple of things beneath the baggy clothes."

If only he'd seen my breasts before I dropped the ten pounds. "They run in the family."

"I approve," he said as he kissed and licked said perky and very happy breasts.

And then all talking ceased, as there was too much steamy kissing and touching and rolling around in the covers. I had just gotten the button on Max's jeans undone when I heard Jack say something loudly in the living room.

This was strange for two reasons. First, Jack's tone was dark, when it was normally light or humorous. And second, Max seemed to notice Jack's unusual mood too.

He lifted his head from his deep dive into my cleavage and angled it toward the door.

And then Jack's voice came again, and this time, his voice was loud enough to decipher his words.

"What do you think this place is, Elise?" Jack said sharply.

"Shit." I sat up and covered my breasts.

For a split second, Max frowned at the absence of the view, and then he looked toward the door. "Were you expecting your sister?"

"No. Though I offered to let her study here while I was working last night. But that was yesterday."

"I was invited," came Elise's sharp response.

I reached for my bra and top and wrangled them on before handing Max his shirt. "We should go out there."

He pulled the T-shirt over his head. "Did something happen?"

"She slept with Jack the night we went to the bar, and she's been acting weird ever since."

Max's eyes widened. "Why didn't you tell me?"

I buttoned the fly I hadn't realized he'd craftily undone. "Do you want to know who my sister sleeps with?"

He cringed. "Absolutely not, but I do if it's my best friend. That falls in the *boyfriend needs to know* territory."

I grinned, because he just called me his girlfriend, in so many words, and it never got old. And then an angry growl of the feminine variety floated back, and I braced for what was to come.

"Where is she?" Elise shouted.

Max and I rushed out of my room right as Elise was making her way down the hall.

Her face was flushed, and she was wearing denim and a fitted top, an upgrade from her normal college-leisure sweatshirt. "There you are." She huffed out an angry breath. "Your bulldog of a roommate wouldn't let me in."

An exaggeration, since she was already inside said apartment. I glanced past Elise to Jack, who stood in the living room, arms crossed and with an angry look on his face. Beside him was some random guy with longish hair and a book bag on one broad shoulder.

"What's going on?" I asked.

Elise waved behind her. "Todd and I swung by to study, like you offered." She emphasized the last part, though her eyes were cagey.

"Right," I said. "Let's assume I believe that's the only reason you brought a guy over. If so, why are you and Jack yelling at each other?"

Jack joined us in the crowded hallway and glared at Elise. "She can't bring over random men."

His comment came across more jealous guy than annoyed roommate.

I looked at Max, who shrugged. "Sorry about that, Jack," I said. "I'll be sure to check in with you first. I think Elise and Todd are only here to study. Elise didn't know I had company." Was my face red? It felt red. If anyone stopped to think, they'd know what Max and I had been up to.

Jack urged me and Max down the hallway and away from prying eyes. "Your sister is welcome to come here, but not men she's dating," he said in a low, tense voice.

I glanced at Todd. He was tall and decent-looking, but I didn't think my sister was dating him or I would have heard. *Pretending* to date him, absolutely. "I don't think they're dating. But...would that be a problem?" I knew Elise's feelings when it came to Jack, but not how Jack felt about Elise. Now was my chance.

Jack looked away and shook his head. "I just don't like it. This isn't a way station."

Jack wasn't immune to Elise spending time with another guy, that much was clear. But I felt awful because Jack was clearly upset.

"I'm sorry. I should have checked in with you before inviting her."

He let out a low, tense sigh. "It's not your fault, Sophia. It's—" He glared at Elise. "Your sister drives me crazy."

Max and I exchanged another shocked look.

Then Max draped his arm around Jack's shoulders, pulling him down the hallway toward Jack's bedroom. "I got this, Sophia. Go check on your sister."

I made my way to my sister, who'd joined Todd in the living room. "Elise, what happened?"

"Your roommate is being an ass."

I pinched the bridge of my nose. "It's his house. I'm the one who's subletting, remember?"

Her lips parted. "Whose side are you on?"

Taking a page from Max's book, I grabbed my sister and hauled her into my bedroom. I shut the door and pinned her with a stare. "Elise, I've never seen you get upset over a guy, let alone combative with one. Do you—" I shook my head, unsure how this would come across. "Do you still have that crush on Jack? Because you're acting kind of crazy."

Elise winced and started pacing. "Maybe. I don't know. But I didn't know he'd freak out if I brought a study partner over."

I gave a disbelieving look. "Seriously? You slept with Jack, then refused to talk to him afterward. You didn't think bringing another man—"

"Study partner!"

I pressed my lips together in frustration. "If Jack likes you too, even if he's not ready to acknowledge it, he would not be happy to see you with another person."

Elise crossed her arms and looked away.

"I mean, seriously, what did you think Jack would do when you brought a cute guy over?" I asked.

She shook her head and started pacing again. "I've regressed, Soph. Ever since I met your roommate, and after that night, I don't recognize myself."

I put my hands on her arms and forced her to stop. "What do you want to do?"

Her eyes grew watery. "I've been stressed out, and I wasn't expecting things to go down the way they did with Jack. I need a break." She looked me straight in the eye. "I haven't told you this yet, but I applied for an exchange student position. Nothing major, just three months in Europe. I thought it would be a good resumé builder. Now I think it's the best way to recalibrate and get my head on straight."

"It sounds like a great opportunity, if you really want to do it." My mind raced with dollar signs. "I'm very close to taking over Green Aesthetic, so I think I could swing the cost."

She smiled gently. "It's a paid internship."

The sense of relief was immense. "Oh, well, in that case, go for it!"

Elise laughed and glanced at the door. "I guess I should rescue Todd."

"What about Jack?"

"I'll apologize," she said. "I shouldn't have shown up without texting first."

I gave her a tight squeeze. "I think apologizing is a good start. When do you leave for the exchange program?"

"In two weeks."

My eyes bugged. "Two weeks!"

She pulled her hair into a ponytail. "I wasn't planning on taking it. Mom's been worse lately, and I didn't want to leave you alone to care for her while you work a gazillion hours."

Sometimes I forgot Elise carried a heavy burden too. "Mom will be fine. Do your exchange program, and I'll handle the home front."

Chapter Twenty-Five

Max

Sophia and I returned to her room, and I stretched out on her mattress with my head near the top.

She lay on her belly across the bottom of her bed, chin in one hand, her face scrunched in consternation. "My sister isn't herself right now."

I rested my head on my hand. "Neither is Jack. He never gets upset over women."

She looked over. "Never? What did he tell you in his bedroom?"

I lifted my eyebrow pointedly. "A best friend never tells."

She plied me with puppy-dog eyes. "Not even your girlfriend? What happened to me needing to tell you things, like when Jack and Elise slept together because it was *boyfriend information*?"

I nodded with pride. "Guilt trip. It's working." I lay back down and stared up at the ceiling. "He didn't say much. Just commented angrily about the man your sister

203

brought." I rubbed my chin. "Thing is, situations that annoy normal people don't bother Jack, so that was unusual. He doesn't get upset, and he doesn't dwell." I tucked her pillow that smelled like coconut, the same scent as her hair, under my head and crossed my arms over my chest, pondering the strange turn of events.

Sophia crawled closer and uncrossed my arms, laying her head on my rock-hard abs. They weren't actually rock-hard—that was wishful thinking and some light humor—but I put in enough hours in the home gym that they weren't soft. "How is that even possible?" she asked. "No one is that patient."

I placed my hand on her leg closest to me. "The short answer is Jack never dates women he might seriously be interested in. Certainly no one good for him. So there was never a need to get worked up. If someone did something he didn't like, he moved on to the next. If someone broke up with him, same thing."

She scratched her forehead. "Why wouldn't he date someone he's into?"

I let out a puff of air. "Who knows? All I can say is that if there was a woman with an ulterior motive within a mile, he would find her and date her. And you know what happens when you pick the wrong people?"

"It doesn't work out?"

"They take advantage." I glanced up, considering the irony. "I suppose that's partly why I didn't trust you at first. I thought you were just another one of Jack's poor choices."

"Hey!" She smacked my arm, and I chuckled.

I gave her an affectionate look. "I guess Jack doesn't always choose bad apples."

"High praise." Her mouth twisted, though I detected the smile behind the sarcasm.

I patted the top of my chest. "Up here. You're too far away."

Sophia inched up, and I hugged her to my chest, kissing the top of her head. "Turns out, you are a mighty tasty apple."

"That sounds dirty."

"It's meant to." I shot her a look that should convey the thoughts running through my mind with her body pressed to me.

She laughed and kissed my neck, feeding into my master plan.

"You missed a spot," I said, gesturing to my mouth.

Her lips parted in surprise. "Using my line now?"

I winked. "Thought I'd give it a try."

Sophia held herself up with her hands just above my shoulders and slowly inched lower until her lips were pressed to mine, her silky brown hair falling around us.

I held back a lock so I could see her pretty face, and she dropped down and nuzzled my neck. "You smell good. Have I mentioned that?"

"No, but feel free to explore."

She straightened and gave me a saucy look. "I will." I received a peck on the lips for my suggestive comment, then, "Why wouldn't Jack choose someone he could be close to?"

I placed my hands on her waist and lightly stroked her skin from her ribs to her curvy little hips. "You sure you wouldn't rather talk about us?"

"Later," she said, yawning as she sank onto my chest and seemed to be settling in for the night. "I'm trying to figure out my sister and your best friend."

I wasn't the least bit tired and far more interested in Sophia's and my relationship than anyone else's, but she hadn't gotten much sleep while considering ownership of the shop over the last couple of days. Thus, I would behave.

But it was a struggle.

"Jack might not date women who are good for him, but he also doesn't dwell when things don't work. Except in his last relationship." My mouth twisted. "That one hurt. I think it had more to do with the vandalism of my building, though. Normally, the only person affected by his poor choices is him."

"The fire starter," she said, her voice growing shallow as though she really were falling asleep.

I pulled a blanket I was partially lying on out from under me and covered her with it. "She was his roommate, until he started to date her and things got muddy. They'd been dating for about a month before Jack and I left for a business trip and the incident took place."

"You guys work together?" she said, perking up.

"Only on one of Jack's businesses."

"He does more than lawyer and design video games? How many businesses does that guy have his fingers in?"

"A few," I said. "It may not look like it, but Jack's somewhat of a genius. Except when it comes to women—no offense to your sister."

"None taken," was her sleepy reply.

"In any case, his ex threw a party with some of the more reckless people in San Francisco's high society and torched the place."

"Your mom mentioned as much during the rooftop party when she asked me if I found Jack attractive."

That must have been the conversation I'd walked in on when I overheard Sophia saying Jack was good-looking. If my mother was involved, who knew what she'd been getting at? Probably trying to find out if Sophia would try to seduce Jack. Basically, what I'd assumed too.

The apple didn't fall far from the tree, it seemed, and now I felt like an ass.

I kissed her head lightly again. "I'm sorry about that. Assuming you were interested in Jack."

"It's okay," came her light voice. "Water under the bridge."

"Considering Jack's ex set fire to the place, I was lucky the damage hadn't been worse. In the end, nothing structural was harmed."

"Jack must have felt awful," she said faintly, as though half awake.

"He did. So guilty, he pitched in most of the money for the renovation, even though he didn't need to. Jack can be stubborn."

She snorted. "Then he's perfect for Elise."

"I was worried Jack had thrown in the towel after Fire Starter, as you called her. Until he rented you the room, and then I worried he'd moved on to a new roommate."

"I guess it makes sense why you might have been concerned about who he dated, given the women he chose and his roommate history," she said.

"For the obvious reasons related to his ex. But also because you're beautiful...and I might have been jealous."

She looked up with heavy-lidded eyes. I wish I could say it was due to sexual arousal, but it was probably sleep-induced. "Jealous?"

I considered hiding it, but what was the point? "Possibly. In any case, Jack seems interested in Elise, so things are getting more fascinating by the minute. She isn't at all his type."

"Elise is sassy," she murmured and closed her eyes.

I nodded. "And smart and hardworking and funny. She's not at all the type of person he goes after."

Jack was the happy-go-lucky sort, who stumbled around relationships the way he ran his multiple businesses. But somehow, he found success in business where he didn't in his relationships. This thing with Elise was decidedly different.

When Sophia didn't say anything after a long moment, I glanced down. Her breaths had turned deep and even.

I tightened my arms around her. She looked incredibly beautiful sound asleep, and I was enjoying watching her hand twitch every other second. I should probably let her rest, though.

I gently shifted, attempting to slide out from beneath her when she made a disgruntled sound and clung to one of my hands.

She wrapped her arms around my waist tighter than one would think for someone so small. "Stay," she murmured groggily.

The only reason I'd considered leaving was for her benefit. But if she wanted me here, I wasn't going anywhere.

Chapter Twenty-Six

Sophia

MAX HAD STAYED THE NIGHT LAST NIGHT, AND IT
would have been amazing—if I hadn't fallen asleep on him.

Darn it! Why?

Though in hindsight, dozing off across his washboard
abs wasn't a bad way to go. But I was disappointed we'd
been so rudely interrupted by my sister and her situation
with Jack.

A note written on one of Max's business cards rested on
my nightstand, along with a foil-wrapped chocolate.

Rubbing sleep from my eyes, I blindly unwrapped the
chocolate, shoved it in my mouth, and read the note.

Sophia,
Early morning meeting and long day of
appointments for Cityscape. I'll call you later.

What do you think about grabbing lunch tomorrow?
   Max

WHY DID I have to sleep so soundly? I'd missed the goodbye kiss.

I stumbled out of bed and hobbled around, preparing for the day, feeling better about signing the contract with Victor after talking to Max. On my way out the door for work, I set the proposal on the counter in front of Jack and his bowl of granola.

"I'll pay you," I said and reached for a banana. No harm in having a lawyer's sign of approval.

Jack glanced at to the proposal, then dug back into his granola with a spoon. "Max already told me. Contracts are child's play—no reason to pay me. I'll get back to you with any changes."

"You are the best roommate ever." Not that I had experience with any roommates other than Elise, but I was sure Jack ranked high.

"Of course I am," he said, though his energy wasn't normal, and I didn't know how to fix things.

"Sorry again about Elise," I said, looking over with a frown.

He waved it off. "She already apologized. Found a note on the front door when I went for a run this morning."

Jack wasn't typically up this early unless he was on his way to bed after a long night of work/gaming. And I didn't remember him going for runs, but then again, he was athletically built, so he must be getting exercise somehow.

He grimaced at his food. "I might have overreacted last night."

I wanted to ask Jack more about Elise, but I assumed he'd shared his feelings with Max last night, and that was what mattered. As long as he talked to someone, because there seemed to be a lot of bottled energy going on. "Okay, well, I'm heading off to work. Don't worry about my sister unexpectedly showing up or staying the night. She's leaving for Europe soon."

His hand paused while lifting a glass of orange juice. He set the glass on the counter, but he didn't look up. "I'm not worried."

Jack's body language didn't match his words, but I wasn't about to push it. "Okay, well, thank you. And I'll see you later."

I raced out of the apartment, balancing the banana, my phone, and an umbrella, as the weather had called for rain, and froze on the landing.

Gwen, Max's ex, was walking down the stairs. The rooftop had a separate entrance, and that meant she was coming from his apartment.

What the hell?

"Oh, hello," she said, and gestured behind her. She was all made up in a red A-line dress with a fitted black jacket, her dark blonde hair floating in waves over her shoulders. "Max already left, in case you're looking for him."

"No," I said lamely.

I knew Max had left because he'd left from *my* bed. But what was Gwen doing at his apartment?

I gave myself a swift mental shake. Even if Gwen and Max's mother scared the crap out of me, with their cold smiles and rich-woman clothes, Max had been with *me* last night, and I had nothing to worry about. "Have a good day," I said and ran down the stairs ahead of her.

I would not be the insecure girlfriend. Max was too cantankerous to be a player. You had to put out loose vibes for that kind of free loving, and he only shared the lighter side of himself with his inner circle. I couldn't see him cheating.

But that didn't explain why Gwen was leaving his apartment.

———

THE NEXT DAY, I texted Max that I was swamped with work and wouldn't be able to grab lunch. I wasn't going to bring up Gwen and his apartment. He'd most definitely been with me the other night, and I wasn't about to start questioning his every move.

Max: I'm deeply wounded to be on the receiving end of your busy schedule.

Sophia: Is this the first time a woman has turned you down?

Max: I plead the fifth.

Sophia: If you think about it, it's all your fault. You recommended Jack look at the contract, and he only suggested one small change. Now it's full speed ahead. Victor wants me to oversee hiring employees.

Max: Need help?

Sophia: Don't you have a company to run?

Max: I like interviewing (devil emoji inserted).

I LAUGHED.

Sophia: If you only knew my nickname for you... Keep your intimidating, handsome presence away. I want to hire people, not terrify them.

Max: Nickname? Suit yourself, but I remain at your disposal for all your future needs.

MY MIND RACED straight into the gutter, and it took a herculean effort to pull it out and get back to work.

I had just wrapped up the last interview and was preparing to close the shop when a tall, handsome figure entered the store.

My heart somersaulted, and an awkward smile pulled at the corners of my cheeks.

There was a reason I'd never dated uber-good-looking men until now. A lot of guys liked the hard-to-get variety, and I absolutely sucked at playing it cool. "What are you doing here?"

Max tucked a hand in his pants pocket—we were going with a navy suit today—and took in the plants that lined the glass wall. They were arranged on hexagonal stands in varying heights that filtered in the sunlight. It was a spectacular sight when I stopped and thought about it.

His brow quirked and his lips pulled into a cheeky smile. "I came to escort you home."

"Our apartment is only an eight-minute walk away."

His gaze followed me as I turned off lights and put design tools away. "I'd hate for anything to happen to my girlfriend on her way home."

I grabbed my bag, walked up to him, and wrapped my arms around his waist. "Like being accosted by a handsome businessman?"

He held me to his large frame. "Especially those handsome businessmen. Unless it's me. Then you may engage in any and all sordid activities with my full approval."

I laughed and rose on my tiptoes to kiss him on the lips.

His eyes gleamed. "I like this reception. Maybe I should walk you home every day."

I tilted my head, looking at him suspiciously. "Don't you usually park near here?"

He had the withering look of a wealthy man who'd been put out. "Only when I must. I've occasionally found golden ticket parking spaces in front of our building."

"I've never seen you park in front of the building."

He held the door for me as we exited the shop. "That's because my luck has been lackluster until now."

"And yet you still parked blocks away," I pointed out.

"Yes, well, now my girlfriend works where I park, and this is advantageous." He leaned in and gave me a lingering kiss right on the sidewalk. "Dinner?" he asked.

I nodded, slightly dazed, and glanced back to make sure I'd locked the store door. My brain fog was in full force with Max around.

He reached for the heavy computer bag I carried and pulled it onto his shoulder. "I hope this doesn't mean you'll be working tonight. I had other ideas." His smile told me exactly what he had in mind—a continuation of the other night—and I was on board.

"Maxwell Burrows, I hope you're not planning on seducing me?" This was my attempt at playing hard-to-get, and I fooled no one.

He reached for my hand, and that was how we walked down the street toward the apartment.

I glanced at him, my heart giddy. "I wouldn't have pegged you for a hand-holder."

Without missing a beat, he said, "There are many things you didn't guess about me, like my rock-hard abs."

The grin that came over my face stretched my cheeks from ear to ear. "I suspected those, but only because I might have felt you up in the kitchen when I was scolding you for stealing my chocolate."

He winked. "Feel me up any time you like. And let's just say, I like holding your hand." A hint of shyness came over his features. "It feels natural."

Being with Max felt natural to me too. And that was the biggest shocker. We were nothing alike, and yet somehow we worked.

We'd made it only halfway home when Max pulled out his phone. I hadn't heard it ring, but it must have vibrated.

He stopped and stared at the screen, his hand tightening around mine. "Fuck." Max's face grew pale, his expression tense.

"What happened?"

He let out a slow breath and closed his eyes. "It leaked."

"You have a leak?" I glanced in the direction of his building. "Where? In your unit?"

He looked at me, confused. "No, not the building. My parents' lost fortune. It's splashed all over the San Francisco news."

Oh crap. "Wasn't that supposed to be a secret?"

He blinked several times as though seeing something he hadn't before. "You didn't tell anyone, did you, Sophia? A friend, maybe?"

My mouth gaped. Was he accusing me of outing his parents? The thought that he suspected me of sharing something he'd told me in confidence hurt.

I dropped his hand, and he reached for it again.

"Sophia, I'm sorry," he said. "I didn't mean to accuse you."

"But you did."

He ran stiff fingers through his hair and let out a sigh. "Only a couple of people know about this, and you're one of them now." He looked at me apologetically. "I shouldn't have asked."

I studied his eyes. "Was your first thought that I'd spilled the truth because I'm not a part of your world?"

He shook his head. "No—I don't know. But I realize how stupid it was for me to jump to that conclusion. Please forgive me." His expression was sincere. He also appeared more distraught than he had at receiving the news.

"I would never willingly hurt anyone, including your parents," I said.

He pulled me in close and kissed my head. "I know that. It's one of the reasons I'm so crazy about you." He leaned back and kissed me on the lips. "I want to finish our date and do an appropriate amount of groveling, but I have to deal with this. There's a meeting with the family publicist happening right now."

I nodded.

"Sophia, I'm serious about us. I intended to ask you to a ball that takes place in just over a week. It's last minute, but

I'm hoping you'll agree to go. I want the world to know the amazing woman in my life."

I felt slightly shell-shocked and uneasy. At the same time, I was thrilled he wanted to introduce me to people. That had to mean something, right? Though my excitement was dampened somewhat by his earlier mistrust.

We came from widely different worlds, and I wasn't sure how well those worlds melded. But the sincerity in his eyes overruled my apprehension.

"At least you know how to apologize," I said, hesitating as I considered his offer. The truth was, I wanted to go with Max and be on his arm, so why hold back? "I'd love to go with you. Just as soon as I figure out what to wear to a ball."

Chapter Twenty-Seven

Sophia

BETWEEN MAX'S TRYING TO HELP HIS PARENTS PUT OUT the fire around their lost fortune and my preparing for ownership of Green Aesthetic, days went by when I hardly saw him. He caught me twice for lunch, bringing a bento box one day and a carne asada burrito the next. The rest of the time, either I worked late, or he was over at his parents' place, going over the details on how to publicly address the financial debacle.

Max's questioning me about the leaked information had bothered me, but he'd been so remorseful afterward, I'd let it slide. Max wasn't the cold person he presented to the world. He was warm and caring, and I was trying to not read too much into it.

The Friday before the ball, I called him while I put away clean clothes in my closet. "How are your parents doing?"

"Nervous. They're waiting until after the ball to give a

formal response. They won't admit it, but I can tell my parents are deeply ashamed and considering moving to another country."

"Seriously?"

"No, but the idea has been tossed around halfheartedly."

I sank onto the carpet of my small walk-in and rested a stack of hangers on my lap. "I'm sorry, Max." His parents didn't have the struggles other people did, but for them, this was big. "How about you? Are you okay?"

The investment hadn't been Max's, but from what I could tell, being a Burrows meant he shared his parents' reputation.

"Investors for Cityscape are getting cold feet, but what's worse is there are rumors suggesting the project's funding is coming from the Burrows family coffers, which isn't the case. However, because of those rumors, the county has put the project on hold until I can prove otherwise."

"What?" I shoved the dresser drawer inside my closet closed a little too hard. "They're preventing a project that will actually help San Francisco?"

"It would seem so," he said.

"That's crap! How can they do that?"

He let out a deep sigh. "The decision is somewhat unprecedented, but the news surrounding my parents isn't giving government officials confidence in my company."

"What can be done?"

"Only time and a lot of legwork will prove that Cityscape is well funded. And time is what we don't have. Not if we want to remain on schedule and within budget."

"So, Cityscape could fall apart?"

He let out a sound of frustration. "I hope not. I'm

reaching out to every contact I have to get the county to reconsider. But enough about this," he said, changing the subject. "I believe I sent you on an errand last night. Did you find something to wear to the ball?"

Max had sent me on a dress-finding mission with Jack. "Jack is a surprisingly good shopping buddy. He waited patiently while I tried on about twenty dresses. Not much commentary from his end unless he liked something. Then his eyes lit up."

I suspected Max had done more than send me with Jack. The dressmaker Jack had taken me to was extra fancy, and there were no price tags! As soon as I touched the fabric of the first dress, I'd started to sweat. It was silk and very heavy. I'd nearly walked right out the door, certain I couldn't afford anything. But Jack had talked me into trying on a few.

Max grumbled, "I would have rather gone with you myself. This situation with my parents can't be over soon enough. Aside from dealing with the city's cold feet, I've spent most of my days talking my parents off a cliff."

"You're being a supportive son," I said. "And that's what matters."

"I'll tell them you think so. So far, they're not impressed and still believe I should do more."

I chewed the corner of my lip and hung a work dress on the rack. I'd finally put the clothes that were too large into a donation bag. "Do your parents know? About us?"

There was a pause. Long enough to indicate what was to come. "I plan to introduce you as my girlfriend at the ball."

So he hadn't said anything.

Just what every rich momma wanted—to publicly learn

their son was spending time with the riffraff. "Is that a good idea? Your mom thinks I'm her plant lady."

"This is all the notice she's ever received regarding my love life. She'll have to deal with the idea of us together, because I'm holding on to you for as long as you'll have me."

I smiled into the phone. "You're pretty tough to put up with."

His voice lowered. "But I haven't shown you all of my charms. Give me a night or two, and you'll be convinced." More grumbling on his end. "Those articles ruined my plans."

"Plans?" I asked.

"To convince you I'm a good guy and to let me stick around."

I laughed softly. "I'm seeing a bit of that. You scored points with the carne asada burrito this week. That thing was amazing." Max was probably the only rich guy who bought his girlfriend lunch from a taco truck. "Speaking of all you've done, I really want to pay you for the dress. The shop lady said the cost had been covered, along with the shoes."

Flutters of panic rose in my chest when I thought about the cost of that outfit with no price tags, but I wasn't about to go into the lion's den of a ball unarmed, even if it took me a year to pay off.

"It's my treat," he said, "so don't spoil it for me."

I twisted my mouth, uncertain. It was strange having a man pay for something other than dinner, but I supposed couples did nice things for each other. And anyway, two could play this game.

"Well, I have a treat for you too. My phone call wasn't only to check in. I also wanted to see if you have time to meet me on the rooftop." I pulled the cell phone from my ear and checked the time. It was after ten p.m., but I wanted to support Max and make him smile.

"I always have time for you."

"You ditched me the day the article came out." Not that I held it against him, but I liked to rile him up.

He made a low growl. "My parents need to put out their own damn fires. I have a girlfriend to take care of."

"Damn straight. Meet me up there in ten minutes?"

———

Max

I CLIMBED the steps to the open rooftop, and the scent of fall and slightly damp air hit me. The night was cool but not too cold, with no rain on the horizon, only typical San Francisco fog. I had no idea what to expect after Sophia suggested we meet here.

But it wasn't this.

The heat lamps were turned on, and there were strings of white lights above lush plants in varying shades of green and red, some with wide, palm-sized leaves, and others with spiky foliage. The rooftop had been nice before, but it looked like an oasis now.

I spotted Sophia at the center of it on the two-person chaise I'd tacked on at the last minute while ordering outdoor furniture. I'd spent little time here since the remodel a few months ago, and now I was patting myself on the back for my amazing forethought.

A two-person chaise was exactly what I needed right now.

My heart sped up as I slowly made my way across the roof patio to the beautiful woman wearing what looked to be soft baby-blue lounge pants and a long-sleeved T-shirt. "You did all this?"

She shrugged slightly. "Not physically. I had help from the shop installers, but I designed it."

I spun in a slow circle and shook my head, amazed. There were a few flowering plants and others I'd expect to keel over in the sometimes-cool San Francisco climate. Nothing I knew the names of, but the assortment and arrangement brought life to the space. "It's incredible."

Sophia patted the spot beside her, not that I needed an invitation. That spot had my name written all over it.

I'd been thinking far too much about Sophia and the interruptions preventing us from having alone time, first from her sister and now my parents. And here, it only took my incredibly smart and talented girlfriend to find the one place no one would look for us.

I eased onto the lounge beside her and nodded at the short tumbler in her hand. "Nightcap?"

She handed the glass to me and reached for another I hadn't seen resting on the table. "Victor gave me this fancy bottle of whiskey or scotch—not sure which—when I signed the contract this week."

She mentioned the name of the maker, and I said, "Whiskey. And not cheap."

Sophia clinked her glass to mine. "To Victor and his good taste."

I glanced pointedly at the plants. "To what do I owe the surprise?"

She waggled her head. "You've been stressed, and I wanted to do something nice for you. And don't look at it as repayment for the dress. I planned this long before."

I typically took care of others, and I suspected Sophia

and I shared that in common, which made this gesture extra special for me.

My breathing increased and a burning sensation tightened my throat. I slowly set my glass aside, leaned over, and kissed her softly. "Thank you. No one has ever done something this nice for me before."

Her expression showed surprise and a little confusion. "Never?"

I shook my head.

"I wasn't entirely altruistic." Her mouth pulled into a sneaky smile. "I might have also used it as an excuse to bring greenery up here."

"Of course," I said and slid my hand around her waist, pulling her closer and kissing her neck. God, I needed this. Being with Sophia took the weight of the world away. "You've made it so nice that this will be the place everyone wants to go. Though I think a few of the plants are going to die."

She half rose and looked over my shoulder a little too aggressively. "What? Where?"

I tugged her back down. "Those plants with the thick leaves." I pointed them out.

"You mean the succulents?" She crossed her arms, blocking all the best bits, but I continued to hug her anyway. "Ye of so little faith. You think I don't know which plants will survive here?"

"I would never think such a thing." After the other day and my mistrust rearing its ugly head the moment my parents' financials hit the streets, I wasn't making the same mistake twice. A man could learn. "You are right, and I am wrong. I will recompense in the form of chocolate."

She harrumphed. "You may know real estate, but I know plant state."

"Plant state?"

She uncrossed her arms and folded them behind her head. "In fact, it's so nice now that there is greenery, I wouldn't mind living here. These heat lamps are ingenious."

I rolled my gaze over her face and down her body. "We could make it even warmer." I gave her a suggestive smile.

Chapter Twenty-Eight

Sophia

I SQUIRMED BENEATH HIS MUSCULAR CHEST, AND HE shushed me. "Don't wake the building."

"You did not just say that cheesy line about getting warmer."

"Say what?" He reached back and pulled his shirt over his head, tossing it aside.

My mouth went dry. Damn him and his physique. "Your body is a menace. Makes my brain lock up."

He hesitated. "Want me to put my shirt back on?"

"Absolutely not, but—" I glanced around. "Should we? Up here?"

"It's private." He tugged my T-shirt down, and his lips whispered over the top of my breasts as his soft hair tickled my neck. "No roommates or mothers to drop by unexpectedly."

My eyes rolled into the back of my head at his light, seductive touch, and then I snapped out of it. Because I was actually considering this. "Did you plan to seduce me on the roof?"

He blinked. "*You* invited *me*, remember?"

I hated it when Landlord Devil was right.

He reached behind him to an ottoman that apparently housed a compartment, and pulled out a lightweight duvet.

My jaw dropped. "You did plan this!"

"Not planned," he said slowly, draping the blanket over us. "But am I taking advantage of the moment? Without a doubt." He looked down my body. "Are you too warm?"

I held back a smile. "Am I too warm with the winter duvet you handily keep up here?"

He grinned. "I'm a planner." His faced twisted. "We need the duvet for privacy, but this top might make your secrets hot. They need fresh air."

I shook my head. "Are you referring to my breasts?"

"You've been hiding them. Thus, they are *our* secret." He nudged his nose along my neck, sending shivers along my skin.

"I'm not hiding them," I said grumpily. "I need to go shopping. None of my clothes fit properly." Max's kisses got my blood racing, but I couldn't stop giving him a hard time. It was too much fun.

Until he did something with his tongue near my nipple and my mind went blank.

He plastered his face along my chest and made his way to my belly, where he slid his head under my top, breathing in.

"Did you just smell me?"

"It's like a garden in here." He inched up. "You sure you're not too hot? Your skin looks flushed."

"Oh, for the love of God." I pulled my shirt up and over

my head, then reached back and unhooked my bra, and it too went over the side of the chaise.

Max stared. "I knew you were overheated. You're all dewy and rosy. Allow me to cool you off." He started kissing my breasts, darting his tongue out in light, feathery touches.

I stroked my fingers through his soft hair. "Nothing about what you're doing is cooling me off."

A masculine sound came from the back of his throat, and he lifted his head. "Want me to stop?"

"No," I said and tried to pull him up to reach his mouth. There was literally no way, though, because he was way bigger and stronger.

It took Max all of a second before he got the picture and inched closer. He leaned down and kissed me, drugging me with his lips.

I slid my palms down his tan skin, moving over dips and ridges until I hit the waistband of his pants and ran my fingers beneath.

His stomach muscles tightened a second before I ran my hand over a very impressive erection.

His lips crashed down on mine, and he reached for the lounge pants I was wearing. "These are going," he murmured. But his touch was gentle as he slid them down my legs, taking my underwear with them.

He slid his hand back up my thigh, caressing the soft inside and the crease between my leg and sex. Until his finger parted the center of me, curled, and did some sort of magic that sent flutters shooting in all directions.

I clenched my muscles so I wouldn't come. It was too soon. That would just be embarrassing.

Max had been teasing me and testing me since the moment we met, and all that pent-up sexual frustration came firing to life. I reached around and squeezed his firm ass, urging his body where his hand had been.

He gripped my hip and rubbed his length against the center of me. His breathing uneven, he said, "Don't get any ideas about trying to leave me; you're mine."

The way his pupils dilated, the gentle, yet passionate touch—it was all there, even without words: I was loved.

There was no reason to hold anything back.

And just because I'm classy like that, I said, "I think it's time your pants came off."

He grinned and unbuttoned the top of his jeans. I helped him tug them off, along with his boxer-briefs.

Wow. Just wow. "How does a businessman have a body like this?"

"I'll take that as approval," he said and moved over me, right where all the good stuff lined up.

Our mouths collided, deepening what already felt like intensely deep emotion. All joking aside, the enormity of being together had my body vibrating.

I wrapped my arms around his shoulders, and he slid his hands down my sides and up the back of my thighs, spreading me until he fit snugly between my legs. He kissed me for long moments until I finally moved my hips, urging him on. He reached for his jeans and pulled out a condom from his wallet.

Leave it to Max to come prepared. Though, technically, I was reaping the benefits, because I hadn't thought of bringing protection up here.

The tip of him entered me, and I bit my lip.

His brow furrowed. "You okay?"

I nodded and hugged him closer until he entered me fully.

Max set a slow pace, lighting up every delicate nerve

ending in me. Somehow, he managed to keep hitting sensitive parts while kissing me and holding me like I was precious.

The sensation in my chest of feeling loved and protected, the sensation he ignited in my body—I lost it. It didn't take long before I cried out, shaking as an orgasm tore through me.

My breathing slowed, and Max shifted slightly, his movements fluid and setting off a whole new arousing sensation. Not enough to reach climax, but enough to have me thinking I might. Especially with the slow pace he was keeping.

Muscles tense, a light perspiration covering his forehead, the dam finally broke. He tensed, and a low moan vibrated against my neck where his face was pressed.

He kissed me while easing in and out, and his chest thumped like crazy against my own.

After a moment, he sank beside me and tucked me against his side. "I'm putting a lock on the rooftop. No one else is welcome."

I smiled against his chest. "Jack might object."

"Just wait and see. Coded deadbolts are going on tomorrow. It's our love nest, and no one else is allowed." He slid his fingers up and down my arm in a lazy caress. For a moment, I thought he might have fallen asleep, and then he said, "What do you have planned tomorrow?"

I lifted my head and looked at him. "The ball?"

His expression fell. "Shit."

"You forgot?"

He rubbed his slightly stubbled jaw. It had to be close to midnight, and he'd started to grow a beard. "I was distracted." His grin was ridiculously endearing. "Might have had a momentary lapse in memory due to passionate sex."

I laughed. "I'm going to remember that the next time I want you to forget something."

He perked up. "Promise?"

I smacked him in the chest, and he rolled over and started kissing me all over my face. "Starting tonight, I'm coming up with a list of things you'll want me to forget," he said as I belly-laughed beneath him.

Chapter Twenty-Nine

Sophia

I WAS *NERVOUS*. NAUSEATED, SHAKY HANDS, HEART-racing nervous.

I stared at myself in the mirror. The dress Jack helped me pick out was classy, in deep emerald silk satin, the length nearly touching the floor. The fit was column, with the waist in the same material cutting in like a wide belt. Pleats in the bodice made my bust look more proportional, and it featured a collar neckline, so there was no cleavage nor leg anywhere. But the gown didn't need to show those things, because it was sexy in its simplicity and cut.

The quality was excellent and more luxurious than anything I'd ever owned. It shouldn't cause a negative stir among San Francisco's finest. And yet I felt like a girl from the Sunset District mingling with people she had no business being around.

It didn't help that Max had called this afternoon and asked if Jack could take me tonight. He'd seemed nervous, and I could tell he was conflicted.

"Something came up," he said. "My parents managed to get a meeting with someone from the city who could help get Cityscape back on track, but I won't be able to escort you to the ball."

Attending the ball without Max ratcheted up my nerves, but I understood how important this project was not only to him but also to the city. "Of course you should go," I said. "Don't worry about me."

Apparently, Jack attended all the balls with Max and his family, as though he were one of the upper class. And if Jack could do it, I could too.

Now I just needed to believe that.

Jack stopped at the door to my room and leaned his shoulder against the frame. With his hair combed back, he looked extremely dapper in a simple black tuxedo.

He nodded slowly and whistled. "Looking good, Soph."

I flattened my hand down the front of the dress. "You promise I'll blend in?"

"No way will you blend," he said proudly. "You'll stand out."

Panic filled my chest, and I swallowed hard. "But I don't want to stand out."

"Too late. All the rich yuppies will try to steal you from Max, and Max will turn into a beast and tear them apart." At my shocked expression, he said, "Not physically. But they'll suffer because Max fights dirty. He'll steal their ill-gotten properties. Do not go up against Maxwell Burrows. Unless you're Sophia Markos, apparently. You've turned my beastly friend into a puppy dog."

And then it occurred to me. "How did you find out we were dating?"

Jack made a disbelieving sound. "That guy doesn't ruffle over anything, and he's been acting like a lunatic from the moment you moved in. I knew there was something going on weeks ago."

Internally, I smiled, and my chest filled with warmth. Max had been giving me a hard time since the day we met, and I'd been dishing it right back. That was the best part about dating him—watching the stoic man turn soft and gooey.

Though only in hindsight did I enjoy this. For a while there, I wanted to drop-kick him.

I reached for a black satin purse that was one of the few items I considered truly invaluable. Passed down from my mother, who'd received it from her mother, it had an understated vintage look with tiny black pearls along the closure. The clutch didn't completely go with my new gown, but it worked. More important, it gave me courage to have something of my mother's with me tonight.

We made our way from our apartment to the street, where a white limousine was waiting. I turned to Jack. "Did you arrange this?"

He scoffed. "Of course not. You do remember who you're dating, don't you?" Jack opened the back door, not waiting for the driver to make his way around. "Your boyfriend insisted. He's been harassing me for the last hour to make sure you're okay and to get you there on time."

We settled in the limousine, and Jack popped the cork of a champagne bottle. "Another of Max's orders—Dom Perignon." He poured a glass and handed it to me, then poured one for himself.

The car was enormous, with supple cream leather upholstery and a bar along one side, where two more champagne bottles were chilling. It was glamorous and exciting, but I wished Max were here too. No matter how thrilling, the experience wasn't as fun without him.

Traffic to downtown was heavy, and it took at least half an hour to make it to San Francisco City Hall. I'd thought it strange to host a ball there—until we pulled up.

The dome was lit in blue, brightening the darkened sky and taking my breath away.

Jack helped me out of the limousine, and we got in line with other elegantly dressed people making their way up the steps to the entrance off Van Ness. If I thought I was nervous at the apartment before, the sensation now grew tenfold. But as soon as we entered the building, some of my nerves dropped away, because *holy shit*.

We passed the pink and ecru marble vestibule and entered what could only be a fairytale. Marble arches along the entire lower level were draped in two-story velvet lilac curtains with gold frill along the edges, while royal-blue velvet drapes covered the arches of the second level. Roman columns and marble statues were carved into the walls of the top of the Grand Staircase, with seven-foot floral arrangements strategically placed on either side. The lower and upper levels were lit by pedestalled chandeliers and the light coming in from the dome at the center of it all.

When I thought about it, Joe DiMaggio and Marilyn Monroe had gotten married here, so yeah, even without the grand ball décor, the place was spectacular.

"I hate these things," Jack grumbled, tugging at the sleeve of his tux.

I swiveled my head to him in surprise. "Then why do you come? Max says you go to all the events."

He shrugged one shoulder. "I work with a lot of these people, and it's the one time I get out and mingle. Gotta put in face time."

He worked with these people? "I thought you designed video games, and your law degree was an added bonus."

"I do, and it is, but I run a few businesses as well."

Okay, maybe Max had mentioned something about Jack having his fingers in multiple businesses. I clearly needed to pump him for more information on the topic when we weren't at a gala.

"Can I get you anything to drink?" he said, peering across the room to a corner where the glitter of barware and staff was set up. "At the very least, these things have great food and drinks."

The people surrounding us were incredibly glamorous, and my nerves kicked back in. "Yes, please. Make it a stiff one."

"Martini?"

I bit my lip. "Maybe not that stiff. Glass of red wine?"

He laughed. "So not stiff at all."

"What?" I said, laughing as well. "I'm a lightweight."

"One glass of red wine coming up." Jack weaved his way across the crowd, and that was when it dawned on me.

I was alone. Like, *alone* alone.

Gah! Why hadn't I gone with him?

I turned and looked for something to do while I waited for Jack. Spotting an object that was right up my alley, I meandered over to a floral arrangement that had a plant sprouting from the center.

Had to give the designer props on originality.

"Sophia?"

My shoulders tensed, and I spun around.

What the hell was my ex doing here?

Paul was dressed in a deep red velvet tuxedo jacket that complemented his hair, which he'd darkened to its natural black. The woman Elise and I saw him with at our favorite dim sum restaurant was on his arm, and she was wearing a light-rose gown with large ruffles along the asymmetrical hem and collar line that looked like some-thing from a runway. She was also glaring darts at my head.

Running into Paul again was shit-poor luck. Couldn't he pretend to not know me? "Hi, how are you?" I said, trying to keep things casual.

He looked annoyed. "Why are you here?"

Heat rolled up my chest, and it was a good thing my dress came to my neck with only the arms and shoulders exposed, because I was pretty sure I'd turned red. Only not with embarrassment but anger.

It was one thing for me to feel I didn't belong at the ball, and another for my ex to assume I had no business being here. "I'm with my boyfriend."

Well, not technically. Max still hadn't shown up, but Paul didn't need the dirty details.

He chuckled. "Your boyfriend? Who might that be?"

This was where things got sketchy, because no one outside of our small group knew Max and I were dating. But Max was about to announce it to his parents tonight. How bad would it be to mention it first to my ex? "Max Burrows. Do you know him?"

Paul's fiancée laughed. As in, bent at the waist, honking loudly in mirth. But Paul didn't flinch. His jaw tense, he said, "Is that so?" He looked around dramatically. "Where is he? I don't see him with you."

I caught sight of Jack dodging bodies and carrying two glasses of wine, and I'd never been more grateful. "He's taking care of a few things. I'm waiting with his friend Jack."

"Hey," Jack said, sidling up and handing a glass of wine to me. "Sorry. Long line."

I gestured to my ex, who was looking Jack up and down. "Jack, this is Paul."

They shook hands, and Jack said, "I've seen you at a few events, haven't I? Park family, right?"

Paul's expression lightened. "That's right. And this is my fiancée." He introduced the woman beside him, even though he'd never bothered to introduce me to her. Not that it mattered. I was well past caring what Paul was up to, and more concerned about Max.

I glanced over the crowd, hoping to finally catch sight of him.

Jack and Paul talked for a few minutes, while Paul's fiancée held his arm and looked anywhere but at me.

After a little while, their conversation wound down, and Paul said, "Good to see you again, Jack." He tipped his chin up at me. "Sophia."

He walked away, dragging his fiancée, who in her five-inch heels scurried precariously beside him.

Jack glanced over. "I sensed tension. You know him?"

"Unfortunately."

He rubbed his clean-shaven jaw. "His family attends these events occasionally. Don't know much about the guy, though."

"He's not terrible. But he's heavily influenced by his family." Was this becoming a theme in my life? Did other people struggle with pleasing the parents of their significant others?

It never occurred to me I might run into my ex tonight. It should have. Paul's family was filthy rich. It made sense that his parents mingled with San Francisco's most influential.

Jack raised his hand, smiling at someone I couldn't see above the crowd, even in my heels.

A rush of excitement filled me, and I rose on my tippy

toes to see if it was Max. I caught a flash of blonde, and my heart sank. Gwen was making her way over.

Jack probably knew Gwen well, since Max and Gwen had dated for a while. They might even be friends.

She walked up in an off-the-shoulder fuchsia gown that dusted the floor, her light hair parted down the middle and straightened. Large diamond ball earrings swung above her shoulders as she held a champagne flute. The woman beside her had short black hair and a midnight silk dress. The two of them together looked like Hollywood celebrities, and I shifted uncomfortably.

Gwen gave Jack a side hug. "You know Sloane."

Jack greeted the other woman and introduced me.

Gwen tilted her head to the side like a curious bird. "How charming your purse is, Sophia." Leave it to Gwen to find the one thing in my ensemble not worth a penny.

"Is it vintage?" the other woman asked. "The Haight has incredible vintage couture."

"It was my grandmother's."

Gwen's friend smiled kindly, but Gwen sent me a sad little look. "How nice," she said, which was the San Francisco equivalent of the Southern "Bless your heart."

Jack's chest puffed up, and he straightened his tuxedo tie. "Sophia looks incredible, if I do say so myself."

I grinned, thankful for my roommate's presence. "Jack helped me pick out the dress."

Come to think of it, Jack had helped me choose a blouse for my date with Victor's son's friend too. Living with a man had its perks.

"Nothing but the best for Max's girl," Jack said, and my back stiffened.

After Paul and his fiancée's reaction to my dating Max

—or disbelief, rather—I was less confident about sharing the information. Particularly with Gwen.

Sloane's eyes widened, and Gwen's placid smile dropped.

"Really?" Gwen said, though her tone was flat. "Did he buy that dress for you?" She looked at my sparkly shoes. They were the fancy kind, with red bottoms. Louboutin, the brand was called. I didn't want to think about how much they cost, but I knew it was far above my pay grade. The entire ball was above my pay grade.

I gave a shaky smile, and Jack grabbed an appetizer off a tray by a passing server, oblivious to the tension.

"He's always doing charities," Gwen said, and I swallowed, my throat suddenly dry.

Gwen was trying to ruin the *Pretty Woman* shopping spree Max had gifted me, and I wouldn't let her. That said, Max had better show up soon, or I was going to kick his butt. I wasn't built for this kind of criticism.

"Jack," Gwen said, her face pulling into a brilliant smile. "Come with me a moment? I want to introduce you to one of my good friends."

Jack glanced at me. "Can it hold off? I'm waiting for Max to show up."

Gwen pouted. "It'll be quick. Promise." She looked over at me. "You're okay, right, Sophia?"

If I said no, I looked unsophisticated and childish, unable to socialize on my own. But if I said yes, I was in what felt like a shark tank of beautiful people who came across more foe than friend.

I would kill Max later, but right now, I'd hold on to my dignity and show I was competent. "I'm fine. I'll be"—I looked around, uncertain—"in this general vicinity."

Jack knew these people better than I did, though I

suspected most of their pettiness went over his head. After a moment, he nodded and said, "I won't be long."

I smiled in return, and Jack moved to walk off with Gwen and her friend.

But not before Gwen's foot caught on "something" and her glass of champagne tipped, spilling liquid down the lower half of my silk gown.

Gwen covered her mouth. "Oops."

Jack's eyes widened, and he hurriedly reached for a napkin off a nearby table. "You okay, Soph?" He handed me the napkin and then looked down my dress, concern filling his face. "Will that come out?"

No, it probably won't, I thought but didn't say.

I dabbed the spot and said, "It's okay," though the spot was black and obvious against the deep emerald of the finest thing I'd ever owned. A crushing feeling filled my chest. I would not cry. I would not let this woman get to me.

I should be fuming with anger. Instead, I was resigned. The more I was around Gwen, the more I saw her true colors. But I wouldn't let her ruin this night. "Go on ahead," I told Jack. "I'll run by the ladies' room and see if I can get this out."

Gwen grabbed a reluctant Jack's arm and tugged him in the opposite direction.

He held up his hand like a phone. "Okay, but call if you need me."

Chapter Thirty

Max

SEVERAL OF THE CITY HALL ANTECHAMBERS AT THE top of the Grand Staircase were closed off by heavy, colorful curtains, and that was where my parents had asked me to meet them. But I was questioning my decision to do so more by the moment. The person from the planning department hadn't shown, and all I could think about was Sophia. The last thing I wanted to do was sit around waiting for this guy.

Finally, a balding man in a sharp tux, with his glittery wife of a similar age, snuck past the curtains and into the antechamber.

"Max, this is Samuel Thompson and his wife," my father said.

Though closer to my parents' age, the man looked slick, and not at all like the workers I was used to dealing with from the planning department.

I'd been trying to reach the person in charge all week to find out how long Cityscape permits would be tied up. Normally, getting in touch wasn't an issue, given my company's reputation and past successful projects. But ever since news about my parents' financial debacle was made public, we'd become family non grata. The only reason society wasn't outright ignoring us this evening was because my mother had planned the entire event.

And it was for charity. San Francisco society had put their trash-talking on hold until *after* the charity ball.

I greeted the newcomers. After a few moments of casual chitchat, my mother engaged Samuel's wife in a conversation about the charity, and I started to mention Cityscape—until my father interjected.

"Max has other projects coming down the pipeline too, including one called Starlight that would turn an entire city block into a work of art. It'll become a destination for tourists and bring in more money than the city has ever seen."

That was a vast exaggeration. Not to mention that Starlight wasn't one of my projects.

I clenched my jaw. Other than tourists looking in from the outside at how the wealthy lived, Starlight would not be a part of the community, nor provide anything useful to them. And I'd made it clear to my father I wouldn't be working on it.

I shot my father a glare that Samuel didn't seem to notice.

"Well," Samuel said, "that certainly sounds interesting. Though Cityscape is more manageable, as it would serve an immediate need. But there's always room to review other ideas..." He looked at me hesitantly. "My understanding is that there's a bit of an issue where the funding is concerned for Cityscape."

"The funding is solid," I said. "There is a rumor about my parents that doesn't involve my business or my company's liquidity." Normally, I wouldn't have put it so bluntly, but my father was pissing me off, and I'd lost all patience.

"Max," my mother said, turning from her conversation with Samuel's wife. "It's so bourgeois to talk about money at a ball." She smiled at Samuel. "Please don't listen to everything you hear. There will be an announcement tonight that should make things very clear where our family stands in the pecking order."

I sipped the champagne I'd been handed, forcing myself to not roll my eyes. Whatever my mother had to announce, I wanted no part of it. Sophia should have arrived by now, and I was eager to find her.

It was clear this meeting was never meant for Cityscape, and I was done here. I held out my hand to Samuel. "If you'll excuse me, I have a guest waiting. My father can fill you in on his Starlight project, and I'll reach out this week to discuss Cityscape."

Samuel hemmed and hawed for a moment. "I'm not the one in charge. I can only pass along a word or two. With the right incentive..."

I didn't allow my face to show emotion, though a sneaking suspicion took root. I glanced at my father, who gave me a short nod.

He'd bought this guy off? For Starlight?

Fuck. I hated this shit. It was why I'd refused to go into politics when my parents and their friends had suggested it. Enough dirty politics took place in business—present company a case in point—and it made me want to shower. Especially when dealing with those who claimed to care, when all they wanted was to line their pockets.

This man wouldn't receive a dime from me. Either my projects were sound or they didn't go through.

"Excuse me," I said and stepped back. "I need to be somewhere."

"Maxwell," my mother cried. "Where are you going?" She followed through the curtain toward the exit, stopping me on the landing that looked out over the main floor.

I scanned the room, searching for Sophia. I had no idea what she was wearing, but it didn't matter. The way I was attuned to her, I'd find her anywhere.

My mother squeezed my arm. "You can't leave yet. You haven't heard the announcement."

I looked at her in confusion. "What is this announcement you keep talking about?"

Her shoulders did the little side-to-side shimmy thing they did when she was pleased with herself. "Using Samuel to get Starlight up and running, as your dad likes to put it, is just the beginning. We have a foolproof plan for solidifying our standing in society."

I sighed and searched the crowd again. "I don't have time for this, Mother. My date is waiting."

Finally, my gaze landed on a woman in dark green with light-brown hair she'd curled in loose waves. Sophia was all the way across the room and standing off to the side. She looked incredibly beautiful in a formfitting gown that showed off how truly stunning her figure was—and her expression was distraught.

Where the hell was Jack? He wasn't supposed to leave her side, but he was nowhere in sight.

I compressed my lips. This was all my fault. I'd agreed to meet my parents because they'd claimed to have a connection who could help with Cityscape. But I hadn't agreed to bribe a man. And now Sophia was alone and upset.

"What do you mean, you brought a date?" my mother said, her voice suddenly clipped. "You mean Gwenny?"

Spotlights crisscrossed over the Grand Staircase below us, and Gwen slowly made her way up, grinning at me.

The fuck?

I turned to my mother, but she was walking away.

Gwen reached the top of the stairs and linked her arm with mine. "There you are."

"What's going on?" I searched for where I'd last seen Sophia. She was still standing there, only now she was staring at me and Gwen, her expression confused.

I tried to free my arm, but Gwen must have increased her kickboxing classes, because she'd clamped on like a vise.

"It's almost time," she said.

A sinking feeling came over me. The spotlights were on me and Gwen, which was probably why Sophia and the rest of the room were staring.

"Thank you all for coming." My mother's voice rang out over the sound system. She stood off to the side, holding a microphone, and appeared slightly tense. "It's been an honor to host the Children's Gala this evening. I couldn't have put together this magnificent ball without the support of the Women in Society team. To everyone here, your generous donations will go a long way toward funding programs for the Bay Area Women and Children's Centers. And now, on a more personal note, I have something special to announce to all you dear friends." She looked straight at me.

She wouldn't do this. Not without my permission. I placed my hand over Gwen's and attempted to pry her fingers off my arm.

"It is my husband's and my greatest pleasure to

announce the betrothal of our son, Maxwell Harrison James Burrows, to Miss Gwendolyn Harper DuPont."

The crowd hooted and cheered, and I felt the blood drain from my face.

Now that I looked more closely, I noticed that everyone was holding champagne flutes like the one I'd been given.

This had been planned. My parents set me up.

Head pounding, I ground my teeth, feeling my heart beat triple time. What the fuck had my parents been thinking?

I tore Gwen's hand off my arm and ran down the Grand Staircase, watching helplessly as Sophia spun around and headed for the exit, knocking into a server carrying a tray of glasses.

The tray toppled, the glasses shattered, but she kept moving to the door without looking back.

Chapter Thirty-One

Sophia

When I reentered the ballroom after unsuccessfully attempting to remove the stain from my dress, champagne was being passed out to everyone in attendance, which I wasn't feeling after having Gwen's poured down the front of me.

Heat burned behind my eyes. I would not cry. This was a fancy date Max had set up, and I needed to hold out a little longer until I found him.

Just as I managed to blink away the tears, I finally caught sight of him at the top of the massive staircase.

Relief filled me. Until I saw the woman he stood beside.

For a moment, I was back at the rooftop party, watching Max and Gwen arm in arm, looking for all the world like the Golden Couple.

Max's face was expressionless as he stared straight at me, his jaw tense, while Gwen beamed up at him.

A loud female voice came over invisible speakers, welcoming everyone.

Max's mother?

She'd spoken of a gala she was planning when I first met her, and this must be it. She went on about donors over the loudspeaker, and then said, "It is my husband's and my greatest pleasure to announce the betrothal of our son—"

The rest of her words turned into a loud buzzing sound inside my head.

Max was getting married? To Gwen?

Memories flashed before my eyes: Gwen at Max's mother's house, sipping tea... Gwen leaving Max's apartment the other day... Gwen's look of surprise when Jack called me Max's girl.

Had they been together the whole time, and I was the idiot who never knew?

The thought cut like a thousand knives to my chest. I wobbled in my heels, the world spinning, my chest rising and falling rapidly.

Even though I hadn't seen much of Max this week, in my mind, we were together. He'd checked in every day and made sure I ate lunch, which I often forgot. When I was with him, my world was lighter. He made me laugh, and he supported me in ways that made me believe I could conquer the world.

But not *his* world.

After everything I'd experienced tonight, it was clear I'd never fit into Max's world.

My hands shook, and I swiveled in a circle, not knowing where to go but knowing I couldn't stay. And locked eyes with Paul.

I'd gone numb after the announcement, and all I could do was stare at my ex.

He was alone this time, no fiancée clinging to him. But Paul didn't look smug. For once, he looked concerned.

I didn't remember leaving the ball, but in the next moment, I was walking down Van Ness, the expensive heels Max had bought me hurting the balls of my feet, my ankles wobbling every time I stepped in the cracks of the concrete.

Max had never taken me out on a proper date. Never introduced me to his friends. No one knew we were together except Jack, who was only marginally a part of Max's society.

Was Gwen Max's official girlfriend and I the secret?

Elise was wrong. A person didn't need to be married to have a sidepiece. They could be so heavily entrenched in the upper crust that outsiders would always be "other."

A wave of dizziness washed over me, and I stumbled. The heel of one shoe scraped the ground loudly before I caught my balance.

Maybe this had been a setup by his family. I didn't know. I couldn't process it. What I knew was that I had no value in the eyes of his parents, nor anyone at the ball—the people he rubbed shoulders with daily. Even if he wanted to be with me, I'd never be welcome.

Tears burned behind my eyes, but they didn't flow. They sat there choking me. I wasn't angry enough to cry, as numbness filled every cell.

It wasn't until I was halfway home that I reached for my phone to call for a ride and remembered I didn't have it. The phone wouldn't fit inside my grandmother's purse, so I'd left it in my workbag.

By the time I got home, my arms were covered in goose-bumps and my teeth were chattering. I crawled up the last steps to my apartment and entered the darkened living room, not bothering to turn on the lights. Inside my bedroom, I kicked off my shoes and fell facedown on the bed, hiccupping before the tears finally came.

The sound of my moaning filled the room. Even if tonight had been one huge mistake, being cut daily by these people would slowly kill me.

I couldn't do it.

My head pounded, and eventually a wave of exhaustion took me under.

———

"Sophia?"

Someone was shaking my shoulder lightly. A second later, the shoulder nudge grew stronger. "Sophia, are you okay?"

Jack. I opened my eyes, and the blurred room oriented itself until I could see tuxedo-clad legs beside my bed.

I pushed up on a shaky arm, still wearing my dress.

Jack crouched in front of me. "You okay?"

"No."

"Elise called me."

I didn't know what time it was. A dozen hours could have passed or none. "Is everything okay?" Elise was avoiding Jack like the plague. She'd never willingly call him.

Jack rubbed his eyelids like he'd been up half the night. "Elise contacted Max when she couldn't get a hold of you. She got his number the night we all went drinking."

That's right. Elise had drunkenly demanded Max's phone number because she "needed someone to pay for drinks while she was in school."

I leaned forward and sank my pounding head in my hands. No matter if it was twelve hours or one, it felt like only minutes had passed since I'd fallen asleep. After a moment, I crawled across the floor to my workbag and dug for my phone.

I'd missed twelve text messages and six phone calls from Elise. Max had called me four times. "What's going on?"

Jack let out a low sigh and ran a hand through his rumpled hair. "I'm sorry, Sophia. You'll have to talk to Max about what happened earlier tonight." He shook his head. "I can't believe Gwen did that."

"I mean with Elise." I tugged the skirt of my gown where it was tangled in my legs, frustrated and wishing I'd bothered to put on sweatpants when I got home. "What happened with Max doesn't matter. It's over."

Jack's expression went from tense to sad. "It's not over. Not for Max. But you're right to worry about Elise. You need to get to the hospital. Your mom had an accident. That's why we've been trying to reach you. Max said he pounded on the door earlier, and when you didn't answer, he rushed off to the hospital, thinking you'd gone there."

———

STILL WEARING the green ball gown, I ran into the emergency room of the University of California San Francisco hospital, half my eye makeup running down my cheeks.

I searched frantically for the front desk while Jack parked out front.

The nurse behind the counter looked to be in her thirties, her hair pulled into a messy bun, with blue scrubs and a cream sweater to combat the freezing hospital air conditioning.

I flattened my hands on the counter of her station. "Can you tell me the room number for Brenda Markos?"

The nurse took me in, her eyes widening slightly before she looked down at her desk. She ran her finger over a clipboard. "Room 224. But there's already someone in there. One person at a time."

And that was when I saw Max walking toward me, his bow tie undone, hair perfectly kempt. He was fucking gorgeous, and I hated him.

"I don't want to see you," I said, rushing toward the door of my mother's room.

He grabbed my shoulders gently, and I flinched.

Max dropped his hands and took a step back, and that was when I noticed the strain in his eyes. "Your mother is stable, but she's with the doctor right now. She had a stroke, Sophia."

My face crumpled and my body shook. "What?"

He reached for me again, but I stepped back.

Max swallowed, his expression pained. "Your sister is getting coffee and should be back any minute. She found your mother on the floor of the kitchen and got her to the hospital right away. It would have been much worse if Elise hadn't found her when she did."

This wasn't real. This couldn't be happening. I should never have moved out.

I crouched and grasped my head.

A second later, I sensed Max crouch beside me, but he didn't try to touch me again. "The best neurosurgeon in town is on her way to see your mother. She'll be well taken care of, Sophia." He let out a harsh breath, and I heard the scratch of his hand running over stubble. "About earlier tonight... Gwen and I are *not* engaged. I'll never forgive my parents for what they did."

This was what he wanted to talk about?

I squinted, not believing what I was hearing. "Are you kidding me right now? My mother is fighting for her life, and you're still the poor little rich boy who can't manage his society parents." I shook my head. "Go home, Max."

His eyes raced over my face, his expression pained, as I stood and moved to meet Elise walking toward us from down the hall.

I gripped my sister in a tight hug, my body shaking.

She pulled back after a moment and looked over my shoulder in Max's direction with a sad expression.

I refused to look back. This wasn't about Max anymore. My priority was to my family.

My sister and I made our way into my mother's hospital room, where I sat at my mom's bedside and grabbed the hand that wasn't hooked up to an IV. Her eyes were closed, and she looked pale. Had those dark circles under her eyes always been there? She looked entirely too fragile.

Tears ran down my face, while Elise spoke quietly in the corner with the doctor.

Screw the hospital rules and their one guest at a time bullshit. They could carry me out kicking, because I wasn't leaving my mom's side.

Elise came over and hugged me. I wiped the tears off my cheeks and scooted over for her to sit.

After a long moment, she said, "Jack told me what happened at the ball. It's understandable you're angry with Max."

"I'm not angry. I'm empty."

Chapter Thirty-Two

Max

I found Jack loitering in front of the hospital and asked him to drop me off at Franklin Street, since I'd raced to the hospital in a taxi. I had it on good authority my parents had returned home, and I had a few words for them.

I walked into the mansion, where my dad was making his way across the foyer from the kitchen, still wearing a navy tuxedo jacket and black dress slacks.

He shoved the roll he'd been eating in his mouth and held up his hands. "I had nothing to do with it," he mumbled around the food. He pulled the bread out of his mouth. "Was your mother and Gwenny's idea. Gwen convinced your mom that you two were still in a relationship and that it was only a matter of time before you got engaged." He looked sheepish when he said, "Your mom thought moving up the engagement timeline was no big deal."

"Even if that were true," I said, my hands balled as I

attempted to contain my anger, "what was the purpose of going behind my back and announcing it to the world?"

My father looked momentarily ashamed. "Like I said, wasn't my idea."

I threw up my hands. "But you did nothing to stop it! What the fuck is wrong with this family?"

My mother rushed down the spiral staircase in a long silk robe, looking peeved. "Maxwell, the neighbors can hear you."

This house was a cavernous black hole. There was no way the neighbors could hear me, even if I cared. "What do you think you're doing, meddling in my life?"

Her mouth parted in shock. "Gwenny assured me moving up the engagement was no big deal."

"Your Gwenny is a pathological liar. You should cut her from your life."

She made the last step down the stairs and stood beside my father, her expression showing the first signs of worry. "We've known Gwen since you two were children."

I pinched the bridge of my nose. "Gwen and I have been over for nearly a year. I'm not dating her. I'm in love with Sophia. Sophia was my guest at the ball, and your stunt sent her running."

My mother looked at my father, who shrugged as though it was news to him.

And right then, the truth struck. This was my fault. I was partially to blame for how this evening had ended. I hadn't bothered to tell my parents about Sophia. I'd planned to spring it on them at tonight's public setting, where they wouldn't dare make a scene. The setting would have served me, and no one else.

I was a selfish asshole.

"Sophia, the plant lady?" my mother said. She pouted.

"She cleans up well enough, but underneath it all is a disaster waiting to happen. She'll embarrass you, Maxwell."

"Like you did tonight?" I snapped.

My mother blinked and pressed her lips together, darting her gaze away.

"Sophia is the woman I love. Get used to it." I spun on my heel, prepared to leave, then stopped abruptly and turned back. "I don't expect you to stop caring about what everyone thinks. You and Dad seem incapable of such emotional maturity. But for once, put your son's needs ahead of your own, or don't bother being in my life."

My mother's jaw dropped, and she looked truly scared for the first time. "Where are you going?"

"To find my girlfriend and hope she'll take me back."

Chapter Thirty-Three

Sophia

TWO DAYS LATER, MY MOM WAS STILL IN THE HOSPITAL, though getting better every day, and I was about to head over and see her. The doctors had run extensive tests yesterday and expected a full recovery, as long as Mom took it easy. Max had reached out several times over the last couple days, but I refused to answer his calls or text messages. I wasn't ready.

Jack said Max was the person who'd found the best neurosurgeon in town, waking the poor woman in the middle of the night, and I didn't know how I felt about that.

"He pulled strings to get the doctor's information," Jack had said this morning. "Made his assistant drive over and knock on her door."

On the one hand, anyone with enough money and power could get someone to show up in their pajamas. I was grateful on my mom's behalf; the surgeon he'd found had taken excellent care of her. But I wasn't comfortable accepting anything from Max right now.

Elise was at home, packing for her internship in Europe. She'd wanted to cancel the trip, given Mom's health, but both Mom and I convinced her it was only three months and to not give it up. I also assured Elise I would take excellent care of Mom, and somehow my stubborn sister had agreed to go.

I didn't want Elise to miss one moment of building a life for herself, and this internship in international healthcare was a wonderful opportunity. She'd been down for weeks, and I was worried. She seemed to know she needed the break too.

I'd swung by the shop this morning, but Victor shooed me out. "Go. Take care of your mom," he'd said, supporting me and giving me time away.

The plan had never been for Victor to immediately drop the business in my lap, so it worked out for me to take a few days off until I got my mom settled.

I entered the hospital room wearing sneakers, a dark, flowy floral skirt, and a cream sweater. "Hey, Mom," I said, carrying a small plant. "A gift from Victor. He sends his well wishes."

They'd moved her from the intensive care unit to a normal room, and she was expected to be discharged tomorrow.

Her face brightened, and she was sitting upright. Her fair skin was paler than normal, but she seemed to have regained some of her energy. "That was kind. Please send Victor my thanks. Everything going okay at the shop? Shouldn't you be there?"

I shook my head and set the plant in front of the window. "Nope. I've got a few days off."

She frowned. "Please don't take time off on my behalf."

That was so like my mother. The woman was in the

hospital after suffering a stroke, and she didn't want anyone to fuss.

The day of her stroke, my mother's speech had been slurred, and Elise and I freaked out. But Mom was lucky, and her speech went back to normal within hours. Everything else seemed okay, except for the exhaustion. She was moving slower than normal.

"Mom, I could use a few days off, and Victor agreed this was a good time."

"Well, if Victor says it's okay. They're letting me out tomorrow, and I'll be able to go home, so you won't need to be around." She worried her lip. "How are my houseguests?"

I groaned. "I assume you're referring to the rats. They've been uninvited."

I sat in the chair beside her bed and reached for her hand, my expression sober. "Elise and I talked about it. You'll stay with me while I get the house packed. If we do it over the next week before Elise leaves, she can help."

My mom's body went very still. "I don't—"

"Time's up, Mom. This is for your health. And for the health of me and Elise."

Her eyes grew watery, and she pressed her fingers to her lips. "I suppose it's time."

It was long past time. But a near-death experience was rock bottom, and my mom knew it.

"It's not safe to live in the house the way it is," I said. "The doctors told us your stroke was due to high blood pressure. He's sending you home with a medley of medications, but your lifestyle is unhealthy, Mom." I swallowed, tears burning behind my eyes. I'd turned into a watering pot lately. I looked up, forcing them back. "I also want you to see a therapist."

"I know, sweetheart." She patted my hand, her eyes red, tears spilling over. "It's hard for me, you know? But I understand."

My mom sank her head back onto the pillow and stared blankly at the ceiling. "I had hoped I could do it on my own. But I just can't bring myself to get rid of anything." She lifted her head and looked at me. "I don't want to be there when you move it out, okay, honey?"

"I'll make sure you're kept busy." I didn't know how I'd keep my mom away from the house without her panicking and racing over to rescue everything, but having her stay with me was a good start.

I rose and kissed her cheek. "I'm going to grab a cup of coffee. You need anything?"

She smiled and closed her eyes. "Nothing for me. I'll just rest a bit. All this lying around is tiring."

I smiled. Thank goodness she still had her sense of humor.

Head bent, pondering exactly how I'd orchestrate the packing of a hoarder house, I walked out of my mom's room and nearly ran into Max holding a massive bouquet of violets and yellow roses.

We stood awkwardly just outside my mom's hospital room.

"Hey," he said, jamming a hand in his jeans pocket. "How's your mom?"

The blue eyes I'd thought cold when I met him were all warmth, and they drew me in the way they always had. But there was too much on my plate. Even if my instinct was to run into Max's arms, I refused to be a part of his world, where they treated me like garbage.

I glanced down and plucked at my skirt, avoiding his eyes. "Better, thank you. She'll go home tomorrow." I hesitated, then said, "Thank you. For getting her such good care. I couldn't have managed it on my own."

He looked away as though frustrated. "Sophia, I want to be here for you and your family. Always."

His expression was sincere. I believed him. But it didn't matter how much I cared about Max. Or even how much he cared for me. I couldn't be with a man whose entire world didn't accept me.

Who I was and where I'd come from would never change. My mother might get better, but she'd always be a poor, widowed woman from the Sunset District. These things were fundamental.

And then something occurred to me, and my spine straightened as I remembered the list of rules Max had shoved under the door after I moved in. I didn't know where things stood with us. Didn't know where I wanted them to stand. But I wasn't putting up with any bullshit. I'd already cleared things with Jack.

"My mom is staying with me while she recovers. Jack offered his room, but I told him my mom will sleep in my room with me."

He nodded thoughtfully.

"I need to get her house cleared out, and it could take more than a week... You don't have any rules you want to throw at me about overnight guests, do you?"

His mouth turned down. "Are you trying to torture me? I was being an ass when I gave you that list, but I thought we'd moved past that. I want to be with you. What happened at the ball was horrible, and I'll forever be sorry for my mother's actions and how I handled things leading up to that moment."

He glanced down, and when he looked up, I realized how tired he appeared—there were two days of stubble on his jaw, and he was wearing jeans and a long-sleeve Henley instead of his usual dress slacks or suit. Even his hair appeared disheveled. Though I always liked that look on him. Still, this wasn't like Max.

"I love you, Sophia," he said, closing his eyes briefly. "I made a mistake in not telling my parents about us sooner, and I wish I could go back and do things differently."

My heart raced at his words, and the urge to go to him was strong.

Keep it together, I told myself. *Don't be weakened by a remorseful man.* Only this felt genuine...

My emotional reserves were tapped, but I couldn't back down. His family... I couldn't forget how they'd treated me. I did not deserve it. Not ever again. I'd promised myself that Paul would be the last man who rejected me as unworthy. In this case, it was Max's family, but was there a difference?

The only problem was, I loved Max, and though I'd cared deeply for Paul, I realized now that I was never in love with him.

Maybe Paul had known I didn't love him the way he'd loved me, and he'd used my mother as an excuse. I didn't know. Either way, the situation with Max was different, and even I could admit that.

"I spoke to my parents and Gwen," he said. "Gwen agreed to tell her friends there is no engagement." His mouth twisted as though he were frustrated. "She wanted to say it had been called off, but I refused, and she agreed to explain there was never any engagement."

He'd shown up at the hospital that night and said as much. "Does it matter? No one will believe you're dating me. I ran into my ex at the ball, and even he didn't believe it."

The skin around Max's eyes tightened. "I don't care

what your douchebag ex-boyfriend thinks. I also don't care what my parents and their social circles think. I care what *you* think, and the rest of them can hang."

He stepped closer, but he didn't reach for me. "Family is important, but I won't stand for disrespect toward my friends, and especially not toward the woman I love."

He reached for my hand, and I let him hold it in his warm, firm grip. Mostly because I longed for his touch.

"Please forgive me," he said. "I should have told my parents about you as soon as I knew I was serious. I also should have cut off all contact with Gwen after she dumped me over my parents' lost fortune."

I shook my head. "Wait—*that's* why you broke up?"

He exhaled heavily. "I'd been thinking about ending things long before that, but the financial debacle was the impetus. Gwen recently had a change of heart, however, which I suspect had more to do with my parents' influence in town. As far as I was concerned, whatever we had was long over."

Paul had broken up with me because my mother didn't fit in his world, and now Max was telling me he'd been dumped because his family name would be tarnished. What the hell was wrong with people? Had they no integrity?

Maybe it wasn't that I didn't fit in Max's world, but that he didn't fit in his world either. And if he didn't fit in his world...then he was in *my world*.

I took the flowers out of his hand. "You should know, I'm in love with you too."

His shoulders sank and he pulled me to his chest. "I'm an idiot, but I promise to be a better idiot."

My chest grew lighter as my heart broke out of its

protective shell. I leaned back. "What every woman wants to hear."

He grinned and kissed me on the lips, quickly, sneaking it in before I could protest. "Those flowers are for your mother, by the way."

I frowned, but he wouldn't let me pull away. "Where is my token?"

Holding me around the waist with one arm, he reached into the back pocket of his jeans and pulled out a red box. "It's not La Fleur au Truffe. That place is high maintenance, with its two-week ordering."

My eyes widened at the pretty red packaging. "You got this in Noe Valley, didn't you? It's a good backup." I opened the box and popped the chocolate in my mouth as fast as I could. "This close," I said, chewing, "I don't trust you not to steal it."

He wrapped his arms around me, lightly smashing the flowers, and held my head to his chest. I breathed in the clean Max scent that felt like home. "God, Sophia, these were the worst days of my life. Don't ever leave me."

We stood there for a minute until he said, "You know, if you moved in with me, your mom could live in your old room while her house is being cleaned. She'd be close, and Jack would love it. He misses having a mom."

I tilted my head back and studied his eyes. He was dead serious. "My mom is a hoarder who's going into therapy for her problems, and you want her to move in *alone* with your best friend?"

He shrugged. "Jack is adaptable. I'm telling you, he'd love it. Or she could move in with us."

I actually could see my mom enjoying being Jack's roommate. She used to love having people over before my dad died.

I blinked several times. "Are you asking me to move in with you?"

"What's this about moving?" a cultured voice rang out.

Max looked over my head and frowned, and I turned.

Max's mother was standing in the hallway in a lavender skirt suit, with her hand on her hip.

Chapter Thirty-Four

Max

KITTY BURROWS WALKED DOWN THE HALLWAY OF THE hospital, black patent leather heels clacking against the linoleum, with a fruit basket in her arm.

"Mom? What are you doing here?"

She smiled at Sophia. "Hello again." Her face grew serious. "Sorry to hear about your mother. I spoke to the doctor, and he says she'll be released tomorrow. Don't worry about the hospital bill. I've covered what wasn't taken care of by your mom's insurance."

I groaned. "Mom, what do you think you're doing?"

She looked at me sternly. "Making amends, Maxwell. Please observe."

She turned to Sophia. "I want to apologize for the announcement at the ball the other night. I should have never gone behind my son's back." She shot me a sorry look before returning her attention to Sophia. "I also should have never listened to Gwen. It turns out she was the person behind the leak—"

"What?" My body tensed. If this was true, I had even more reason to hate my ex.

My mother adjusted her designer purse on her forearm. "Gwen wasn't making any headway with you and thought to force your hand. It seemed she'd decided that being a part of a scandalized influential family was better than not being a part of it. But no need to fret, Maxwell," my mother said. "I've taken care of everything. We might be broke—"

"You're not broke," I said.

"—but we have a handful of connections left, and connections are power. Gwendolyn is taking a nice, long trip across the Atlantic. Turns out she has family in rural Holland who can use her expertise in... Well, who cares. She's gone."

I stared at my mother, impressed.

"Thank you," Sophia said hesitantly. "But I can't let you pay my mother's hospital bill."

Mom waved her off. "Already done, dear. I expect you over for tea sometime next week, yes? I'd like to get to know the love of my son's life."

She might be pushy, but she wasn't wrong. I looked down at Sophia and smiled.

My mother made an annoyed sound. "You two. I can see this will get nauseating quickly. I better meet your mother, Sophia, if we're to spend this much time together."

And like a bulldozer, my mother plowed through the middle of Sophia and me, forcing us to part or risk being run over by patent leather.

She entered the hospital room, a bright smile coming over her face at what I assumed was Sophia's mother, but I couldn't see past the privacy curtain.

Sophia blinked rapidly. "What just happened?"

"You've been added to the fold," I said thoughtfully.

This was indeed a plot twist. "That was my mother groveling."

"Wow."

It *was* wow. This was a big concession on Kitty Burrows' part. I'd planned to pay the hospital bill, but my mother paying was...kind. She'd been thoughtful, in her own way, and that gave me hope.

I guessed I'd have to pay my parents a visit and thank them.

Sophia and I talked about her mom and the house she wanted to clear out.

"I have movers you can use," I said. "I'll reach out today."

"Really?" she said. "One place I contacted never returned my call, and the other said they were booked for the next two months. I'd decided to pack myself, with Elise's help, but it makes me dizzy just thinking about it. There's a lot of stuff..." Her face crumpled. "As much as it pains me to admit, I need help. Especially if I want to get it done quickly and to replace the flooring and paint the walls. I don't want to miss the opportunity to do maintenance on the house while my mom is being agreeable."

"What will you do with all of her things?"

"Burn them in a bonfire?" she said with an impish look that quickly faded. "But that won't fly with my mom, so I'll put it in storage."

"All of it?"

She seemed to ponder that a moment. "The furniture needs to be cleaned, but otherwise it stays, or my mom will have a heart attack after her stroke. If there's anything else I don't think she'll miss, I'll sneak it out, but most of it will go in boxes and storage until she's ready to part with it."

I pulled out my phone and typed out a text. "I'll take the week off and help you."

"What?" She looked distressed. "You can't. What about work?"

"I already have, and the company will be fine. We're in between projects, with Cityscape on hold indefinitely. I've emailed everyone I know to get it to move forward again, but it's a waiting game right now. Besides, I haven't taken a week off in five years. I could use a vacation."

She gave me a dubious look. "And you're going to spend it with me dumpster-diving through my mom's home? That is awful."

I pulled her back to my chest, exactly where she belonged. "Not awful. I'll be with you. Besides, someone has to make sure you are properly supplied with chocolate and taco truck food."

Her eyes lit up. "Ooh, tacos. Can we get some? I skipped breakfast."

My mouth turned down. "We need to do something about your forgetfulness when it comes to feeding yourself. As soon as you move in, I'm hiring a chef."

She pinched my waist. "I never said I'd move in."

I laughed. "But you did. You sealed it with a kiss."

"Stop using my weaknesses against me!"

The sound of my mother laughing floated out from the hospital room, and Sophia's and my eyes grew round.

"What are they doing in there?" she said.

I glanced at my watch. They'd been talking for at least fifteen minutes while we chatted about the move, and it was making me nervous. "No good can come from those two together. You've seen my mom's salon? She's a high-end hoarder. They're probably plotting a shopping spree."

"Or to hit a garage sale."

I sent her a panicked look. "Don't joke. My mom has a guy who finds her 'collectibles' at estate sales."

More happy laughter floated out from the room. "This is so weird," Sophia said.

"Agreed." I nodded toward the exit. "Let's grab lunch while they're busy plotting world collectible domination."

Chapter Thirty-Five

Sophia

Two weeks later, I raced home after receiving a text message from Max.

> Max: The mothers are plotting something.
> Regroup at your apartment, stat.

Given what we'd recently learned about our mothers' past, I was terrified.

It turned out Kitty Burrows and my mother had gone to elementary school together and were childhood acquaintances. In between my mom's virtual therapy sessions (to be held in person once she was fully recovered), Kitty called on my mom while she lived at my place, and you'd think they were two peas in a pod, sitting on Jack's couch and chatting about old times.

I speed-walked up the street in my white tennis shoes and noticed a man with a lightly wrinkled tweed sports jacket and a beer paunch standing out in front of our building, which caught me off guard. He was looking through one of the windows to our apartment, and that was a tad creepy.

"Can I help you?" I asked.

I'd spent the day interviewing candidates for coordinator positions. Victor had a pile of great applicants, and I honestly wanted them all, but would have to whittle it down to two.

"You live here?" the man asked. He didn't look like a mass murderer, and it was the middle of the day. Maybe this was an innocent query?

He glanced down at his notes. "I'm a reporter. I'm looking for a Maxwell Burrows. I have a few questions for him."

So, not an innocent query.

Without responding, I texted Max that another reporter was outside.

He replied immediately with a one-liner.

Max: Ignore.

"I'm sorry," I said and walked toward the steps to the apartment. "I can't help you."

"Look, lady," the man said. "I've got a deadline, and I need something on this guy. I hear he's as ruthless as his society parents. The world needs to know what he's up to."

I stopped and spun around. The news cycle had

barraged Max and his parents over the last two weeks, turning them into villains. Though I didn't always understand his parents' motivations, they didn't seem like bad people, and Max was innocent. "Max Burrows is working on a real estate development this city desperately needs. But your people's quest for the next shocking article flatlined it, and now San Franciscans are going to lose out on affordable housing. How do you live with yourself?"

His eyes narrowed. "What project did you say it was?"

I crossed my arms. Cityscape was dead, according to Max. No amount of communication had taken it out of planning department purgatory. What could it hurt to mention it? "Cityscape. Affordable housing for over a hundred residents. But you probably don't care about that because it's not a juicy scoop."

I turned and hefted my bag higher on my shoulder, making the slow trek up the stairs to my apartment.

"Don't be so sure about that," the man called.

When I glanced back, he waved in a salute and hurried over to a beat-up silver sedan across the street.

I shook my head and finished my hike to the flat.

When I walked in, I hefted my bag onto the counter and toed off my shoes. "Hey, that reporter..." I started before the words died on my breath.

I'd expected Max and Jack to be watching sports or knocking over furniture with their virtual reality headsets on, but that wasn't what I found. "What are you two doing?"

Jack was in the corner of the living room with his back against the wall, a ping-pong ball in his hand, and one eye closed as he squinted and lobbed it at one of my tea mugs. He missed.

"Dammit," Jack grumbled.

Okay, so I'd left out one or two mugs. Or eight. Shit, this was a lot even for me. But I'd been busy!

Max was standing partway in the hallway, one leg lunging toward the living room.

"No cross bounds!" Jack yelled, and Max inched his foot back.

Max went for the underhand lob at a bright yellow mug I'd left next to the TV.

I rarely watched TV, so I wasn't sure how that one had ended up there. I scratched my head. Probably why I'd lost the mug to begin with.

The ball rimmed the ceramic edge, but it stayed inside. Max pumped his fist in the air.

"That's cheating," Jack said. "I saw your foot."

"Ten feet away," Max argued. "I was within regulations."

I put my hands on my hips. "Excuse me."

Max walked over and wrapped his arms around my waist. "Did you bring home any chocolate? We ran out."

I glared. "You mean you went into my stash and cleared me out."

He blinked innocently. "I can't help it if you don't maintain a steady supply."

I ground my molars. "It's impossible to keep a steady supply with you around. When did you say you were returning to work? It's been two weeks."

He sank onto the couch and kicked socked feet up onto the coffee table. "Cityscape is dead, and I'm deciding on my next project. I've got time."

The chocolate situation was dire. I hated to admit it, but I'd need to buy cheaper chocolate if I wanted to pay my rent and keep my boyfriend around. "What did you want to say about our mothers?"

"Oh, that." He sat forward, resting his forearms on his thighs. "Apparently, your mom somehow snuck my mom over to her house in the Sunset before the movers came and packed everything up. They dumpster-dived before we could get to it."

I pressed my hands to my face, horrified. "No. Was your mom disgusted?"

He shook his head slowly, a sly grin on his face. "That's the funny thing. She wasn't."

Weird. "Well, how much did my mom try to keep? I wanted most of that stuff to go into storage."

"One item," he said.

I tilted my head, confused. "One? That's all?"

Max nodded. "My mom had her collector fellow go over there with them, and they found one item worth a bit of money. Kitty is holding it in her parlor until your mom can sneak it back into the house."

My face heated. After all the work Elise and I had put in to cleaning my mom's house, my mom was sneaking around like this? Did she need to go to the therapist three times a week instead of two? "Are you kidding me?"

Max patted the couch beside him. "Maybe you should sit for this next part."

I lumbered over and sank beside him, my exhausted body falling into his side, where I snuggled up because he was warm and cozy, and he smelled delicious.

He draped his arm around my shoulders. "Turns out your mom had an original Picasso ceramic worth about thirty thousand dollars."

I sprang forward, and he tried to pull me back. "What?"

"The jar with the green nose."

I squinted like I was farsighted. "No way. That's just some weird jar my mom kept in the living room. The only reason Elise and I didn't break it playing indoor beach ball is because my mom put it on the top of a bookshelf."

"It's real. They authenticated it."

"There was actually something worth money in that house?" I twisted my mouth, considering why this was the first I'd heard about it. "I'm assuming my mom didn't tell me because she was afraid I'd get rid of it."

"According to my mom," Max said, "they had a bit of fun sneaking back into the place, and your mom didn't want to get caught. But since I'd threatened serious consequences if my mom failed to share things with me ever again, she fessed up."

I nodded, mentally putting things into perspective. "This is actually not terrible news. She controlled herself and kept it to one item. And bonus, it has monetary value."

Max smoothed down my frazzled hair. It got that way toward the end of the day, and I liked it when he petted me because he didn't seem to know he was doing it. "Thirty thousand dollars' worth of good news, if you ask me."

"Agreed," Jack chimed in while aiming his ping-pong ball at another mug. "I'll take the ugly jar if your mom doesn't want it."

Max frowned. "Stop pretending to be hard up. Your net worth is bigger than mine."

What was that? I never took Jack to be strapped for money, but he lived in a heavily subsidized apartment and ate my food. How could he have more than Max?

Something to probe Max about later.

"You know," I said, poking Max's chest lightly, "I won't need to move in with you if you're always here." I was prodding him because if we spent more time at his place, he'd be forced to supply *me* with chocolate instead of the other way around.

His face brightened. "You finally agreed?" He stood and moved toward the bedroom hallway. "My mom kidnapped yours for a dinner date, so they won't be back for a couple hours. Let's start packing now, and you can be up there tonight."

I'd already decided to move in with Max, despite the chocolate thievery, because he made me happy, and he fed me. And I was in love with him. But I liked it when he got excited over the little things, like packing up my room.

Max stopped abruptly in the hallway and pulled his phone from his pants pocket. "Huh," he said after a long moment.

I helped myself to the popcorn the guys had set out and made my way to his side. "What is it?"

"My phone is blowing up. There's a Flash News article about me."

The reporter! My shoulders tensed, and I stopped breathing. Crap! "What does it say?" My voice came out shaky, but I was trying to play it cool.

He looked up. "It's about Cityscape."

That was insanely fast. How did the reporter post it so quickly? And why? There had to be any number of tawdry stories more interesting than this one.

I held up my hands. "Okay, look, I can explain. The reporter outside—"

Max glanced at his phone again, and his brows rose. "Cityscape is back on."

"What?" I reached for the smartphone.

Samuel Thompson: Max, this is Samuel. Cityscape is greenlit.

My jaw dropped. "Holy shit."

He slid the phone back into his pocket. "You were saying?"

"Uh, well, you see, I might have mentioned Cityscape to a reporter. In my defense, I didn't think he'd care about the project. And you said yourself that Cityscape was dead."

He nodded slowly, an intense look in his eyes. "So you complained to the reporter about the assholes in the planning department, and you got my project back on track."

My lips parted. "Maybe?"

He bent and grabbed the back of my thighs, hiking me over his shoulder.

A rush of air left my mouth on a *gah*.

"We're out, Jack," Max said, speed-walking past the living room. "Gotta show my girlfriend my appreciation for her tenacity. With my tongue."

I looked up at Jack, horrified. "No!" I smacked Max's back. His tongue had been added to the list of my favorite things after he did some acrobatics with it in bed last night, but still! "He didn't mean that!"

"Yes, I did," Max said.

Jack's laughter filled the air as Max climbed the flight of stairs to his apartment faster than any human should be able to with another person on their back.

Epilogue

Sophia

"Really?" Max said as he moved my last boxes into his apartment. "You called me Landlord Devil?"

Despite Max's eagerness, it had taken more than six weeks for me to finally move in with him, but work was killing me softly with training the new hires and projects pouring in, so I'd kept pushing off the move until now. But this was just the official move in. I'd been sleeping over at Max's nearly every night.

"*Call.* I call you Landlord Devil. As in, it's my current nickname for you."

His head tilted to the side. "I like it. It's appropriate."

"Isn't it?"

Max reached down and picked up a pair of pink underwear. Not the ones he'd seen on Jack's couch the first day, but still, they were pink, and they'd somehow fallen on the floor.

His face pulled into a naughty grin. "Did you plant these?"

"No!" I reached over and tried to grab them. "They must have fallen out of the laundry this morning."

"Be honest—you planted them." He held my underwear over his head, blocking me when I tried to reach for them. "What if I left my boxers around the house?"

"I'd envision you naked," I said.

He nodded in appreciation. "Good point." He absently tossed the panties behind him. "Maybe you should stop unpacking and come back to the bedroom with me."

I put my hands on my hips. "My panties aren't going to get put away if I go back to the bedroom."

"I've decided being neat is overrated. Your panties want to be free, and I'm here to support their movement. Why don't we start with the ones you're wearing?" He sauntered toward me, all casual like, but there was intent behind his movements.

I giggle-screamed, and he chased me around the couch.

"They want to be free, so let's help them," he said, catching me by the waist and kissing my neck.

"You first!" I shouted and darted out of his reach.

He froze for all of a second, then started shucking his clothes.

At the first flash of Max's naked skin, I wrapped my arms around his neck and jumped in his arms, but he'd been standing on one leg at the time, trying to get his pants and shirt off at the same time in his haste.

We fell back, and Max twisted so we landed on the couch.

"Ooof," I said, then peered down at his shirt wrapped around his neck. "Can I help you with that?"

He winced. "I think I sprained something."

"Please tell me it wasn't your penis."

The look of horror on his face was hilarious. "Don't put

those sorts of images in my head." He rolled me over and kissed my mouth. "My body is in perfect working order—"

"I thought you said you sprained something."

"—and I'm about to prove it."

Also by Jules Barnard

Landlord Wars

Never Date Series

Never Date Your Brother's Best Friend (Book 1)

Never Date A Player (Book 2)

Never Date Your Ex (Book 3)

Never Date Your Best Friend (Book 4)

Never Date Your Enemy (Book 5)

Cade Brothers Series

Tempting Levi (Book 1)

Daring Wes (Book 2)

Seducing Bran (Book 3)

Reforming Hunt (Book 4)

About the Author

Jules Barnard is a *USA Today* bestselling author of contemporary romance and romantic fantasy. Her contemporary series include the Never Date and Cade Brothers series. She also writes romantic fantasy under the same pen name in the Halven Rising series *Library Journal* calls "...an exciting new fantasy adventure." Whether she's writing about sexy men in Lake Tahoe or a Fae world embedded in a college campus, Jules spins addictive stories filled with heart and humor.

When Jules isn't in her sweatpants writing and rewarding herself with chocolate, she spends her time with her husband and two children in their small hometown in the Pacific Northwest. She credits herself with the ability to read while running on the treadmill or burning dinner.

Stay informed! Join Jules's reader group for writing updates: **julesbarnard.com/newsletter**

Made in the USA
Las Vegas, NV
25 May 2023